THE SIEGE

PART TWO

KRIS MICHAELS

WWW.KRISMICHAELSAUTHOR.COM

CAST OF THE KINGS OF GUARDIAN

The Cast of The Kings of Guardian

Jacob King (Code Name: **Alpha**, and is known as *Skipper* to Alpha Team)

He is married to **Victoria "Tori" (Marshall) King**. They have four sons, Talon, twins Trace and Tanner, and the baby, Tristan.

Joseph King (Code Name: **Fury**)

He is married to **Ember (Harris) King**. They have one son, Blake, and a daughter, Beth.

Doctor Adam Cassidy (Known as **Doc** to Alpha Team)

He is married to **Keelee (Marshall) Cassidy**. They have one daughter, Elizabeth (Lizzy).

Jason King (Code Name: **Archangel**)

He is married to **Faith (Collins) King**. They have three sons, Reece, Royce, and Rogan.

Jared King (Domestic Operations CEO. **Dom Ops**)

He is married to **Christian (Koehler) King** (No Code Name). They have one son, Marcus.

Jasmine King (Jazz)

She is married to **Chad Nelson**. They have a daughter, Chloe, and a son, Chance.

Jewell Reynolds- King (Code Name: **CCS**)

She is married to **Zane Reynolds** (Code Name: **Bengal**)

Jade DeMarco-King (No Code Name, and she's not happy about this.)

She is married to **Nicolas (Nic) DeMarco**. (Together they are Domestic Operations Chief Operations Officers)

Doctor Maliki Blue (Mercy Team)

He is married to **Poet Campbell**, who is also **Mercy Team.**

Frank Marshall (Owner of the Rocking M Ranch)

He is married to **Amanda King.**

Justin King (Code Name: **Magus**)

He is married to **Danielle "Dani" (Grant) King.**

Drake (Simmons) Marshall

He is married to **Doctor Jillian (Law) Marshall.**

Dixon (Simmons) Marshall

He is married to **Joy** (Code Name: **Moriah) Marshall.**

Mike White Cloud (Code Name: **Chief**)

He is married to **Tatyana (Taty) Petrov.**

Kaeden Lang (Code Name: **Anubis**)

He is married to **Sky Meyers**. They have one daughter, Kadey.

Isaac Cooper (Code Name: **Asp**)

He is involved with **Lyric Gadson**.

Ryan Wolf (Code Name: **Lycos**)
He is married to **Bethanie Clark**. They have one son, Ethan.

Dolan McDade (Code Name: **Thanatos**)
He is married to **Eve Salutem**.

Luke Wagner (Code Name: **Tempest**), now a Sierra Team Member
He is married to **Pilar Grantham**.

Dan Collins: (Code Name: **Smoke**)
He is married to **Charley (Charlotte) Xavier** (Code Name: **Bambi**)

John Smith (Marshall Ranch Foreman)
He is married to **Shae Diamante** (Former Mossad).

Doctor Jeremiah Wheeler (Guardian Psychiatrist)
He is married to **Eden Wade**.

Roman Alexander (Code Name : **Reaper**)
He is married to **Harmony Flinn**.

The founder of Guardian and employer of the people mentioned above:

Gabriel Alexander (David Xavier, Code Name: **The Saint**, previously known as **Archangel** before Jason took over as CEO of Guardian Security.) He is married to **Anna**. They have four children, **Gabrielle**, the oldest daughter, twin sons Deacon and David (David goes by Ronan), and **Charlotte** (Charley).

CHAPTER 1

1 *500hrs, South Dakota, The Hollister Ranch, north of the Marshall Ranch and the Annex:*

"What the fuck?" Andrew Hollister lifted in his stirrups and searched for the aircraft he heard. It didn't take long to see the smoking trail in the sky.

"Shit, is it on fire?" Ryan Conklin, his ranch foreman, spoke from a few feet away.

"It's going to crash on our land. Come on." Andrew put his spurs to Jasper's ribs and the horse leaped, ready for a run. He topped the ridge about a mile away with Ryan right behind him. As he reined in his horse, he watched the plane detonate against the ground. A fireball billowed into the air seconds before the sound of the explosion hit them. Andrew lifted his eyes, instinctively looking for what had caused the plane to crash.

"Parachutes." Ryan pointed into the clear blue sky.

"They're coming down too fast." He snapped his eyes to where the billowing black plumes of smoke lifted into the pristine blue sky.

"You go to the plane. I doubt there will be any survivors if they didn't bail, but we need to check. I'll head over to the parachutes and try to administer first aid. Call the old man and let him know what's up. Get the ATVs out here. These guys are going to need medical."

Ryan's weathered face crinkled in confusion. "Medical?"

"They jumped too low. They're going to fuck up their legs at a minimum. Get the old man to call the doctor and get him heading this way."

"I'm on it." Ryan's horse spun to the north and Andrew reined Jasper to the southwest.

Andrew gave Jasper his head and tickled his ribs. The horse set out at a hard gallop and Andrew lowered over his neck, letting the thoroughbred stallion fly.

As he let the horse run, he batted away memories of his time in the service. This was South Dakota. There were no hostiles here. A mechanical issue probably caused the crash. He looked over his shoulder at the plume of black smoke. *Mechanical my ass.* That plane was in flames on the way down. He felt the stallion start to tire and pulled him up a bit, slowing the pace now that the animal had spent himself and would obey his commands easier. He moved the reins slightly and the horse veered to the area where Andrew believed the first parachutist would land. They scaled a low, rolling hill and he pulled Jasper up. The horse danced, wanting to run, but even with his hooves prancing, he stayed in one place.

Andrew caught sight of the plume of material and headed Jasper in that direction. He was out of the saddle and running to the man less than a minute later. The horse would stay ground-tied to where he left it. He pushed the chute out of the way and winced at the angle of the guy's leg. The damn thing wasn't supposed to bend that direction.

"Okay, man, we have help on the way."

The guy grabbed his denim shirt. "Find Fallon."

"The other guy? I'm on it. First thing I need to do is get you immobilized."

"It was a surface-to-air missile," the man panted, his face ashen and white.

"Son of a bitch." He knew it. He'd seen that type of damage before. Andrew propped the guy's head up using some of the parachute and a flat rock. He unhooked the harness and used the man's emergency knife to cut it from his legs. If the wind picked up, the man could be dragged, and with his leg that fucked up, it wouldn't be pretty.

"Phone, do you have a phone?"

"Yeah." Andrew handed the device to the man. The guy dialed and put the phone on speaker. The sharp squeal at the other end of the connection stopped both Andrew's actions and the man's. "That can't be." He hung up and tried again.

"Reception is spotty here at best, but I think that line is disconnected." Andrew finished running his hands over the man's other limbs. He grabbed two good-sized sticks before he trotted back over to his horse and dug in his saddlebags. He came back with two lengths of leather and splinted the leg to immobilize it. To the man's credit, he didn't yell as Andrew worked. He damn near passed out but didn't let out even a whimper. Andrew stood up. "Good news is I think your leg is the only thing fucked up. How close were you to the ground when you jumped?"

"Too damn close." The man's eyes closed. "Fallon pushed me out. Man, I didn't see where he landed."

"I did. I'll go check on him. Do not move." He reached for his phone, taking it from the man's stomach where he'd dropped it, and jogged to Jasper. He mounted as his call connected.

"What?" his father's voice rasped viciously across the connection.

"One of the parachutists has an injured leg, a closed fracture, but it's busted to hell. I put it in a splint. I'm checking on the other one." He pointed the horse's nose in the direction of the other chute and Jasper galloped, happy to be moving again.

"I called the doctor, he's on his way." His dad's words softened.

"The guy said it was a surface-to-air missile that took them out."

"What the hell? Is he fucking drunk or just insane?"

Andrew answered, "Lucid and I don't think he was lying. I saw that plane on the way down. The ass end was gone, and it was on fire."

"Son of a bitch. All right, I'm calling Marshall.

He has connections. Maybe he'll know what the fuck is going on."

"Send out the ATVs. We'll need the two with the beds and carrying boards to get them in to the ranch."

"Already done."

Andrew hung up and once again dropped out of the saddle at a dead run. The second man was covered by his parachute. After finding a way under the material, Andrew checked for a pulse, which was there and, thankfully, strong. The guy had a huge knot on his head and was bleeding from his nose and maybe the ear. The blood was smeared and clotting, so telling where it had come from was near impossible without moving the pilot's head. There was no way he was going to do that. He'd seen head injuries ruin not only careers but lives, as well. Carefully, he ran his hands over the man's limbs. Nothing protruding. Self-Aid and Buddy Care was drilled into him, and God knew he'd used it overseas. Way too fucking much. He grabbed some dead scrub brush and rocks and fixed a makeshift shade, shielding the guy from the afternoon sun. He checked the man's pulse again. Still there, still strong. The longer the man stayed unconscious, the more he worried about brain swelling or internal bleeding. He'd met both of those bastards up close and personal, too. Traumatic brain injuries were too fucking common when things exploded.

At the thunder of hooves, Andrew looked up. Ryan reined his mount to a stop. "Nothing alive on that plane. Your pap has people coming. Maybe thirty or forty minutes out. He alive?"

"Yep, but unconscious. The other one has a fucked-up leg. Stay with him and make sure he doesn't move, all right?"

"On it." Ryan's mount scooted over the hill in record time. Andrew glanced down at the unconscious man. "Don't fucking die on me, man. I'm not losing another guy. You copy?"

The only thing that moved was his horse. Jasper found a patch of long grass and made himself at home. Andrew cut the man out of his harness using the knife secured to the pilot's boot. They weren't wearing insignia, but he recognized a flight suit for what it was. He recognized the type of men these were. He'd fought alongside people like them.

Andrew watched the man's chest lift and fall. "What the fuck happened up there?" Andrew asked the man as he looked up into the limitless blue

South Dakota sky and began the long wait for help to arrive.

He heard the ATVs before he saw them. Jasper lifted his head from grazing as one crested the hill and then slowed dramatically as it came down the other side. "What do we have?" Dusty, one of the hands that had been hired while Andrew was in the military, jogged to his side.

"Head injury, which means we treat for spinal injury, too. We need to immobilize him."

Dusty didn't waste any words. Instead, the man jogged back to the ATV and pulled open the back bin. "Head or entire body?"

"Head and core at a minimum." He didn't know how badly the man had fucked himself.

"Got it." Dusty made his way over with several boards. "If we can roll him to his side, making sure not to let his head get screwy, we can lay him on this. Then, we can get him to the bed of the ATV and wrap him up so he can't move."

Andrew nodded, and the two moved together to get the man onto the six-foot sheet of wood. The fly-fly boy's feet hung off by four or five inches, but it was the best they could do. "Where did you learn first aid?" Andrew asked as they lifted the man.

"Rodeo. Not the televised ones, the little ones in podunk towns. Even with the clowns charging in to distract them angry bulls, some of the old boys got messed up," Dusty grunted as they lifted the man.

They hefted his weight to the back of the ATV and strapped him down. "Go slow. He hasn't regained consciousness."

Dusty jumped onto the front of the ATV and cranked it up. "That ain't no good. I'll get him back to the ranch."

"I'll help Ryan with his guy and then I'm heading to the crash site. Tell Senior I'll be in after I make sure there isn't any fire danger."

"Got it." Dusty released the brake and the ATV moved forward. With utmost care, the guy made a wide arc and headed back toward the ranch.

Andrew watched the vehicle until it dipped behind the hill. He looked up at the sun that lowered into the western sky. *Had the fucking war followed him home?* He lifted his straw cowboy hat and wiped at rivulets of sweat. It wasn't like he needed any other reminders of his time overseas. He had the scars and dealt with the disabilities daily. He didn't need fucking reminders.

Grabbing Jasper's reins, he swung up into the

saddle. "Enough whining, Hollister. Get your ass in gear."

Jasper's ears helicoptered toward him as he spoke. He patted the stallion's neck. "Come on, boy." He leaned forward and clicked his tongue, and the horse lunged into motion.

CHAPTER 2

Nine hours earlier, 0600hrs, Mountain Standard Time, The Marshall Ranch, Hollister, South Dakota:

Frank Marshall pushed his foot against the wood of the porch and set the swing into motion. He glanced over as his wife, Amanda, came out of the house. Her hair was pulled back in a ponytail that hung to the middle of her back. The black hair was streaked with grey, but she was movie-star beautiful without a lick of makeup. He stopped the swinging motion, and she handed him his cup of coffee and then sat down beside him.

He lifted his arm and she leaned into him. "This

never gets old." She motioned to the view in front of them.

"A lot of sweat and tears in this land." He set them swinging again and took a sip of his coffee.

She made a noise of agreement. "What's on your agenda today?"

Frank grunted. Not much. He'd been relegated to supervisory duties, which he hated. Between the twins, Keelee, and his ranch foreman, John, there wasn't much for him to do. "Talked John into riding to the west. We'll need to ride the fence before we bring the cattle down this fall."

"Don't they use the ATVs to do that now?" Amanda chuckled when he grunted again.

"Using helicopters and ATVs to do a roundup, too. Scares the weight off the damn animals," he grumped, but deep down, he had to admit it took a lot less time and effort. Still, seeing the old ways that he'd steadfastly held to go by the wayside was kind of like watching an old friend die of neglect. Sad.

"New technology," Amanda sighed. "Is it terrible of me that I'm glad we get more time together?"

He tightened his arm and kissed her head.

"Nope. Just don't want to become irrelevant in my own home."

Amanda lifted and twisted in the swing to look at him. "You'll never be irrelevant. How many times a day do the twins, John, or even Keelee ask your opinion or want you to settle a disagreement?"

He smiled. "With those boys, there will always be an argument."

"Exactly," Amanda chuckled and lifted her hand to his face. "But beyond that, I will always need you." She leaned in and kissed him.

The woman's lips were his downfall. He pulled her a bit tighter and lengthened the kiss. "Damn," he whispered as the kiss ended. "What you do to me."

She opened her eyes slowly. "That feeling is mutual, I assure you." She lifted one eyebrow. "Maybe tonight we should revisit these feelings?"

"It's a date."

"Which means you'll be home on time?" She narrowed her eyes at him.

"When was the last time I was late for a date with you?" He leaned in and kissed her again. "Never." He answered for her.

"Just making sure." She smiled and snuggled

back under his arm. He took a sip of his coffee and felt ten feet tall and bulletproof. His wife, a woman he could in no way deserve, loved him as much as he loved her. Life had a weird way of filling in the gaps. He gazed across the vista and drew a deep breath. For most of his adult life, he'd thought that he'd be alone. After Elizabeth, he'd tucked in and dug deep, being the best dad he could be for his girls. Not once did he think that he'd find someone to love him. Figured it wasn't in the cards. But Lady Luck had dealt him a pat hand with Amanda. He wouldn't change a damn thing.

"Awww... Am I interrupting cuddle time?"

Frank grunted at Joy's taunt.

"Good morning." Amanda sat up.

"Morning. Can I borrow some coffee? Real coffee? Dixon only has that hazelnut shit. I can't deal with it anymore. The smell makes me want to puke." Joy leaned against the porch railing.

"Of course. I'll go get you some." Amanda was on her feet and moving before either he or Joy could object.

"I could have gotten it." She turned to look at Frank.

He grunted. It wasn't in Amanda's nature to let others do. "You've been gone."

Joy grunted in return, which meant she'd been on assignment. From all accounts, she was as deadly as they came. It wasn't his place to approve or disapprove of what she did for Guardian. Judgement was something he didn't condone so he wouldn't practice it himself.

Amanda returned with a small can of coffee. "I'm surprised Jillian didn't have any."

Joy took the red can and tossed it into the air, catching it effortlessly. "She and Drake are on a health kick. Herbal teas only." Joy shivered exaggeratedly. "I need my caffeine."

"Coming from a vegetarian, the health kick taunt is funny," Amanda laughed and Joy wrinkled her nose.

"Maybe. I'm told I'm a contradiction." She gave a whistle, and Sasha, her little white poof of a sidekick, raced across the yard, yapping.

"You're wonderful, Joy. Don't ever change." Amanda bent down and pet the mini-mutt.

"Couldn't. Not in my nature. Thanks for the fix. I'll pay you back." Joy turned and jogged down the stairs, Sasha following her owner.

"You don't have to, we have plenty," Amanda called after her and received a raised hand in the air as acknowledgement. She sat down next to

Frank.

"The smell makes her ill." She slid her eyes toward him. "Are you thinking what I'm thinking?"

Frank took a sip of his coffee. "Wasn't." But now he was. How would that work? Joy as a mother. He'd have to wrangle himself around that concept.

Amanda took a drink of her coffee. "Tori said the boys' school break was coming up when I talked to her over the weekend."

"Good. Been a while since they've been out." Frank pushed the swing and set them in motion again.

"There's Mike." She dipped her head in his direction. He worked out every morning, usually with Dixon and Drake, but since Joy had just got home, Dixon wouldn't be with them.

"And Drake," he said as Drake jogged around the old barn and then raced to catch up with Mike. They sprinted out of view, each one trying to win the race back to the Guardian side of the ranch.

"We are truly blessed." She dropped her head onto his shoulder.

He grunted in agreement. Their life was damn good.

Joy Marshall opened the coffee can and grabbed on to the counter. "Damn." The smell of the coffee made her stomach roll. She swallowed hard and pushed the nausea down. She'd been feeling off for a couple of weeks. Moody as a bitch, too. She put the plastic lid on the coffee and shoved it into the refrigerator, slamming the door. "Stupid," she grumbled and headed back across the massive living room to her and Dixon's part of the house. She stomped down the hall and into the bedroom. They'd torn the damn thing apart last night. She'd been gone for almost two weeks, and they were both eager to make up for lost time.

The shower was running, and since she'd thrown on yesterday's clothes to go borrow the damn coffee her fucked-up stomach wouldn't let her make, let alone drink, she pulled off her T-shirt and bra as she approached the bathroom. Her shoes, jeans, and panties dropped where they came off. To hell with being neat.

She opened the shower door and saw her husband in all of his soapy wonder. Those muscles moved against each other, bulky yet so damn nimble. A corner of her mouth twitched up. He'd almost worked his way to a ten last night. Not that she'd admit it to him. He was magnificent when he tried to reach perfection. She watched as the white foaming suds slid down his body. The Adonis belt that led to his cock caught her attention. She moved up and trailed her fingers down the ridge.

"I didn't satisfy you last night?" his deep voice rumbled around the shower stall.

"That was so long ago," she chuckled and moved in front of him.

He opened his eyes and blinked several times, the water dripping from his reddish-blond lashes. "Did you get your coffee?" He wrapped his arms around her and pulled her into him. She went willingly.

"I did, but I decided I didn't want it after all." She lifted up on her toes and linked her fingers around his neck. "Brace yourself, Quick Draw." That was the only warning she gave him before she tightened her arms and lifted her legs, literally climbing his big body like a jungle gym. He grabbed her ass and lifted her up, settling her at his waist.

His lips crashed against hers. The kiss a continuation of the hard, fast-paced fucking they'd done last night. It was what they both enjoyed. He moved, and her back was against the wall of the shower. Braced between the cold stone wall and his hot body, her libido went nuclear. This man drove her insane. He fucked like a stallion and fucking loved her on top of it.

He fisted her hair and tugged. She groaned when his wet stubble scratched her neck. It shouldn't feel so damn good, but it did. One arm supported her, and the other unwound from the grasp he had on her hair. He found her breast and pinched her nipple. She jolted so hard he stopped and looked at her. "Don't stop." Her breasts were sensitive this morning, but she couldn't care less. Dixon stared at her for a moment. "Don't you dare fucking stop." She ground the words out and pulled him in for another kiss. He didn't let her lead; instead, he overpowered her kiss and assumed control. Fuck, she let him. This space, next to him, was the only safe place in the world for her. With him, she let go of needing to be in control. He hefted her up a bit and with his free hand centered his cock under her. "Yes." She hissed the word as he entered her. "Hard, Dixon. Hard and fast." She whispered the words as she bit his earlobe.

He obliged. The hard length of his cock moving

in and out at a rapid-fire pace ignited every nerve ending in her lower body. Her breasts rubbed against the hair on his chest as he thrust into her. Overloaded in sensation, she tightened in anticipation of the edge, that point where it was almost painful but so fucking sweet. Dixon slowed, and she grabbed his shoulders, her nails digging into his skin. "Don't, not this time."

He laughed and pulled out slower. "This time, every time."

She groaned, "Vicious bastard."

"Wanton bitch," he responded and lifted her again, repositioning her higher on the wall.

"Fuck me like you mean it." She shifted her hips and groaned when he drove into her to the hilt. "Fucking perfect."

"Yeah, you are. Perfect for me." His hips sped up, and this time, he didn't stop. She tightened; her body bowed to the point of breaking. Shattering in a magnificent orgasm, she gasped for air as he came inside her, crushing her against the wall.

Her stomach rolled and saliva filled her mouth. "Let me down. Now."

"What?"

"Oh, shit." She bent to the side and heaved.

Dixon let her down but held her as she dropped to her knees, still heaving.

When her stomach finally stopped trying to emergency evacuate via her throat, she leaned back into her husband, who was sitting on the floor with her.

"Son of a bitch. I must have picked up the flu."

Dixon made a non-committal sound. She opened her eyes and tipped her head back. Fucking mistake. She bolted forward and started with the dry hacks again. Fuck.

When she finished, she was as fucking weak as a newborn. Dixon stood up, turned off the water, and draped a towel over her. The asshole picked her up like she wasn't an assassin and cradled her next to him as he took her into the bedroom. "Rest." He covered her with the comforter and moved her wet hair from her face.

"I'm fine. Just need some sleep."

"Then sleep." Dixon's words came a split second before his lips touched her forehead.

She would have responded, but damn it, she was tired. She just needed a few moments. The fucking flu. Just what she needed.

Dixon shut the door and shoved his legs through the jeans he'd taken with him. He zipped up and padded down the hallway. Palming his cell phone, he dialed Adam's number.

"It's early, man," Adam grumped at him.

"Joy's been vomiting. Dry heaving. She's as weak as a kitten."

"I'll be right down. Wait, does she know you're calling?"

"Do you think I'm stupid?" Dixon huffed. She'd kill him.

"As long as you take the blame, my friend. I don't want her pissed at me. I enjoy my life."

"Har, har. You're not coded, you don't have anything to worry about. Just get down here."

"I'll be there in ten." Adam disconnected the phone and Dixon dropped into one of the recliners.

Drake walked out of the kitchen. "Didn't mean to eavesdrop, but I couldn't help hearing that she's sick."

"Flu. She thinks she picked it up on her last mission." Dixon scrubbed his face. "D, I've never seen her like that. I'm shook, man."

"I can tell." Drake dropped onto the ottoman,

sweaty from his morning workout. "Adam coming over?"

"Yeah. She dropped to the floor and, man, it was serious. Like she'd been on a four-day bender, but she rarely drinks, you know?" Dixon clasped his hands together. His wife was one of the strongest people he knew. Having her go down like that was unnerving.

"She's sleeping now?"

"Yeah."

"Come on. Let's grab a cup of something hot and wait for Adam. Have you eaten yet?"

"No. I know you're trying to be helpful, but I'm just going to sit here and quietly freak out, okay?"

Drake stared at him for a minute. "It sucks sometimes. Loving them so much."

"Wouldn't trade it for anything in the world." Dixon flopped back in the chair.

"Me either."

Dixon glanced around and then his eyes darted back to his brother. "Where's Jilly?"

"She went to her lab. Woke up with an idea that she wanted to get down. Figured since Joy made it home last night, you weren't working out. Chief and I did the circuit."

Dixon nodded. "Yeah, thanks. What do we have to do today?"

"Not much. The next class doesn't start until the beginning of next month. John and Frank are riding fence the old way today."

"It will take three times as long on horseback." Dixon shook his head. "But good on John for being game."

"John learned from Frank, so the old way was the only way he knew although he's damn good at adapting." Drake chuckled. "Figured I'd take a look at that project Jillian and I have been talking about building."

"You're serious about a new house?"

"Well, yeah. This is fine for us now, but Jillian and I are serious about adopting, and we're looking to foster older kids that are at risk of aging out of the system."

"Not younger ones?" Dixon glanced out the window to look for Adam and then looked at the clock on the wall. Five minutes. Shit. He was going crazy.

"Neither one of us are that sure about how to take care of the young ones. Older ones are where we think our comfort zone lays. Plus, working on the ranch will build character. It didn't hurt us to shovel shit." Drake shrugged.

"No, it didn't. Builds character and muscles," he agreed and popped up on his feet when he heard boots on the porch outside.

Adam opened the front door and walked in without knocking. "Thanks for dressing up for my visit, man." Adam whapped him on the stomach and headed to the back bedroom. Dixon fell into step beside him. "Sorry, my man, I'm doing this solo and blaming you. Wait here." Adam closed the bedroom door in his face. Drake laughed from the other end of the hall. Dixon lifted the bird to his brother. The man laughed harder. Fucker.

Dixon leaned back against the wall and waited. And waited. And fucking waited. Adam exited the room thirty minutes after he entered it.

"What the hell? Is she okay?"

"She's sleeping again."

"Is it the flu?" Dixon trailed one of his closest friends.

"No." Adam stopped in the living room. "I think she wants to tell you, though."

"What? Is it... cancer?"

Adam barked out a laugh. "No. Nothing terminal, I assure you. Just let her sleep. I'm going to have the lab test a blood sample I drew. And no, I won't charge you extra for making me draw blood. My nurse is far better at it than I am."

"Blood test. Holy fuck, man, what is wrong with her?" Dixon ran his hands through his hair.

"Dude, go get in bed with your woman. When she wakes up, she'll tell you. I can't. HIPAA violations and all that shit."

Dixon stared at Adam. "Since when do you care about that?"

"Since your wife can smear me across the ranch. Yeah, I think that's the exact point I started caring. I'm going home to my wife, breakfast, and a shower. You're welcome." Adam walked out the door.

He heard Drake's feet shuffle into the room. "You are damn good at being in position to listen." Dixon turned around. Drake was wearing basketball shorts and had a towel hung around his neck, fresh from the shower.

"Dude, I took a long shower trying to give you your privacy. Why the fuck was he being all secretive and shit?"

"I don't know." Dixon scrubbed his face again, his morning stubble stiff under his palm. It wasn't like Adam at all. Hell, he knew how many stitches were in the Skipper's shoulder and how many pieces of shrapnel Adam had pulled out of Chief that time in Afghanistan.

"Best do as he said. I'll head over to Jillian's lab and give you two the house."

"Thanks, man."

Drake started to walk away but stopped. "Whatever is going on, she's going to be okay, Dixon. We'll make sure of it."

He turned and stared at his brother. "Whatever it takes."

"As long as it takes." Drake winked at him and headed back to his side of the house.

CHAPTER 3

O 630hrs, *Mountain Standard Time, The Marshall Ranch, Hollister, South Dakota:*

Keelee Cassidy watched her husband's truck pull back up their drive. It was rare that he was called out suddenly, which usually meant someone from the staff was ill, but in this instance it was Joy, Dixon's wife. She poured him a cup of coffee, mixed in a teaspoon of the caramel creamer he loved, and moved to the kitchen door to wait for him.

He smiled and accepted the coffee, giving her a kiss in return. She sighed, closed her eyes, and leaned into him. "Is everyone okay?"

"Yep. Where's Lizzy?"

"Already down at the barn with Kadey. They wanted to check on Ethel and Lucy." Kadey and Lizzy were almost inseparable and had been for years. "Those girls have every intention of winning the blue ribbon at the county fair. I keep telling them only one may win, but they swear they don't care which one wins as long as it is one of them."

"Those girls are spoiling those calves, and yeah, there will probably be some hurt feelings if one wins and the other doesn't, but you live and learn," Adam sighed and took a sip of his coffee. "So, we're alone?"

"For the time being, why? What's up?" She leaned back against the counter and smiled up at her man as he stepped up against her.

"Me." He set the coffee down on the counter.

"Oh, dear, Doctor, whatever shall we do about that?" She ran her hands down the front of his chest. His pecs flinched under her touch. She loved that her man still worked hard on his body. It reaped her benefits that she'd never tell a soul about. Her man was a stallion between the sheets.

"Perhaps we should adjourn to the bedroom and lock the door." He moved her off the counter and started backing her down the hall.

She wrapped her arms around his neck. "Afraid two twelve-year-old girls are going to bust in and spoil your fun?"

He growled a bit in the back of his throat as he dipped down to kiss her. She opened as his tongue delved into her mouth. They bounced their way into their bedroom, ricocheting off walls. She heard the lock click into place when they finally stumbled into the bedroom. Adam's hands were under her T-shirt and lifting it off her, forcing her to raise her arms from around his neck. She found the hem of his shirt and tugged it up over his rock-hard body. She held on to him as he unfastened her jeans and slid them down her legs, her panties traveling with them. She stepped out of the denim while unbuckling his belt and unfastening his jeans. He toed out of his boots, sending them backward a step or two as he lost his balance. They laughed, not breaking the kiss.

Finally out of the clothes, he backed her to the bed and carefully lowered her to the mattress. His hot cock nestled against her abdomen as they kissed. His hips started to rut, slowly at first. She slid her fingers from his hair to his shoulders and then trailed them down his spine. Gripping his firm ass in her hands, she lifted up against him.

She wanted him in her, and foreplay wasn't necessary. She was hot and wet for him because he always affected her that way.

He lifted her leg and pushed up. With one of his legs folded on the bed and the other on the floor, he pulled her closer to him and entered her. She grabbed his arm as he stroked in. Rolling her eyes up to the ceiling, she sighed at the feel of her husband inside her, the pull of his body as he exited and the push as he entered her. His shaft ignited sparks that fueled the fire that always burned for him. He dropped to his arm, keeping himself over her. She pulled his eyepatch off and tossed it somewhere on the bed. He didn't need to hide his injuries from her. He was perfect for her.

As he lowered for a kiss, she wrapped her legs around his. They moved in concert, each one taking but together giving each pleasure. She clung to him as she orgasmed. The tight grip of her body just before she exploded resonated throughout her core. The ultimate sensory experience, perfect in its way, always melted her into a pliable mass of complete contentment. She felt Adam climax. The bliss they shared in these moments made all the other complications and problems in their life somehow more manageable.

He dropped beside her and pulled her into him. "Okay, we need to do that more often."

"Sex?" She squeaked the question. She thought they had a pretty robust sex life. Was she mistaken?

"Morning sex," Adam chuckled. "Sex with you anytime is fantastic, but damn. That was sunshine *and* fantastic."

She chuckled and snuggled into him. "How's Joy?"

"Oh, she's going to be fine." He wrapped his arms around her. "What do you have planned for today?"

She got the hint; he wasn't going to talk about anyone he'd treated. She sighed and thought about all the things that had to get done. "This morning, going over the books. The feed store in Hollister is going to open next month. That will save us from having to truck what we purchase from the south."

"And help the new business in the process."

"Yep. This afternoon, Sky and Lyric are coming over, and we are going to go down to the main house and make an anniversary cake for Taty and Mike. Shae said they weren't going to celebrate it."

"And you just couldn't let that happen, could you?" Adam chuckled. His rumbling laughter vibrated under her ear.

"No! It is a special occasion. Why wouldn't they celebrate?"

"I have no idea. You could ask them."

She lifted and whapped him with a hand. "Men. You just don't understand."

"And we never will." He reached up and pulled her down to him. She relaxed into the kiss.

A knock on the door sounded a second before the knob rattled and Lizzy yelled, "Mom?"

She sat up immediately. "Yep? I'm changing."

"Okay. I'm going to Kadey's. Her mom said it was okay."

"She did, Miss Keelee!" Kadey's voice echoed after her daughter's.

Keelee dropped back onto the mattress. "All right. Be good."

"We will!" both girls answered at the same time.

They laid in silence, listening to the two girls as they walked through the house. The kitchen door slammed shut. Adam lifted up and glanced at the clock. "What time do you have to look at the books?"

Keelee pushed him back down onto the bed and straddled him. "Whenever I get to it." She leaned down and kissed her husband. "Tomorrow. The day after. Next week."

Adam laughed and spun them so he was on top of her. "Perfect." He lowered for a kiss, and she wrapped her arms around him. It really was perfect, wasn't it?

Dixon laid on his side in their bed and stared at his wife as she slept. She was his world. Her rough exterior and abrasive personality didn't fool him for a second. Inside, she hid the scars that the world would never see, but she'd allowed him access to them, and even with the heartbreaking story of her past, she'd survived. In some ways, she'd flourished, and in others, she'd... managed. Regardless, what she was completed who he was. They weren't a typical suburban husband and wife. They'd never be that type of couple, but what they were was perfect for them. He never wanted that dynamic to change.

Joy being sick was shocking. She'd never even had a headache that he knew about. Having her dry heaving in the shower had fucking sent a chill down his spine.

"You're staring."

He reached out and moved a piece of long

black hair from in front of her face, pushing it back behind her ear. "He wouldn't tell me what's wrong with you. I'm worried."

Her eyes opened and she stared at him. "I'm sorry I scared you." She whispered the response. That was how he knew she was being completely honest with him. Whispered words between them were private and cherished by both of them.

"What's wrong?"

He moved closer to her, and she closed her eyes, putting her hand on his chest. "Don't move the bed."

He froze. "Babe, you're scaring the hell out of me right now." He barely breathed, not wanting to make her ill again.

"I'm fine. I promise. This will pass." She opened her eyes and stared up at him. "I'm pregnant."

Dixon blinked and opened his mouth to speak but snapped it shut. *Pregnant.* He drew a breath and then released it. If he was scared before, he was fucking terrified now. What if she didn't want the baby? What if she wanted an abortion? "Are you okay with that?"

An extremely rare smile spread across her beautiful face. "I am. Are you?"

He let out a whoop and moved to hug her. Her

eyes bulged and she rolled out of the bed, running toward the bathroom. He heard her heaving and shot into the bathroom. He grabbed her hair and held it out of the way as she leaned over the toilet. "What part of, 'Don't move the bed,' didn't you understand?" She said the words into the porcelain throne and then heaved again.

"I'm so sorry, babe. I'm thrilled. You'll make a fantastic mother." He stroked her back. She would. Her past was something that Joy would never allow to happen to her children. She would be a fierce mom.

She moaned and grabbed her hair. "Washcloth."

"On it." He stepped over her, wet a washcloth, and handed it to her. "Is this morning sickness?"

She buried her face in the cool cloth and grunted. "Saltines and ginger ale. Adam said that would help settle my stomach."

"Shit, we don't have that."

She lifted her face from the cloth and arched an eyebrow at him.

"On it." He stood and headed back into the bedroom. "Wait. We should get you back in bed first." He turned from the doorway and walked back to her.

She lifted a hand. "I'm going to sit right here. Crackers and ginger ale, Quick Draw."

"I'm heading into Hollister. Do you want anything else?"

"I don't *want* that." She put the cloth over her face again.

"I should ask Amanda…" He stopped his words in mid-sentence at her hissed response. "No?"

She lifted her face from the cloth. "How about we adjust to the news before we spread it around?"

He cocked his head at her. "Drake?"

"A day or two, Quick Draw. Give me a day or two to get my head around this."

He walked over to her and bent down. "I'll give you as long as you need. I love you. You are going to be a fantastic mom."

She closed her eyes. "I'm going to fuck up, but I'm going to try my best."

He dropped a kiss on her head. "We have a history that will not be repeated. We will be good parents. I know that in my heart. I'll be right back."

He jogged out of the bathroom and grabbed a T-shirt and socks. His boots were in the entryway. So, maybe it was a damn good thing Drake and Jillian were building a new home. It was going to get noisy in this one. He smiled as he slammed his feet into his cowboy boots. He was going to be a dad. Nothing like his sperm donor and everything like Frank Marshall. Damn, it was a fantastic day.

0700hrs, Mountain Standard Time, The Annex side of the Marshall Ranch, Hollister, South Dakota:

Mike White Cloud draped his towel over his shoulders after a quick shower. His wife wasn't home yet, which meant that the mission she was working in Russia had run longer than anticipated. Of course, *she* wasn't in Russia. She was in the communications center across the Annex, acting as an instant translator. Taty taught Slavic dialects to Guardian assets. She also filled in during emergencies.

The team's linguist had taken a bullet to the leg and was holed up, waiting for the rest of Omega Team to finish their mission and pull him out. The team was working its way through the migrant refugee camps on the Belarus-Poland border. The man they were searching for had been photographed three days ago in one of the camps. It was Omega Team's mission to secure him and bring him to the United States. Mike didn't know why; the team's mission was a need-to-know situation. He didn't need to know any more than he currently did.

He pulled on his jeans and T-shirt before he combed and braided his hair. It reached the small of his back now. He pulled on socks and shoved his feet into his well-worn cowboy boots. Standing up, he rolled his shoulders and glanced around the magnificent house he shared with his wife. Never in his wildest imagination would he think that he'd end up with a family. The Marshalls, which included Dixon, Drake, and by marriage, Adam and Jacob. Of course, that family would be hollow without his woman, Taty. She filled the emptiness he'd held for so long. He was rich beyond his wildest imagination, and that had nothing to do with the quality of his bank account, which was also more than he'd ever imagined acquiring.

He closed his eyes and opened his soul, thanking the powers that moved through the universe for his fortune, and sent those spirits his pure, unadulterated gratitude. Acknowledging the good things in life wasn't to be taken for granted. He'd been on the other side of these blessings. He knew how fortunate he was, and he'd always take time to acknowledge the positive position in which he found himself.

He made his way to the kitchen and poured two large thermal cups full of coffee. Capping both, he made his way over to the comm building and let himself in, working through the entrapment area, punching in codes, and leaning forward to let the retina scan do its thing. When the door popped open, he was greeted by the world's best assistant. Shae smiled and jogged her head toward the back of the facility. "She's been there since I got here about an hour ago."

"Thanks. Why so early this morning?"

"John was up at four. We worked out, he sent the hands off to fix that water pump and check the tanks in the northern pastures. We ate breakfast before six and he went back out to do the hands' work so he could ride with Frank today. I was ready to come to work, so here I am. So, I'll get everything done early and take Velvet out this afternoon for a ride. It's going to be a beautiful day."

"You spoil that horse." Mike smiled at the woman. The love she had for the animal was endearing.

"I don't spoil my horse any more than you spoil

yours." Shae lifted an eyebrow at him. "Tell me I'm wrong."

Mike jerked his head to the side. "I think I hear my wife calling me. Excuse me."

Shae laughed and stepped out of his way. "We have a meeting with the Rose at ten."

"Got it," he acknowledged as he headed down the hallway. Shae was indispensable. Efficient in the extreme, and with her background, she knew what needed to be worked immediately and what could wait. Instead of putting out multiple fires every day and working long into the night to catch up on the administrative end of the job, she allowed him to focus on what was important and either farmed out duties to the twins or handled the situation herself. Shae was a gift that he took time to give thanks for, too.

He lowered, punched in the code to unlock the door, and waited for the lock to pop before he pushed the heavy door open with his shoulder. Taty glanced at him and smiled but quickly moved her eyes back to the video feed. He dropped into an empty chair beside her and placed her coffee onto the workstation. She grabbed it but stilled. "The woman said she knows who you are looking for. The man told her to shut up. Separate them and question the woman."

She pressed the button to mute the comms. "Thank you. It has been a frustrating night."

"It happens," he acknowledged. He'd lived through many an operation that left the team without a resolution.

"Thank you for this." She leaned over and kissed him quickly before snapping up and hitting the button. "The man is threatening her. Give her an earpiece."

Mike leaned forward and watched the fuzzy video feed. His wife spoke in rapid Russian to the woman. The look of relief on the woman's face was immediate, and a conversation ensued. Finally, the woman gave the comm back to the Omega Team member that had handed it to her.

"She is your primary's wife. The man who is threatening her is their escort. They paid money to him to get them into Germany. He is trying to extort more money. Her husband will go willingly to the United States. They have a daughter and a son that must go, too. She will lead you to them."

Mike leaned back in the chair and took a sip of his coffee. His wife had filled in a couple times for missions, but her primary job was teaching specific

Slavic languages to operatives who needed to traverse the countries without being pegged as a foreigner.

She hit the mute button, and together they watched as the team, dressed as refugees, escorted the woman through the crowd gathered at the fence line hastily constructed by the Polish government. "Did you work out this morning?" Taty asked as they both watched.

"Of course." He nudged her with his leg. "Our bed was cold without you in it last night."

She turned and smiled at him. "I'll make it up to you, my love."

"I'll hold you to that promise." He smiled and bent over to kiss her. He didn't let the kiss linger; her mission was the priority right now. He would wait. "I love you."

She sighed and kissed him again. "I love you, too. Now, go to work and let me finish. I'll stop at your office before I go home and crawl into that cold bed."

"Woman, the thoughts that just went through my mind should heat up those sheets from here." He waggled his eyebrows at her.

She laughed and waved him away. "Leave

before you talk me into ignoring my responsibilities."

"Is that a possibility?" He growled the question and narrowed his eyes. Wanting her as much as he did, he might consider it. No, actually, he wouldn't. Neither of them would jeopardize a mission or the team for such a thing, but the innuendo was enticing.

"No. Now go. Tell Asp I'll meet him at two. I need some sleep." She gave him a sexy, lazy smile and leaned away from him, lifting her coffee cup between them.

"I'm going." He stood, bent down, and kissed her again before he adjusted himself in his jeans. He'd take his time getting back to his office so he was presentable to mixed company. Taty keyed the comms and spoke to the team as he closed the door.

"Hi, Daddy!"

Kaeden turned from the kitchen counter as his daughter and Lizzy tromped into the kitchen.

"Hey, you two. Where have you been?" He pointed to the table. "Pancakes?"

"Yes, please!" they both answered as one.

"We were out with Ethel and Lucy," Kadey answered as they sat at the table.

"Which one is bigger today?"

"They're the same," Lizzy answered. "Mom says she's going to get us halters for them."

"For cows?"

"Yup. We have to show them, so they need to learn to follow a lead." Lizzy said matter of factly.

He mixed up the batter that Sky had made earlier and poured four small cakes on the griddle. "Yeah, and Mom said she'd get us purple shampoo for them so we can make sure Lucy's socks and Ethel's coat are super white."

He turned and narrowed his eyes at his daughter. "You're joking, right?"

They shook their heads in unison. "When you show calves, you have to make sure they're perfect."

He flipped the small cakes. "Frank lets you do this?"

"Grandpa says it builds character," Lizzy said and then giggled. "I just think it's fun."

"Lucy and Ethel are cows, not dogs." He reached for two plates.

"So?" Kadey asked.

Kaeden shook his head and laughed. "So, I hope you have fun."

"Oh, we do! By the time school starts again, they'll be really big." Lizzy danced in her chair.

"Bigger than Brantley's calf," Kadey added and did the same jig.

"Brantley?" He paused plating the pancakes, looking back at his daughter and her best friend.

"Brantley Olsen," Sky spoke as she came into the kitchen, fresh from her shower. She leaned up and he dropped a kiss on her lips. "He lives just outside of Hollister and his dad is letting him raise a calf to show, too."

"Oh." Thank goodness. He was probably going to have a heart attack the day Kadey became interested in boys.

"Yeah, and he's really cute, too," Kadey chirped in, and both she and Lizzy giggled.

He sent a look toward Sky. "Cute? The calf or Brantley?"

The girls dissolved into laughter. "Brantley!" they both answered.

His gaze whipped over to his wife. Sky laughed, shrugged, and turned to make her tea. He was so screwed.

"Here you go." He put the pancakes in front of the girls and started another batch.

"Dad, we saw Shae this morning. She's taking Velvet for a ride this afternoon. Can we go with her?"

"What did Keelee say?" They'd agreed long ago to let Keelee approve or disapprove of all things ranch. Neither of them was up on the safety aspects of living on a ranch although they'd learned the basics.

"We haven't asked her yet 'cause she's going to ask if it's okay with you," Lizzy spoke with her mouth full.

Kadey nodded her head, her eyes pleading with him to agree.

He glanced over at Sky, and she nodded. "Okay, if Keelee says you can."

"Cool. Maybe she can ride with us, too," Kadey said.

"Yeah, that would be fun," Lizzy agreed.

He loaded two more pancakes each onto the girls' plates and moved over to lean against the counter with his wife. "When did they grow up? Boys? Cute?"

Sky dropped her head back and looked up at him. "They're twelve. They can't stay little forever."

"Are you sure?" He wasn't ready for his baby to be a teenager or, God forbid, date.

"Pretty sure." Sky nodded and took a sip of her tea. "Can't stop time."

"Boys?" She laughed at him as the girls chatted about those damn cows and what color halters they wanted for each. "I'll keep them away."

"You won't."

"I can. I have the skills." That was a fact.

Sky put her tea down and wrapped her arms around his waist. "I'm sure you do, but terrorizing teenage boys? Really? Don't you have better things to do?"

He stared down at her and answered honestly, "No." He needed to have a plan in place. "Dating my daughter? Nope. She isn't going to date until she's… hell, at least thirty."

She laughed and shook her head. "You can't stop the inevitable."

He glowered down at her. "I can sure as hell try."

"Go to work and stop being a grump." She toed up and kissed him. He turned to her and held her waist, deepening the kiss.

As she lowered, he breathed, "I'm not a grump."

"You're not." Sky cast a look at the girls, who

were lost in conversation. "You're a sexy beast who is magnificent in bed."

He felt his eyebrows pop.

She smiled wickedly. "Someday, Kadey is going to have someone like you that wants her like you want me."

He dropped his hands and groaned. "Wicked. You are wicked. You will pay for that."

Sky laughed, drawing the girls' attention. "That was my plan."

Kaeden grabbed the tote he took to work every day. "It worked. You two stay out of trouble."

He winked at his wife and left to a course of goodbyes. *Boys*. Seriously? He needed a plan.

CHAPTER 4

"So, five bedrooms, four on the upper level and ours on the ground floor." Jillian stared at the blueprints over Drake's shoulder. They'd just finished lunch and were taking a moment out of their day to look over the newest set of plans for their house.

"Yeah. I know we want to help as many kids as we can. Aging out of the system is traumatic, but we need to start with one." Drake turned and pecked her cheek. "We don't want to bite off more than we can chew."

"Frank said we can use any of the rooms upstairs in the main house if we get approved before the house is ready." They'd have to be foster parent-certified to take the kids before they turned eighteen. Keeping them after their birthday was entirely on them. She swiveled him on his stool and sat down on his leg.

He pushed her thick blonde hair from her shoulder and smiled, shaking his head. "Don't you think that defeats the purpose of taking them when they are aging out? We want to provide a stable environment for them, not move them around."

She grimaced. "You're right, I'm just so..."

"Excited?" Drake laughed at her. "My silly Jilly."

She rolled her eyes. "Don't call me that, and I was going to say optimistic. I think we can make positive impacts on these kids' lives."

"I do, too. I can't get what the child protective agency worker told us out of my head. Foster parents literally kick them out because they don't get any more funding."

"Not all of them. The Wilsons were trying," she reminded him. They'd visited with several parents that had agreed to meet with them. The Wilsons had too many kids in the house, but the older ones had learned to be scarce when anyone from Child Protective Services was around. They shared two small bedrooms downstairs, one for boys and one for girls. The Wilsons were on a pension and couldn't supply more than room and a meal at night, but at least the children who'd aged out had that. It was more than most. Jillian had sent them a five-figure check and had asked them to let her know when they needed more.

"Yeah, and I saw how much you sent them." Drake pulled her in and kissed her. "You have the heart of an angel."

"I don't. I just have more money than I could possibly need." And she did. With the money she'd received for selling her inventions, she could fund the Wilsons without noticing the difference.

"Which is why you're the one making the determination on where we are going to build. We can huddle up here with everyone else. The valley behind the Annex is still quiet, but this is still a community where the kids will have supervision even if we aren't around. If we build further out…" He let the statement trail.

She turned and laid her head on his shoulder. "Do you honestly think I'd put more distance between you and Dixon?" She felt guilty enough about suggesting a home of their own.

He ran a hand up and down her back. "This is a joint decision. It's time we start our own family, in our way. Like they are."

"What?" Jillian's head popped up, clocking Drake's chin. She grabbed her head and rubbed it while her husband groaned and grasped his jaw. "Ouch, damn it, Drake, you can't do that." Tears formed in her eyes.

"Do what? I think I chipped a tooth. Shit." He shoved his finger into his mouth and ran it over one of his molars.

"They're starting a family?" She put pressure on the knot that was forming on the top of her head.

Drake's eyes opened wide, and he stared at her. "It's an assumption. Maybe a logical guess, but yeah, I think so."

"Really? What led you to that conclusion? Damn, you have a hard jaw." She moved a bit in his lap.

"You have a hard head. I'm going to have to make an appointment to see the dentist." Drake whined.

"They fly out whenever we need them, so spill." She dropped her hand and stared at him, waiting for him to answer.

"Dixon called Doc over to the house this morning. Joy was throwing up. I just figured it was the flu, but then Doc leaves and doesn't tell D anything. Tells him Joy is fine and that she'll let him know what's going on. So, I put one and one together and got two." He shrugged. "I wonder if I can get the guy to fly out today." Glancing at the clock, he sighed. He stuck his finger back into his mouth. "Chipped for sure."

"Oh, poor baby." She leaned down and kissed his cheek. "I think you're right."

"I know. It's sharp, too." He frowned and replaced his finger with his tongue.

"Not about that," Jillian chuffed and put her hand under his chin. "Let me see." He opened his mouth, and she ran her fingertip along the side of his molar. "It feels smooth to me. Oh…" Drake's mouth closed, and his tongue swirled around her finger. She gently tugged her digit out of his mouth and leaned down to cover her lips with his, melting into his hard chest when there was a cough from the doorway. Jillian groaned and lifted away.

Amanda cleared her throat and, flustered, looked down at her boots. "Sorry to interrupt, but you did say you'd help with the surprise party we're throwing for Taty and Mike?"

"I did and I will. Drake and I were just talking about the new house."

Amanda's eyebrows lifted. "Talking. That's not

what we used to call kissing in my day." The woman's laughter was joyous and irresistible, and both Jillian and Drake joined in.

Jillian stood and pointed to the blueprints. "We actually just decided to accept your kind offer of letting us build in the valley. What we want to do for these kids will require space for them to become independent, but we'll need the support of our family."

Amanda walked in and glanced over Drake's shoulder. "This is the first floor?" She asked.

"Yes, here is the front porch and it wraps around the west side of the house so we can watch the sunset. The kitchen is over here on the east side of the house." Drake pointed out the family room off the kitchen and the great room at the center of the home then showed her their suite on the other side of the home.

"If I could suggest one thing, you'll need a mudroom." Amanda tapped beside the back door that led into the kitchen. "I swear it saves my sanity. Muddy boots, coats, a sink to wash up in if necessary."

"Great catch." Drake grabbed a pencil and made a note on the blueprint.

"Bring these over tonight. I know Frank would

love to look at them." Amanda glanced at her watch. "I'm going to pop into Hollister. I need vanilla. You can't make a cake without it. I have no idea how I'm out of it, but I am. Would you like to drive with me?" Amanda asked Jillian.

"I would. I want to pick up a few things." She put her hand on Drake's shoulder. "Do you need anything?"

"If we're bringing the blueprints over tonight, I'd say taffy," Drake chuckled. "Knowing Frank, he'll go through a bag before we finish this."

"True. I'll grab a couple extra bags. It won't go bad the way he goes through it," Amanda chuckled. "I'll go get the keys to the truck. We need to go and get back. Everyone is meeting up in the kitchen at two to bake the cakes. Sky is going to let us help with the decorations tomorrow. I've practiced with a piping bag until I can't see straight, and I still can't get my border piping to look like hers."

"I'll be right there." She watched Amanda leave before she turned back to Drake. "Rain check on what we started."

"Always." He dropped a quick kiss onto her lips and turned to roll up the blueprints.

"We're really doing this, aren't we?" She drew a

deep breath and smiled, puffing the air out with a punch. "We're going to be part of the solution."

"We are going to do our best." He dropped the rolled sheets of paper into the tube and capped it. "One step at a time. Foster approval and a house."

She nodded. "So, a year, year and a half?"

"That's realistic. Eighteen months is doable as far as construction is concerned. I can work on the house during the winter."

"You know everyone else will show up to help." She waited for him, and they walked out of her office together.

He made a face. "Not sure if that's a good thing or not."

"It's a good thing. Everyone pitches in around here, you know that." She hip checked him and laughed when he almost bounced into the wall.

"Woman, you are abusive today."

"So not abusive. You used that chipped tooth excuse to get me to snuggle up. Admit it."

"Me?" He blinked several times and pointed to himself. "How could you suggest such a thing?" Laughing, he bent down, wrapped an arm around her waist, and lifted her up to his mouth. "Go. I love you."

"I love you more."

"That could never happen." He smiled at her.

God, she loved this man. He was her protector, her shelter, and her best friend. She kissed him, and he let her slide down his body. Oh, the feel of that man did things to her. Sexy things. Amazing things.

He lifted an eyebrow as if he knew where her mind had wandered.

"Rain check." She waited for his nod before she spun around and almost floated over the path to the main house. Happiness had settled into her bones and warmed her more than the sun in the sky. It was a fabulous day.

"Where's Taty?" Asp stood in Mike's doorway, holding a bag of cookies. One of the chocolate cookies with vanilla frosting popped into Asp's mouth as Mike looked up.

"Shit, I was supposed to tell you that she'd meet you at two. She worked all night."

Asp lumbered into the office and dropped into a big wingback chair Mike had against the wall. "No worries. Lyric is hanging with Sky. Something about baking a cake at the big house." Asp flipped another cookie into his mouth.

"How are you not five hundred pounds?" Mike leaned back and dropped his pen onto his desktop. It was obvious Asp had settled in for a conversation.

"Fast metabolism and I work out." The man shrugged. "Burn more calories than you consume, you know the gig."

"Dude, you consume a lot of calories." He nodded to the bag of cookies.

"Not true. Here I do. At home? Not so much. Lyric is experimenting with vegan food." Asp dipped his chin and leveled his stare at Mike. "*Raw* vegan-type food." He shook his head. "I'll be lucky to survive these phases."

"So, you like, what, eat raw broccoli?" He'd eaten food when he was deployed with his team that was questionable, but raw vegetables only? Not his ideal, that's for sure.

Asp nodded and popped another cookie into his mouth. "Bingo."

"Damn. You should ask Taty to teach her how to cook some of the dishes from Georgia, and not the state, the country." His wife's food was simple and delicious.

"God, no. Lyric would convince Taty of the benefits of a vegan lifestyle and then you'd want to kill me. No, thanks. Believe me, I know my woman. She's passionate, but her interest fades quickly, and she moves on to the next thing that interests her. Life is never dull with that one." Asp leaned forward, placing his elbows on his knees. The bag that held the cookies hung empty from his fingertips. "I wanted your opinion on something."

Mike cocked his head. He and Asp weren't exactly friends, more like acquaintances, so the comment was curious. "Go ahead."

"I'm thinking about leaving the Shadows. Tempest did it. He works with Sierra Team. What are the chances of getting a position here at the ranch? Lyric and I love it here. The place we have in Jacksonville is all right, but neither of us considers it home."

Mike blinked and leaned forward. "Man, I don't know. We've stopped building since the Rose has come up to full speed. The majority of what we do now is limited to rehab and recurring training for single operatives and our investigators. The Rose has the team traffic. Have you talked to Anubis? He and Zane are running the Shadow operations. Alpha oversees the section, but the Shadows are their baby."

Asp shook his head while staring down at the floor. "No, because I was wondering if we could set up a sniper school here."

"A sniper school?" Mike leaned forward again. "You mean for the teams?"

"No. I mean for anyone who needs the skills. The Shadows, teams, single agents. Billy and I were shooting the shit last night, and the idea started. Both of us are snipers. Military trained. We can teach it, and this country has the weather, freezing in the winter and scorching hot in the summer. It's a skill that's in demand. Believe me, Billy and I are comparing notes. We're busy. We'd still be available to go on missions. If need be, we could recruit John to do a class or two. The guy has mad skills, but as we push people through, that operations tempo should reduce. Most of the missions Billy is used for are overwatch situations. Making sure teams get in and out without a problem. You know my background and what I do. It's selfish for us, but helpful for Guardian, too." Asp sat back in his chair and stared across the desk at him.

"Damn. That makes sense." Mike chuffed a lungful of air. "All right. I'll talk to Anubis and

Bengal. If they think it has merit, we'll approach Alpha, and if he buys in, ask him to push it up the chain." He was always working to remain relevant and reinvent the usefulness of the Annex. The center was his baby, and he made sure they were earning their keep.

Asp stood up and extended a hand to him. "Thanks, man. I appreciate you hearing me out."

Mike rose and took it. "A great idea. I have a meeting with Anubis at three. We'll talk about it then."

"Perfect. I'll head down now and practice conjugating my verbs. Your wife is picky."

"She'll keep you from getting in trouble. Listen to her," Mike said as Asp headed for the door.

"Believe me, I know. Later." Asp left, and Mike dropped back down into his chair. He glanced at the clock. An hour and a half until his meeting with Anubis.

Anubis had just finished his updates with the Shadows and sent the information to Bengal for his five o'clock brief with Archangel. He glanced up at the monitor on his wall and buzzed in

Mike. The man was always early, but that was all right.

He pressed another button, releasing the interior door, and watched through the video feed as Mike made his way down through the maze to his office. Anubis' door opened, and he stood. "Early. You bored on the other side of the complex?"

"No. Far from it, but I was approached by one of yours today with a proposal." Mike sat down in the chair in front of his desk.

Anubis did a double-take at that comment. "One of mine? Asp? He's the only one here."

"That would be the one."

He blinked and sat down. "What on earth did Asp proposition you about?"

Mike leaned forward and explained the request. "I think it has merit."

Anubis leaned back and scrubbed his face. "It does. Yeah, that's something to look into. Did he say why he wanted to ditch the day job?"

"No, and I didn't ask. I'll leave that to you. I don't have the need or the want to know that information. But what I do want are your logistical projections for the next quarter."

"That's an easy one." He grabbed a folder from the top of his desk. "Here you go. Minimum requirements. The Rose is making my life extremely comfortable." He smiled. "The new document section Fury has up and running has streamlined everything. Drops from Arizona to D.C. reduce the amount of work we have to do. All I need are salary and upgraded equipment when necessary."

"What about someone to help you? Working all these nighttime calls has to suck." Mike glanced at the small budget sheet in the folder.

"That isn't an option right now. Bengal and Fury take the calls when I need a night off." Anubis leaned his forearms on his desk. "Each one of those operatives is my responsibility. If they need me, I'll be here. Sky understands. She rolls over and goes back to sleep when I hit the tunnel."

Mike shifted in the chair. "Having Asp here would ease that demand, and you do know the emergency access tunnels aren't supposed to be used except for an *emergency*, right?"

Anubis bobbed his head. "Yup. Tornadoes, World War Three, and mosquitoes. All emergencies in my mind. Have you seen the size of the mosquitoes this year? I think I saw one fly away with one of Frank's cows in its claws."

Mike chuckled and shook his head, his braid

falling over his shoulder. He flipped it to his back, laughing, "Wimp."

"Damn straight." Anubis laughed at the jab. He'd itch for days.

A warbling tone stopped the laughter from both of them. Anubis was out of the office on Mike's heels, and they slammed down the hall to the facility's communications room.

Chief flipped on the speakers as he brought up the equipment. The words that followed froze the blood in his veins.

"Mayday, mayday, mayday. Guardian Flight 343, mayday, mayday, mayday. A surface-to-air rocket hit us. Go! I'll hold it as long as I can."

"That's Fallon." Mike whispered the words.

"Fuck that!"

"And Mack." He knew the pilots well.

"Mayday, mayday, mayday. Guardian Flight 343, mayday, mayday, mayday."

"I've got it! Strap up! We're losing altitude fast! Mayday, mayday. Guardian 343. We were hit by a surface-to-air missile..."

They scurried when Mack gave the coordinates. Chief called up the latitude and longitude.

"Shit, they were almost here. Get CCS on the line. I'm making a copy of the transmission and sending it to Jewell, Code Red," Mike spoke as his fingers flew across the computer system. Anubis picked up the phone and pushed the direct line to CCS.

The phone rang and he put it on speaker, freeing up his hands. They both paused when the ringing ceased. "What the fuck?" Anubis hung up the phone and punched the line again.

Nothing.

"Hold on. There, it's sent to Jewell. There might be a problem with the switch." Mike moved to the wall and picked up the phone, dialing the area code and number. An electronic scream blasted through the handset.

They looked at each other. "Try it again." He waited, a tendril of gut-clenching adrenaline weaving through him. The squelch rang out again.

Both of their cell phones vibrated. Fuck, they'd forgotten to take them off before they entered the comm room.

He pulled his phone up and looked at the face as the software transcribed the call to text.

"This is a recorded message from Operator Two-Seven-Four. Armageddon Protocol. Repeat, Armageddon Protocol. Heaven is under siege. Emergency recall of all

operatives. Rerouting all comms through the Rose. May God bless us all."

"Fuck, call the—"

"Rose," Mike finished for him and punched the numbers in.

"Status?" Joseph's voice rang out sharper than an acid-tipped spear.

Mike answered, "Unknown. Our inbound aircraft was shot down by a surface-to-air missile. I'm sending radio comms recording to your location. I can't get through to D.C., and what the fuck is with the info from Operator Two-Seven-Four?" Mike's words spilled out as Anubis called up the cameras and defense systems around the ranch. He checked them every morning and evening. He never fucking thought he'd be checking them for a reason.

Anubis could tell they were put on speaker on Joseph's end as the din of the Arizona office became louder. He hit the keyboard and pounded in his passwords. The video feeds were up, but where the hell were the security systems? He retyped his password and sighed when the program came up.

Mike stood and pointed a remote at the television on the side wall. It lit up, already tuned to the national news channel.

Joseph's voice snapped out, "Unknown. Stand by. Gabriel, did you hear that?"

"Yes, I'm trying to raise Charley and Smoke, but neither are answering their phones. There is no connection to the facility in D.C."

"Son of a bitch." The whispered words drew his attention from the monitors. He blinked, trying to comprehend what he saw. A plume of smoke lifted to the Washington, D.C. skyline. A jostled cell phone video popped up. *Oh, God.*

"Turn on your television. National news. Fuck, all of them are covering it." Chief's words cut through the conversation.

"Pull everyone in," Mike said over his shoulder. Anubis hit the floor and ran to the next room where he punched the tornado alarm that would send everyone's family and essential personnel to their emergency tunnels. The staff that was still here at three on a Friday, which was minimal, would go to the tornado shelters built under the buildings where they worked.

Anubis slammed back to the comm room and skittered to a stop as he heard Maliki Blue yelling, "I saw it. Rockets. From all four directions." The doctor stopped and coughed. "Poet is trying to find an entrance. Sonya said there were three more. I have a couple Guardians and we are looking, too. The back, by the theater, is still standing to a degree. I'm heading to the main entrance. We need someone to coordinate with local law enforcement. A fucking zoo here. No responders yet." No one could miss the fact that Maliki was running as he spoke. "Watch out!" There were shouts in the background. "Another building just went down."

"Our people?" Joseph demanded.

"I don't have a clue. Hundreds of people out here looking like zombies. We need an on-scene commander. I have to get to the injured."

"Call in regularly," Joseph snapped.

"As I can. Lives matter more than updates." The phone went dead.

"We need to get the families. Mountain Protocol. Chief, hunker down. Is Anubis there?"

"Right here." He sounded off.

"Open the Pit. Get everyone to safety. Nobody topside. Not a soul."

"We already have."

"Anubis, recall all your assets and get an accounting of all teams OCONUS. Suspend all overseas operations; they can't work without satellite support. Keep this line clear. This will be our primary contact line."

"Copy," he said just as an explosion shook their building. Alarms on the security system went wild and the alert screamed from the control room. Both he and Mike jerked their attention to the monitors. "Fuck!" He raced to the alarm system and set off the external alarm, a five-minute, wavering tone. War. Another explosion rocked the solar arrays, a third hit several of the wind turbines.

"We need to get underground and gather everyone." Chief grabbed his arm. "Nothing we can do to help if we're dead. Everyone knows what to do and where to go. Let's hit it."

Anubis cussed vehemently as he glanced at the monitors. "Shoulder-fired rockets." He pointed toward the cafeteria on the monitor. As if in slow motion, they watched the building explode and disintegrate. "God, I hope anyone in there took cover. Let's go."

He and Mike pounded down the hallway to the tunnel access point. He prayed Sky and Kadey were already underground. As much as they'd practiced this event, he'd never dreamed they'd ever have to do it for real.

CHAPTER 5

Shae laughed at Lizzy and Kadey as they brushed down their horses. The girls were filled with energy and giggles. She loved it when they rode out together. They filled her with joy, and while she was an authority figure to them, they confided in her about their crushes and curiosity about boys. She always encouraged them to talk to their moms and gave advice she knew wouldn't be controversial.

"Have you curried them?" She led Velvet to the door of the barn. They were turning the horses out to pasture.

"Yep." The girls exited the barn where they'd stowed their tack. The first thing Velvet did was roll in the dirt. "Little devil," Shae muttered but smiled at the horse. "Let's put the halters away. Then we can go up to the big house and see if we can help with the party."

"Party?" both girls parroted.

"Mike and Taty's anniversary. They weren't going to celebrate it, but someone got wind of that and totally took over."

"My mom, I bet," Lizzy laughed. "She's all about celebrations."

"Could be." Shae wasn't going to point any fingers, but Keelee and Amanda had taken the bull by the horns, as they said in this part of the country. They walked into the tack room.

"I wonder when we'll get the halters for Lucy and Ethel." Kadey handed her the red halter she'd used, and Shae placed it on the proper peg.

"Soon, I would suspect." The girls were in love with the calves. The red one was Lucy, the blonde one was Ethel. The girls had hand-raised them and the calves followed them around like pups. "I haven't seen them in a week or so. Have they grown?"

"Yes!" Kadey jumped up and down. "Hurry up, Lizzy, let's go see them. They're in the small barn still. Grandpa Frank said since he wasn't using the stalls we could keep them there as long as we want."

"We need to turn them out and let them graze." Lizzy hung her halter on its peg.

Shae smiled. Grandpa Frank was a softy. He'd had John get a couple hands to clean out the small structure, repair the ancient stalls, and run fencing from the smaller building to the east paddock so the calves could graze.

They wandered over to the little red and white building. The brilliant blue skies held only the faintest wisps of white clouds. "Mom asked Dad if he wanted to go to Silvan Lake Sunday. If they go, you're coming with us, right?" Lizzy asked Kadey.

"Yep. Dad has to stay here all the time for work. If he takes vacation this year, I want to go to a theme park. The ones in Florida. Have you ever been, Shae?"

"No. I've never had the inclination to go to a theme park. Is it fun?" She laughed when both girls stopped walking and spun to look at her. "What? Tell me why I would want to go be elbow to elbow with people when I have this." She spun with her arms open.

"Shae, you have no idea what you're missing.

They have all kinds of rides and shops and candy, plus, they have the princesses!" Kadey laughed. "I don't care how old you are, princesses are awesome."

Shae shook her head slowly and drawled, "Not as awesome as princes." She laughed and sprinted to the barn. The girls followed, laughing.

They spent a good half hour in the barn with the calves before Kadey and Lizzy turned them out to graze. Just as they were about to leave, the tornado siren sounded. Shae froze, the warning so at odds with the day that a shot of adrenaline pulsed through her body. No, there was no storm. But... She spun and stared out the partially open door. "Shit."

"There aren't any clouds, Shae. Why is the siren going off?" Lizzy headed toward the door.

"No! Lizzy, come here." Shae snapped the words and both girls jumped at her tone.

"What's wrong?" Kadey grabbed Shae's hand, her voice trembling as she spoke.

"I don't know. Come on, over here." She reached out to Lizzy, who flew in her direction. "Here, you two get in here, pull that hay bale apart, make it fluffy." If she had to, she could hide the girls under the hay and make a stand.

She watched as the girls pulled apart a bale of

hay and started to spread it. She reached down and pulled her jean leg up, slipping her nine mil pistol out of the holster at the top of her boot. There were snakes on the ranch, and she'd been caught once without a gun. Never again. Shae bent down so as to not be seen through the windows and made her way to the back of the small barn. She peered out the door that stood ajar. Nothing. Grabbing her cell phone, she looked down for a second.

That's when the first explosion happened. The air rippled with the percussion.

"Damn it." She moved to the other side of the building and peeked out. A plume of smoke lifted into the brilliant blue afternoon sky. Another explosion, followed by two more, happened within seconds.

"Shae?"

At Lizzy's words, she held up a hand and hissed, stalling anything else the girl was going to say. Her big blue eyes were terrified, but there was nothing Shae could do to reassure her at the moment. There were four... no, five men wearing ghillie suits coming toward the ranch from the southeast. She moved and glanced at the back of the main barn that had an emergency access point in the tack room. Fuck, they'd been in that room. If she'd just stayed out longer like the girls wanted, they'd be safe now. *Or you'd all be dead in the pasture.* She batted that thought away and dipped low to look out the door.

The men were still about a thousand meters away, but if they went now... It was a risk she had to take. "Come here now!"

Both girls were by her side in an instant. "We have to run back to the barn. I need you to run as fast as you can. No sounds. No cries, nothing. There are men out there that will hurt us. Do you understand?"

They both nodded.

"Okay, remember, no sounds. None." She stared at each one of them and then cast a glance at the men who were approaching. "Come on. Kadey, hold Lizzy's hand." She carefully opened the door and ran in a crouch, holding Lizzy's hand with her left. She ran on her toes to dampen the sound of her feet and bent over, keeping her head down. The girls, bless them, kept up with her. They entered the main barn, but she slowed them down, careful to make sure no one else was in the structure. The ranch hands that John had hired full-time were working on a water pump up in the north pastures. They wouldn't be back until tomorrow afternoon. It was why John was up so early this morning. He'd wanted to make sure they had everything they needed. She listened carefully before she darted across the building and pulled them into the tack room.

"Why are we here?" Kadey whispered. Shae held her finger to her mouth and glanced at the wall that blocked the tunnel access. She moved the tack on the peg that she would release to access the portal, careful to make no sound when the leather and metal came to rest by her phone.

"Check the barn," a man's voice said from outside the structure.

Shae placed her pistol on the feed bin because she needed two hands and unlatched the peg.

"Who the hell does that guy think he is?" another male voice said from inside the barn.

"Shut up," a third voice rasped. "Clear."

"It's a fucking barn, of course, it's clear."

"I said shut up."

Shae listened to the two men and picked up her pistol after sliding the peg to the right. She let the peg drop gently. A metallic click resounded through the barn. She slid the wall and lifted the hatch quickly. "Now." Training the gun at the door, she watched in her peripheral vision as the girls scurried down the ladder.

"Over here," the loudmouth said. He was right outside the tack room door. As the latch lifted, she emptied her clip, moving the impact point of her bullets six inches each shot. Hoping she dropped the loudmouth and caused the others to be cautious, she moved.

Twisting to go down the ladder, she hit the switch to slide the wall back into place and slammed the hatch shut after her. Blindly, she found the latch and spun it, locking the portal shut. She had no idea if the wall made it back before she shut the hatch, but she fucking made sure that the lock on the underside was secured.

"Shae?" Lizzy's scared voice echoed through the darkness.

"Take a couple steps away from the ladder, girls." She heard the shuffling and then the lights in the tunnel came on. Checking again to make sure the locking mechanism was set, Shae shoved her empty pistol into her waistband and skittered down the ladder. She knelt at the bottom, dropped her empty clip, and removed her spare from her other ankle. She slapped it in, pulled the charger to the rear, and loaded a bullet. She pointed it to the ground and moved forward. "Come on, we have to move."

Whoever was out there had explosives. What Shae needed now was distance and locked emergency doors between them and those bastards. She grabbed Kadey's hand. "Hold on to Lizzy's hand." Immediately, the girls complied. She moved them down the tunnel at a steady pace, not wanting to exhaust the girls but needing to get to the next door before the people above could figure out what was going on.

"Do you think our moms and dads are okay? Grandma Amanda and Grandpa Frank?" Lizzy, the bolder of the two, asked about five seconds into their trek.

"Everyone knows what to do when they hear the siren. Get to safety. Here, we're shutting and locking this door, too." She dropped the girls' hands long enough to secure the door and ensure the iron bar engaged correctly. God, she prayed John and Frank had heard the siren or the explosions. There were outlying access points. Not many, but...

The girls grabbed her hands again, and they were off. "What about the dogs and Ethel and Lucy? Our horses!"

"The animals will be okay. These men aren't after the animals." Shae kept the girls moving; they needed to get to the Pit. There they had weapons, comms, video, and a way to strike back.

"Why are they after us?" Lizzy asked as they kept moving. The girls jogged to keep up with her fast pace.

"I don't know." But she would find out. This was a safe space—*her* safe space—and she would fight to keep it that way as would every able-bodied Guardian on ranch soil.

Fuck, able-bodied.

The clinic.

There were always recuperating Guardians at the clinic. Those explosions... What would she take out if she was attacking? Power, comms, and access to any help, which would be the flight line and the road into the ranch from the highway.

An explosion above them shook the tunnel, and the lights flickered on and off.

"Shae!"

"Don't worry, just dust settling," she spouted, hoping they were reassuring words. Still, she powered through the section of underground pathway.

"What is exploding?" Kadey jogged forward and looked up at her.

Shae looked up. Where were they? How far had they traveled? Surely, they were on the Guardian side of the ranch by now. "I don't know."

"I'm scared." Kadey's words were quiet, but Shae heard her.

She stopped and kneeled in front of the girls. "We are all scared, but being frightened isn't a reason to make bad decisions or stop thinking. We're doing everything we can to reach your moms and dads. I will take you to them, but right now, we need to move. Let's run, that will give us something to concentrate on instead of being scared, okay?"

Both girls nodded. "Let's go find your parents." Shae let them lead off and fell into a slow jog behind them. She stopped them to shut and secure another door. The more metal between them and those men, the better. Once she was done, they started out at a jog again. *God, would this tunnel ever end?*

CHAPTER 6

"**W**hat the fuck is happening?" The disembodied voice of the rat bastard he was serving under echoed through Ferguson's earpiece. He stood at the corner of the barn and watched as the human mouth, also known as Bell, lifted his head from behind the stall wall where he'd taken cover. Whoever was in that room knew how to scatter a crowd.

He clicked his mic. Fucking shoddy-ass equipment wasn't voice-activated. Once again, he was working with a bargain-basement budget. "Unknown defender inside the barn. Stand by," Ferguson whispered into the comms before Bell could start his mouth. He caught the man's eye and motioned for him to go right; he'd come in from the left. There hadn't been any sounds or any more bullets flying their directions, but that didn't mean there wouldn't be.

He quietly crossed the long hallway that split the barn in half. Peeking into the small pens, he let out a held breath. Empty. Thank God. He hated horses. They scared the shit out of him. Three thousand pounds of stomping hooves. Not his gig. He reached the cover he was aiming for, a solidly constructed wall just before the room from where the bullets were fired. He made sure he was behind the shelter and waited for Bell to move. As the man clanked and lumbered from his position, Ferguson waited for more gunfire. Bell was incompetent, and he was saddled with the fuckwad, so why not use him as bait? That scenario sure as fuck beat getting holes drilled into his ass.

Bell fell against the wall, his unsecured equipment making enough noise to draw the first bullet. And the second, third, and fourth. Idiot.

He motioned for Bell to open the door. The man shook his head and pointed at the holes that had appeared the last time he'd tried. Ferguson leveled his M4A1 at Bell and lifted his eyebrows, the message clear. The man opened the door or he'd get a 5.56-millimeter hole through his chest.

This asshole was more of a liability than an asset, and Ferguson didn't have any qualms of sending him to his maker.

Bell's eyes narrowed, and for a second, it appeared like the stupid son of a bitch was thinking about the option. He reached over and slowly moved the latch of the door. Ferguson fought to stop the roll of his eyes. If the damn man would open the door, Ferguson could go in and take out the shooter. It took forever, but finally, the door swung open slowly. Ferguson kicked the door as soon as he could and it slammed into Bell, which was what he wanted. Bell was an idiot, but he was an idiot with a gun, and he didn't want the fucker to come in and bust a cap in his back. At the same time the door gave Bell a flat nose, Ferguson pivoted and dropped. There was nothing in the room. He lifted and slid along a tall cabinet and lifted the lid, pointing his weapon in. Nothing.

He clicked his mic. "Clear. Shooter is gone."

"What do you mean, gone?" the so-called leader of this bullshit mission asked.

"Gone, as in not here. No way to exit, but not here," Ferguson spoke but kept his back to the wall and an eye on Bell. The asshole sauntered into the room, his M4A1 still on 'Fire,' finger on the trigger. Yep, still a threat and still an idiot.

Bell examined the entire room then opened the bin and shoved his mug in, no lead-in weapon and no regard for his own mortality. "They have to be here," Bell mumbled. It was the first semi-intelligent thing the man had said all day. Ferguson listened to the selector of Bell's weapon flip. A quick glance confirmed the weapon was now on 'Safe.'

With that knowledge, Ferguson stopped to study the room. Everything exactly in place... except there. He moved forward and examined the peg that held nothing. There was a pile of leather on the bin he'd cleared. He narrowed his eyes. *Why?*

Stepping closer to the wall, he examined the floor. Nothing. He reached out and grabbed the peg. It was solid. Frustrated, he slammed it with his fist. The peg slid and dropped. A click of metal sounded. His gun was pointed at the door as it opened. He turned his mic on. "We have rats."

"Rats?" Bell shrieked like a girl and jumped back.

"A tunnel, fuckwad." Ferguson did roll his eyes this time.

"Oh, why didn't you just say that?" The man moved closer and bent down, tugging on the latch. "I think it's locked."

You think? Ferguson moved back and waited. Their fearless leader would arrive soon. He didn't trust them and they sure as fuck didn't trust him. If he didn't need money like yesterday, he wouldn't have hired on for this shit. He'd been a mercenary for ten years and never once had an op in the United States.

Bell placed his M4A1 by the wall and put some muscle into opening the access point. Ferguson pulled out a cigarette and lit it, pulling the tar and nicotine into his lungs with a grateful inhale. He didn't like this mission. If it wasn't for the pay that he was promised, he'd have exited stage left when he was told they were heading to the middle of the country. But he'd ended up owing money to people in New York. He owed big money, and he always paid his debts. So, here he was, in fucking South Dakota, in a ghillie suit that stank of mildew, watching a moron try to open a locked hatch.

"I'm coming into the barn," his fearless leader announced over the comms. Damn, now he couldn't shoot the guy. Ferguson pulled another toke off his cigarette and crossed his feet at the ankles as he leaned against the wall.

"Where is it?" the man's voice thundered through the barn.

"Keep coming. Open door on the right," Ferguson called out. Bell grunted and strained, now using a reverse grip. *Yeah, that's going to do it, bud.*

Hound barreled through the door, stopped, and assessed the situation. "Hidden by a fake wall?"

"Yup. Not an amateur escape system. What did we get into?" Ferguson lobbed the question at the man who was leading them.

Hound narrowed his eyes. "Lob a couple grenades on that bitch, it will open."

"Doubt it," Ferguson said. "That's thick, not an internet purchase reject shit like in Afghanistan. Might damage it, but it won't open it." He'd seen shit like this before. "Big money involved here."

Hound nodded. "Then we'll go big." He keyed his mic. "Bring me a rocket."

Ferguson sucked in another drag off his cigarette. The bastard was mental. "You'll blow this building up, and even then, you might not get that thing open."

Hound turned on him. "Like I care?"

Ferguson shrugged. He didn't give a shit, but he was going to be well out of range. Shrapnel didn't have any discretion, and he had the scars to prove it. He dropped his cigarette and ground it under his boot. "Everything else cleared?"

"No. Too many fucking buildings on this side of the hill. Milton, Kaiser, and Aster are clearing the rest. Casey has destroyed the power grids, comm building, and a couple other buildings, and is working through the rest now."

Ferguson had heard the explosions. Trigger happy assholes. They were supposed to be looking for a specific person, not destroying the damn place. Again, he didn't give a fuck, but it was sloppy. Sloppy work got people like him killed. Well, it was a damn good thing he was a survivor. If shit started to go south, he'd ghillie himself out of range and find a way back to New York. At least he spoke the language this time.

He wandered out of the room that smelled like leather and started out of the barn. That was when he saw the fur huddled in the corner of one of the stalls Bell was supposed to clear. He went in and took a look—a collie, and she was old. *Damn*. He glanced over at the open door. Fuckers could destroy whatever they liked, but he wasn't about to kill a helpless animal.

People were one thing, dogs were another.

He slung his M4A1 over his back and bent down, extending his hand. "Hey, old friend." The dog's tail whapped against the straw. "What say you let me get you out of here before they blow themselves up?" The dog licked his hand. "Good girl."

He grabbed a length of twine and attached it to the old lady's collar. The dog got up and happily followed him out of the barn. He drew a breath and searched for a shack that those fuckers wouldn't think was worthy of blowing up. *There.* About three hundred feet. He followed the path and pushed open the door. The inside had been reno'd. Two pristine stalls were loaded with fluffy hay... or straw... or whatever the fuck people who did this for a living called the shit. He opened one and led the dog into a stall, closing the gate behind him. "You'll be safe in here."

He'd just closed the door behind him when Hound stuck his head out of the big barn. "Anything in there?"

"Nope, just a falling down shed." He stayed by the door. If that bastard targeted the damn thing, he'd have to drop him. The dog rated higher on his list of things he'd like to be around than any of the men he was currently working with.

Over his comms, he heard Bell say, "I'm set up. Are we ready?"

"Stand by. Aster, get yourself clear." Hound jogged over to where Ferguson was and acknowledged he was clear.

"You're not blowing it?" Ferguson smirked.

"Fuck, no." So, his hired supervisor wasn't a total idiot. Good to know. "Ready," Hound said over his comms once he stood next to Ferguson.

Ferguson counted under his breath, and at five, the flash of detonation spread through the boards as they expanded. He and Hound ducked as splinters of wood exploded through the air. When he stood up, half the building was gone. Small flames around the detonation site fed desperately on the shattered wood.

"Where was that fucker when he shot the rocket?" Ferguson searched for Bell.

"Fuck if I know." Hound looked around. "You don't think the asshole was still in the barn, do you?"

Ferguson pulled out his pack of cigarettes.

"Yeah, I do. That was not the sharpest tack in the box."

"Fuck." Hound sighed and nodded at the pack of cigarettes. "Bum one from you?" Ferguson held out the coffin tack and lit it, too. "Guess we should go see if we can get in."

"Why are you here, man?" Ferguson asked as they walked forward.

"Money." The answer never varied for those in his business. They walked forward in silence.

"Stateside is new territory." Ferguson shook his head and pointed to the left. A leg stuck out from under a piece of wall.

"Not to my liking, but when you are between hell and a hard place, you do what you have to do." Hound sighed, reached down, grabbed the piece of smoldering wall, and pushed it up, the cigarette braced between his gritted teeth as he moved the heavy object by himself.

Ferguson sank into a squat. He looked up at Hound. "He's D.R.T."

"What the fuck does that mean?" Hound grunted against the strain of the weight.

"Dead right there. Half his head is gone."

The wall fell without warning. Ferguson stood

and took a look at the mess Bell had made. "The tunnel was over that way."

They walked through the debris. Hound belted out orders to others who checked in as they searched for the hatch. Ferguson found it and used a fractured piece of lumber to move some of the smoldering debris from the top of the hatch.

"Well, what do you know? It's open." Ferguson reached down and angled the piece of wood through the handle and pried it up.

A ladder down to a lot of nothing.

"Get going," Hound said to him.

Ferguson cocked his head and looked up at his fearless fucking leader. "No backup?"

"I'll be on your six."

"Who's going to run this shit show?"

"Fuck if I care. If we find the guy the boss wants, we're rich. Fucking beyond rich."

Ferguson stood up. "You don't say? How come I didn't know about this when I signed on?"

"Meh, need to know basis and all that shit."

"Keeping the money for yourself?"

Hound smiled, but it looked more like a sneer. "Not anymore. Are you in or not?"

"I'm in, but not with you behind me."

Hound's smile morphed into a snarl and his

eyes narrowed. "That's why I like you, Ferguson. You're the only fucker in this outfit that has a brain in his head."

He lifted an eyebrow. "I like my brains in my head, too. After you."

Hound barked out a laugh and slung his M4A1. "Don't mind if I do.

Five minutes later, they stared at a door that looked like it had been borrowed from Fort Knox.

"Well, fuck me," Hound sighed.

"Rather not." Ferguson wasn't particular as to who he fucked, but he'd draw the line at Hound.

"Can't blow it," Hound replied, ignoring Ferguson's comment.

"It could collapse the tunnel," Ferguson agreed.

"But we have a direction. If you can't chase the rats, you look for their nest." Hound turned to exit the tunnel.

"Who the fuck are these people?" He didn't get it. Farmers or ranchers with tunnels for emergency egress? That shit did not compute.

"Heard they were connected to Guardian," Hound's voice floated back to him, the metal tunnel making the words easy to hear.

He stopped dead in his tracks. "Guardian?"

Hound turned on him and stared at him. "Yeah,

why? Don't tell me you're going to go all pansy-ass on me now."

Ferguson cocked his head and lifted an eyebrow. "Not likely." He stared down his new acquaintance until Hound nodded and turned to lead again. Ferguson did what any normal, semi-sane mercenary would do. He flipped the lever on his M4A1 and shot Hound, dropping him in that metal tube. He walked up to the guy and kicked him over. Yep, D.R.T. Ferguson was many things, but stupid wasn't one of them. Guardian would retaliate and wipe out every last one of the people on this piece of property. There was no winning against that organization. He'd seen them system-atically dismantle some of the wickedest sons of bitches on the planet.

He made it up the ladder and out of the tunnel. Three men were about a hundred feet away. "Is everything else clear?" He barked the question as he lifted from the hole.

"This side. The house is empty, and the rest of the outbuildings are empty," one of the men answered.

"Hound said to report over the hill. He's checking out the tunnel." *Or decomposing in it. Potato, potato.*

"What about you? What's down there?" One of the men motioned to the ground.

"I'm waiting for him up here and relaying orders. The only thing down there is access to a bunch of cow food. Hound is rigging it to blow. Now, you want to discuss this further?" He lifted his M4A1, putting the men at the business end of the barrel.

They moved out with that. He watched as they crested the hill. When they did, he put up the hood to his ghillie suit and did a one-eighty. No fucking way he was going to be a part of this op. He pulled out his compass and shot an azimuth. Time to get the fuck out of dodge. He knew which direction more troops were coming in from and he was damned if he was going to run into them. North. He'd head north and then east. Or maybe just north. Canada couldn't be that far away.

CHAPTER 7

"Do we need three tiers?" Sky looked at the pans on the counter. "If we do, I'll need a four-inch round. I have the ten- and six-inch ones. Amanda, where are the smaller pans?" Sky turned with two six-inch pans in her hand.

"Check the cupboard next to the mixing bowls." She moved the flour canister from the counter. "Lyric, will you grab the eggs from the counter?"

"Got them." Lyric spun and grabbed the bowl of eggs she'd gathered and washed this morning. "What flavor are we making it?"

"Taty loves almond." Keelee poured herself a cup of coffee from the pot that was always full.

"Almond? Blech." Jillian gave a shudder and jumped off the counter, bouncing over to the fridge. She grabbed a soda and then bounced back to the counter.

"It can be overpowering if you don't edit what you add, but I know what I'm doing." Sky laughed. "I've eaten some cake that tasted like you were chugging the bottle of artificial flavor. Subtle is the key." She carefully measured a small amount of the extract and poured it into the mixture.

"I think we ate the same cake," Jillian snorted and popped the top on her soda.

"Mom, we need some milk." Keelee broke the eggs into a small glass dish.

"Got it." Amanda headed for the refrigerator and pulled out a gallon jar of full cream milk. She shook the container to mix the cream into the milk before she set it next to Keelee.

"What are you doing drinking soda? I thought you were on a health kick," Joy said and lifted herself onto the counter next to her sister-in-law.

"No, *he's* on a health kick, I will never give up my soda. Drake told me you were sick as a dog this morning." Jillian wagged her eyebrows at Joy.

Amanda caught the look Joy gave Jillian and hid a smile as she gathered the rest of the ingredients they'd need.

"Drake was exaggerating, and it was the last

part of a twenty-four-hour bug." Joy shrugged it off. "I'm not contagious, in case anyone is freaking out."

Keelee snorted. "We're all healthy as horses. No need to freak about a bug. You want coffee?"

Joy shook her head and turned a paler shade of green. "I'm good."

Amanda stopped by the cupboard, pulled out a sleeve of graham crackers, and opened it. She took out one and munched on it before she placed it by Joy and Jillian. "I love these things. They were the only thing I could eat when I was pregnant with Jewell. Settled my stomach right down. Now I love them just because."

"Do you have any cheese crackers?" Keelee asked. "The ones with the cheese baked in? They were my best friend when I was carrying Lizzy. Aunt Betty used to keep them all the time."

"How is Betty enjoying life with her daughter?" Lyric asked from across the kitchen.

"Loving life and the grandbaby. She's a full time nanny and couldn't be happier." Amanda chuckled and pointed to the cupboard where she kept the fish-shaped goodies. "Cheesy goodness is still in that cupboard." Keelee dropped the eggshells in the compost bucket before she skittered over and grabbed a bag of the crackers.

Sky snorted. "For me, it was rice cereal treats. It was all I could stomach. It didn't matter if I was offered a steak dinner. If I didn't have a rice cereal treat, my stomach revolted."

Jillian handed a cracker to Joy and took one for herself. "Oh! We decided to build our house in the little valley."

Keelee spun. "Excellent! When will you start taking in kids?"

Amanda watched the relief spread across Joy's expression as the women switched topics. She brewed a cup of peppermint tea and walked to the counter where Joy was listening to the conversation. Jillian, being the animated person she was, jumped off the counter and paced around the kitchen as the other women made the cake batter. Amanda slid the cup near Joy. "Helps with the upset stomach."

Joy narrowed her eyes. "You know." Her gaze darted around the kitchen, making sure no one else was listening.

"I suspected. Never let your stomach get too empty." Amanda patted the woman's hand. "This will pass."

"Thank God," Joy sighed and nibbled on the cracker.

"Where's Dixon, and why aren't you in bed?" She asked the first part out loud and whispered the second half. She'd suffered from morning sickness with Justin and Jared. She was in bed most days of her first trimester. Thank God Chance was such a good husband and daddy.

"Dixon is with Drake," Joy answered in a conversational tone and then whispered, "I couldn't stand to be in bed any longer."

Jillian chirped from across the room. "They were going to go over to harass Isaac until the transport plane comes in."

Lyric snorted. "Not very smart."

"Oh, they took food," Jillian laughed. "Gummy bears and sour worms."

"Isaac loves sweets. He'll endure anything for candy. Maybe they can team up on Billy. That man needs to be annoyed."

As the women talked, Joy swallowed hard and reached for the tea. Amanda chuckled under her breath.

"No, I doubled up my fist and slugged him across the chin. Set him on his butt, too." Lyric mimicked the action, and the women broke into laughter.

"Where are Kadey and Lizzy?" Amanda asked as she took the mixing bowls that were now empty to the sink.

"Riding with Shae," Keelee spoke as she put the cakes into the oven.

"I saw them coming into the barn before I walked up here," Joy said, nibbling on her graham cracker.

"What kind of icing are we doing, Sky?" Lyric asked as she grabbed a dishcloth and dried the bowls Amanda was washing.

Sky looked up, panicked. "Italian meringue buttercream. It is the easiest to pipe. Has anyone checked on Mike and Taty's schedules to make sure they won't be coming over?"

"Taty has a class with Isaac at two. It's late because she worked last night," Lyric said as she set another dry bowl onto the counter.

Jillian picked it up and returned it to the cabinet Amanda had taken it from. "The plane is coming in, so Mike will be busy when it gets here."

"Cool. Until then, he's meeting with Kaeden, so we can cool, crumb coat, stack the cakes, and ice them tomorrow?" Sky asked no one in particular.

"Sounds like a plan," Amanda agreed. "We can put the cake in the second refrigerator." She nodded to the pantry off the kitchen. "I've cleared room."

Everyone stopped talking as the long, steady wail of the tornado alarm sounded. "What the hell?" Keelee slapped her hands together, ridding them of sugar, and headed toward the back door.

"Don't go out there." Joy hopped off the counter and grabbed Keelee before she reached the door.

"Why not?" Sky froze, her hand, lifted to measure sugar, visibly shaking.

"It's not right," Amanda spoke. "Something's wrong."

Jillian came to her and stood right beside her. "What do you mean?"

Just then, a long warbling tone replaced the steady stream. "Everyone needs to get into the tunnel." Joy snapped the command. She spun and clutched her stomach. "Fuck, not now."

"The girls!" Keelee spun and broke the hold Joy had on her. Amanda grabbed her daughter-in-law. "They're with Shae. We all know she'll take care of them. When that alarm sounds, we need to take cover. She'll take care of them and get them out of sight."

"There are no tunnels at the damn barn!" Keelee shook her arm.

"Yes, there are. There are access points throughout the ranch. Shae knows it, too."

Amanda felt Keelee turn even as she twisted to ask Joy, "There are?"

"Yeah. One in the barn." An explosion snapped everyone's head toward the Guardian side of the complex. "Shit. I'm not getting into the logistics of it right now. The one thing all of you can do to help is to get into the tunnel and follow it to the end. I can't protect you otherwise." Joy ran to the sink and heaved.

"Protect us?" Jillian asked.

"I don't have time to explain." Amanda swept her gaze across them all. "Keelee, trust Shae to take care of the girls, but unless everyone gets into that tunnel, those girls might not have moms—"

Another explosion rocked the Annex side of the ranch.

Lyric pointed out the windows. "Are those men? With guns?"

Joy moved across the room faster than Amanda thought possible. "Ghillie suits. They're hunting us. Everyone, go now."

Amanda grabbed Keelee's arm and Sky's hand.

"Trust Shae, she'll protect them." Terrified for her granddaughters, her family, and Frank, she did the only thing she could. Follow the plan. "Come on." She went behind the bar and lifted the fake floor, opening a door that led to steps. "Everyone down, inside. The lights will turn on automatically." She helped Jillian down, then Lyric. "Keelee, Sky, you have to get in." She pleaded with them.

The sound of a round being chambered in a rifle swung everyone's attention back around.

Joy turned and faced the kitchen but spoke to them in a low, measured, deadly tone, "If you don't get the fuck in the tunnel, you'll be responsible for all of our deaths, and I, for one, want to meet the kid I just found out I'm having, just like you want to see your kids again. Now, fucking move your asses!"

Amanda waited for them to pass. "Joy, come on."

The woman walked backward. Another explosion rocked the Guardian side of the complex. "Fuck, who is this fucking stupid?" Joy spun and trotted to the hatch. "Go." She motioned for Amanda to go down the stairs and stepped down into the system, too. "Will the floor go back over the door?"

"Yes, it is on a hydraulic slide." Amanda reached up to hit the release button on the door. "I couldn't lift the door, so Frank had the slides put in. Assists me with opening and closing. The floor goes back into place as soon as the door secures." They both walked down two steps until the door sealed overhead. Amanda flipped the switch and prayed the slide worked.

Joy followed her down the stairs, the rifle in her hand like it was an extension of her arm. She walked beside Amanda, acting as if there was nothing to see here and all things were as they should be.

"You damn near outed yourself up there," Amanda whispered to her daughter-in-law.

Joy grunted. "If it would have saved those two mommas from being killed or worse, I would have read them my resumé."

"Congratulations, by the way. You'll be a fantastic mom." Amanda smiled softly.

"Yeah, well, let's live through the night before we start any prognostication efforts." Joy glanced behind her. "Where does this come out?"

"The Pit."

"Any other tunnels run into it?" They walked

through a door, and Joy handed Amanda the rifle as she shut and secured it.

"Why did you close it? What if someone else is trying to get away?"

"We were the only ones at the house. Anyone else coming would be the enemy." Joy spun the latch and took the rifle from her. "Are there?" Joy looked at her.

Amanda blinked. "Are there what?"

"Any other tunnels that join with this one," Joy spoke slowly and stared at her like she was going senile.

"Yes, further up. I never asked where they came from, but I assumed from this side of the ranch." She frowned. "Which should have led me to ask where the access points were. Why didn't Frank tell me?"

"How often are you alone at the barn? At our house? Shae and John's? If he thought for a second you needed to know, he would have told you. We were told because it is our responsibility to make sure everyone here makes it to safety. Shae knows. She's former Mossad, she's damn good. The girls will be all right," Joy spoke but looked over her shoulder. She turned to see the rest of the women, who'd backtracked to find them.

"I'm in the barn all the time." Keelee's brow furrowed.

"Never alone." Joy pointed down the tunnel. "Let's go. They'll be wanting to do a headcount and send people out for those who haven't shown up yet."

"What do you do for Guardian?" Keelee asked, looking at Joy.

"What they tell me. Can we walk? I'm going to puke, and I really would prefer to do it in private."

"When did you find out you were pregnant?" Lyric asked as they all started to walk again.

"This morning," Amanda supplied for her. Even in the artificial lighting, Joy looked slightly green around the gills.

"Congratulations." The word was murmured by each of the women.

Joy grunted. "Hell of a way to celebrate."

They moved through another door, and Joy handed Keelee the rifle this time. Joy closed and secured the door, moving to take the weapon again.

Keelee shook her head. "You don't look so hot. I'm a dead shot. I'll hang on to this."

Amanda lifted an eyebrow when Joy gave up

the weapon. The woman probably felt like death warmed over.

They moved forward. No conversation, little sound. When they reached a Y intersection, Amanda stopped and looked down the tunnel.

"Shh." Joy's prompt froze everyone. She grabbed the rifle out of Keelee's hand and dropped to her knee, the barrel pointed down the new tunnel. "Get back." Amanda retreated immediately and drew Jillian and Sky back with her. Keelee and Lyric hustled back, too.

Amanda could see Joy from where she was standing. The long drape of her black hair hung to the side, shielding her face from her view but not the exacting way she held the rifle, ready to kill to protect them.

"Oh, thank fuck," Joy spoke and dropped the weapon seconds before she landed on her hands and knees, retching up the remnants of the graham crackers she'd eaten earlier. Keelee looked around the corner and vaulted over Joy. "Lizzy!"

"Momma!"

Sky jumped over Joy and was on her knees, hugging Kadey.

Shae moved past the girls to where they all huddled around Joy. Jillian was holding her long hair back from the mess. Shae stopped in front of where Joy was swaying on her hands and knees and crouched down. "Damn, girl. Hangover much?"

Joy looked up at Shae and whispered, "Fuck you."

Shae gave her a measured look. "You okay?"

"Never better," Joy nodded.

"Liar." Shae called her on her obvious issue and holstered her pistol before she reached down for the rifle. "I've got our six unless you need me to carry you."

Joy sat back on her heels, letting Shae take the rifle. "Try it and see where that gets you."

Shae looked around until her eyes landed on Amanda. "How much further?"

A sense of helplessness washed over Amanda. "I don't know for sure. I've only been down here once and that was years ago. I'm sorry."

The sound of a muffled explosion from one of the tunnels snapped everyone's head back the way they'd each come. It was the first time an explosion had originated from the ranch. "It's okay. Doesn't matter how far. Let's go." Joy powered to her feet. "Watch your step."

Amanda walked beside her daughter-in-law

and said a prayer of thanks for Lizzy and Kadey's safety. She also sent up a prayer for Frank and John. They'd have heard the explosions, wouldn't they? They'd know not to charge back into danger.

God, she hoped so.

CHAPTER 8

Adam Cassidy strolled down the hall with a smile on his face. Dixon was going to be over the moon when he found out he was going to be a dad. The test Adam had in his hand proved his suspicions were correct: Joy was rocking a positive blood test. He stopped in the hall and sighed, looking around his little hospital. Right now, they were minimally staffed. The surge of operations overseas had slowed, and with fresh teams to relieve those in the theater of operations, his business had slowed to a trickle, which was fine with him. They had three people here to rehab and none on critical care protocols.

"Hey, Doc."

One of his patients, Liam, stood in his doorway as Adam passed.

"Out for a walk?" Adam extended his hand.

The man transferred his cane and shook his hand. "Yep. Have to work up an appetite." Liam laughed and patted his flat stomach. "I'm going to be the size of a Mack truck by the time you spring me from this place."

"You have another week to suffer through PT and our calorie-laden offerings." Liam's leg wound had become infected while overseas. The damage to the muscles of his calf was extensive, but the man had a positive attitude with a family and a desk job waiting for him. He was motivated to get the rehab done and be gone.

"I'll do it standing on my head," Liam laughed and headed down the long hallway.

"Lord, no. On your feet, please." Adam chuckled at the wave Liam gave him.

He stepped into the next room. "Hey Andie, how are you today?"

The woman glanced up at him. "Itchy. Really freaking itchy."

"Casts do that. No coat hangers, that will tear up your leg." Adam picked up the wire hanger from the hospital bed.

"But Doc," she pleaded while making scratching movements with her fingers.

"I've got you." He held up a finger and ducked out of the room. Heading to the locked medication room, he searched the cabinets until he found what he was looking for. He held up a can as he entered her room. "This will fix you up." The anti-itch cast spray was instant relief. He showed her how to insert the small straw into the spray top and insert that into the cast. The alcohol relieved the itch, and a drying agent controlled the moisture to help eliminate itching.

She followed his instructions and flopped back on her bed. "Oh, I think I love you."

Adam belted out a laugh. "If I had a nickel for every time someone said that when I've produced this remedy..."

"You'd have a million dollars?" Andie quipped.

"No, probably a quarter." Adam shrugged. "How's the head?" She'd had a wicked concussion, and they'd been following protocols, but concussions were something he watched carefully.

"No headache today. Of course, that could be because I was going crazy with itching." She shrugged.

"Remember what happened to you?" He lifted a penlight and examined her eyes.

"Kind of. I remember being thrown backward into that building. I don't remember going on that mission with the team that day. Can't remember anything after chow the night before." She closed her eyes. "Doc Wheeler said it may never come back, which sucks. You know?"

"Far better than you can imagine." He pointed to his eye. "Lost this due to a head injury. I went through hell trying to get back to normal, but you get there."

Andie nodded. "I'm lucky. I mean, Ranger didn't make it. Which is what I think bothers me the most. I just wonder if there was something I could have done to help him. I'm the medic." She shrugged her shoulders and lowered her eyes.

"I've read the reports your skipper and the rest of the team put together, Andie. There was nothing you could have done. He was taken out by a sniper on the other side of the road. Even if you weren't knocked unconscious, you couldn't have helped." Adam leaned against the wall. Spending time with his patients was what he loved about his little hospital.

"Yeah, that's what Doc Wheeler said, too, but

there is something here that keeps telling me there was something more." She held her hand over her heart. "I just know there was." She looked up at him.

"Trust your gut. Go after the answers, but don't let it drive you crazy. You'll remember or you won't, but you *can* get answers. Firsthand accounting of the events from your team, the medics that treated you and Ranger." He got it. He'd let depression whip his ass for far too long before he'd decided to fight for a life.

"Yeah. Yeah, I guess you're right." Andie laid back against the pillow and adjusted the hoodie she was wearing. "How long until I go home?"

"You got someone waiting for you?" Adam knew she didn't. She lived alone. No family.

"No, but I have a bed that folds you into it and a kitchen where I can cook what I want when I want it." Andie snorted. "Something that won't put a thousand pounds on my hips. Speaking of which, I get to learn new exercises today. Meagan is going to show me how to keep in shape even with a bum leg. She's a good PT."

"She is. We're lucky to have her. Don't overdo it, or you'll have to stay longer." Adam opened the laptop on his station and plugged in his notes.

"I'll be good," Andie chuckled. "I need the sounds of traffic. All the silence around here—"

Adam stopped typing as the eerie monotone sound of the tornado warning siren pierced the peacefulness of the Annex. "What the hell?" He strode to the window and stared out. Not a cloud anywhere.

"Doc, my inner oh-shit meter just pegged." Andie stood up, propping her crutches under her arms.

"Mine, too. Time to take a walk." Adam motioned for her to follow him. He pointed down to the end of the hall. "Meet me there and take Liam back with you."

Andie nodded, grabbed that damn spray can, and swung down the hallway, pegging the floor in a smooth, steady fashion. Adam ducked into the next room as his nurse on duty jogged down the hall.

"What's going on?" Caroline, his nurse, asked in a panicked tone.

"Don't know. Get next door to the rehab center and make sure everyone takes cover. I'll move everyone here."

"Cover as in cover, cover?" Caroline's voice rose dramatically.

"Yes. Get them underground. Everyone." Adam turned to his last patient. "Blocker, we have to move, and now."

The man nodded. Adam grabbed the IV and attached it to the wheelchair that was in Blocker's room. Then, he carefully helped the man out of the bed. He settled him into the chair when the siren changed tone. "Fuck," Blocker grunted. "War."

"Yeah." Adam glanced out the window in the direction of his house. Fuck about summed it up. Keelee knew what to do. She'd get Lizzy into the tunnel. *Son of a bitch, what was happening?*

He wheeled Blocker out and down to the end of the hall. "Liam, give Blocker your cane and use his wheelchair to push him."

Liam looked at him as if he'd lost his mind. "Where the hell am I pushing him to, Doc?"

Adam moved past his patients and opened the storage closet.

"We all can't fit in there, Doc," Andie said, looking around him.

"Not here." He opened the back of the closet and called the elevator.

"Well, shit. You got tricks up your sleeve, Doc."

"Guardian does." The door opened to the elevator. "All of you, get in. When you get to the bottom, get everyone out and stand by. I've got to get some meds and I'll be down." Blocker's IV wasn't going to last and he needed IV antibiotics, not the stuff Adam had stored in the Pit in case of emergencies.

An explosion rocketed everyone into motion. Adam sprinted to the medicine room and grabbed a cart. "Fucking hell." He loaded as much as he could gather into the silver cart and then exited. He stopped and lifted his boot, knocking the keypad off the wall. If the fuckers wanted drugs, they'd have to work for them. The second explosion blew out the clinic's windows. Adam ducked but kept his ass moving. He'd shut himself in the closet when the third explosion hit. Jamming his finger against the call button for the elevator, he begged the piece of metal to hurry. "Come on, you son of a bitch." Okay, so he wasn't begging, more like commanding. Finally, the door slid open. "What the fuck?"

"Doc, get your ass in here." Dixon grabbed him as Drake grabbed the medical cart.

Adam hit the button. "Why in the hell did you come up here?"

"To get you." The 'duh' wasn't said, but the tone was implied from Dixon's attitude.

"Where are Jillian and Joy?"

"The main house." Dixon and Drake said at the same time, which was no longer weird but almost comforting.

"Joy will get the women to safety."

"Not a wimp in the lot. They'll make it," Drake agreed.

Dixon shook his head. "I should have made her stay at home."

"She'd have to get here from there. This way, she's with the women." Drake tried to comfort his brother.

"She's sick as a dog," Dixon sighed as the elevator opened into the Pit. They spilled out, and Adam found his patients.

His nurse jogged in from the other direction. "They're down. What's happening?"

Chief and Anubis walked into the main area. Taty, Asp, and Billy followed them into the main room. "Sitrep. Listen up."

Anubis ran down what he knew, which wasn't much. "Which means we follow emergency procedures to the letter."

"Sunrise protocol," Dixon and Drake stated at the same time.

Anubis nodded. "Exactly. Right now, we need to get our people accounted for. Asp, you and I will work with Taty and Billy to account for Annex personnel."

"Dixon, Drake, and I will head to the ranch side and get our people," Chief said as he marched past. Double D fell in behind the man.

"Take weapons," Anubis called after them.

"On it," Mike replied but didn't break stride.

"Damn straight," Adam echoed. Fuck, he wanted to go with his team, but he had patients who needed him. Well, *a* patient, but Blocker was enough to keep him rooted and not following the rest of Alpha Team as they headed out.

"Adam? I'm sure everyone is okay." Caroline stood beside him.

"They have to be. But, until we find out for sure, we need to set up Blocker in a room. Moving him wasn't ideal. We'll need to monitor him closely. I have what I could gather, but we may have to get inventive with his care."

"Then we get inventive." Caroline drew a breath and straightened her shoulders. "Not the first time I've had to work under adverse conditions. I just never dreamed it would happen here."

Adam walked with her to where her patients were waiting. "No one did." He glanced up at the massive underground complex they were walking through. Strike that. Someone had prepared for the worst-case scenario.

"Found him. Bastard's dead. Shot in the back of the head. Fucking Ferguson had to have taken him out." Kaiser stepped up and off the ladder leading down into the hole as he spoke. Milton swore under his breath. Casey had sent them to get Hound after Ferguson had told them to go away. An absolute clusterfuck of an operation, now compounded by the fact that their leader was dead.

"Or someone came back down that tunnel, shot Hound, and took Ferguson," Aster, a man he'd worked with before, spoke as he stared down the hole.

"Shit. This mission has been a question mark since the inception." They had a sprawling ranch and complex with absolutely no one to be found. Hell, there was a fucking cake baking in the oven at the main house, but not a person anywhere. A ghost town.

Kaiser cinched up his ghillie suit pants. "Casey is the next in command."

"Damn." Milton spat the word out. Casey was

an insane motherfucker who'd rather level this place than do what he was told. They'd been told to find a man. A single man, not blow the place to hell. What if that son of a bitch killed the guy? If the fucker lost them their payday, he'd do for Casey what had been done for Hound. The asshole. He leveled his stare on Kaiser before he asked, "Does that tunnel lead anywhere?"

"Yep. To a sealed steel door. Ain't no way to get through unless you blow it."

"Blow up an underground tunnel?" Milton looked at the man.

"I'm not recommending it, just the only way to get through. That, or maybe a torch. A big one."

"What direction was it heading?" A tunnel system would explain why there wasn't anyone in any of the buildings.

Milton recalled the briefing Hound had before they got on the plane. Intel said there should be about thirty people, maybe more. That bastard Casey had to be told to leave the women alone if there were any. The fucker was told point-blank by Hound in front of everyone. All the sick mother did was lift his eyebrows. From what Hound said during the brief, the money behind the operation wanted the kill. Obviously, it was personal. Well, good luck. Milton stared down the hole. Damn it. The people were probably holed up behind that door down there. That was his bet.

A tunnel system. Holy hell, a system that big… well, that would be a massive undertaking. Lots of money. He glanced back at the log cabin mansion. Not impossible based on what he was seeing but fucking improbable. Next to no chance, which is what he was going to report to Casey.

"Yo, man, did you hear me? I said that way." Kaiser pointed toward the flight line, not toward the buildings Casey had destroyed or cleared on the other side of the hill that separated the two entities. Milton blinked, trying to remember what he'd asked. Ah, yes. Direction.

Milton lifted his mic and lamented the ancient comms they'd been provided. Again. "Casey, Hound is dead. We have a tunnel. Believe the occupants may be holed up behind the door underground. We need a torch."

There was a long pause before Casey's voice came back to him. "Go through the garages and outbuildings over there. Should be something you can use. I'm calling the site secure. Outposts report nothing. We have two teams on the exterior cordon. Work the fucking door."

"Are you calling the money?"

"Don't have the number. Hound didn't trust me." An evil laugh floated over the comms. Milton lifted his eyes and watched his men shake their heads. Yeah, nobody trusted Casey. Their new leader continued, "Figure they'll contact us when they get tired of waiting. Until then, we kill anything that sticks its head out of their fucking holes."

"He wants them alive," Milton reminded his superior.

"I never heard him say that. Did you? Matter of fact, no one said shit to me, so I'm doing this like I would any operation. Secure the objective. We did, this land is ours. If the fuckers don't like it, they should have taken a more hands-on role with this part of the operation. Casey out."

Milton rubbed the back of his neck. "The objective was one man. Not to claim this property. I heard Hound tell Casey that." He nodded to Kaiser. "Go frisk Hound. See if he has a cell on him."

Kiser slithered down into the hole without a second's hesitation. Aster glanced at him. "You calling the money?"

"If there's a phone? Hell, yeah. Casey got one

thing right, though. Money should have been hands-on. This operation feels off. Way off."

Aster nodded and glanced out toward the rolling hills. "Maybe Ferguson did cap Hound and walk out."

Milton rolled his shoulders. "That's probably what we should do."

Aster turned his gaze back to him. "Can't. Need the money."

"So do I, my man. So do I. Morals don't feed you or pay the bills," Milton agreed.

"I got a feeling about this one, Milt." Aster kicked the ground. "We probably ain't making it out."

Milton narrowed his eyes at his compatriot. "There is no one here. An empty plot of land with people so scared they are hiding underground. This is a cakewalk." Except for Hound and the blabbermouth they'd found under the smoldering barnwood wall. Hell, he couldn't even remember the guy's name. Burn or Bull or something like that. At least he was finally quiet.

Aster shrugged. "Whatever."

Milton heard Kaiser in the hole. "Got one."

He grabbed it from Kaiser's hand as soon as the man surfaced. There was only one number listed.

He pushed the button and waited for the damn thing to connect. He wasn't going to let Casey ruin his payday, and besides, it would be night before long. Rats had a way of surfacing at night. He wanted to know what his orders were from the money's mouth.

He looked at Aster. "Take Kaiser and find a torch."

The men turned to leave as the phone was answered.

CHAPTER 9

F rank Marshall stared at the vista. "Damn. Nothing like it."

John Smith sighed beside him. "Have I thanked you recently for taking me in?"

Frank grunted. "No need to thank me. You've worked your ass off." John had shown up not knowing the difference between a cow's nose and its tail, but the man learned damn fast. Frank had put him through a crash course so he could bluff his way through a casual conversation and then the man put his head down and learned how to be a damn fine rancher.

"Yes, but not many would have given me the protection and the chance to make a life for myself." John leaned forward and rubbed the neck of his mount. "And because you did, I met Shae. Lots to be thankful for."

Frank reached into his shirt pocket and withdrew two pieces of saltwater taffy. He handed one to John and unrolled the other from its wax paper square. He popped the candy into his mouth and gazed up at the sky. "Best be heading back if we want to be home by suppertime." They'd traveled out farther than he'd set out to go, but they'd inspected all but the farthest pastures. The young ones could take the four-wheelers out and check those.

"The fenceposts here need to be replaced." John pointed to the dry rot at the ground. The barbed wire was still tight, but several of the posts had snapped at the base. Frank had counted fourteen in this pasture that were broken and at least twenty that were close. "Thirty-seven posts." John pulled his phone out and jotted the information down.

"Why do you carry that out here? No reception." Frank turned his mount, and they started the long ride back to the ranch.

"For things like this. I keep records of what pasture needs what, when it was last inspected and by whom, the condition of the grass, how many head can graze it for how long."

Frank grunted. He kept records like that, too, but in his head. Times changed. A cowboy's management methods changed, but tending to cows, well, that never really changed. Keep them fed and healthy. Cows weren't just his business; they were his legacy to his family. Since John had come on board and Keelee had hitched up with Adam, he'd slowly and carefully grown his herd and bought up more land. Enough so, when the day came that he wasn't on this earth any longer, Keelee, Tori, Dixon, Drake, and Mike would have equal shares of one of the wealthiest ranches in the country.

"Thought any more about bringing in a herd of bison? The market is up for them."

Frank drew a breath. "Not for me. I know cows. Bison have their own issues."

"Thank God," John chuckled. "I was just starting to feel comfortable with what I'm doing. Keelee wanted to look into other income streams."

"She's good with looking forward." His daughter always had the ranch's best interest at heart even though he had to rein her in every now and again. Bison. At least it wasn't ostriches.

They made their way back by a different route, checking fences and making minor repairs as they rode. Frank looked at the sky and then at his watch. "Damn near five. We have at least an hour ride to make it back."

John grunted as he stretched a length of barbed wire. Frank waited until it was taut before he drove a U-nail into the wooden post. John released the wire and stood up, rolling his shoulders. "I'm game for a more direct route. My stomach thinks my throat has been slit."

Frank chuckled and handed over a piece of taffy.

"Thanks." John unwrapped it and popped it into his mouth. "I never understood your fascination with this stuff until I started riding out with you. Keeps you going."

Frank grunted. He had a sweet tooth, that was the truth of the matter. This damn candy was his one vice. He mounted and waited for John to stow the equipment in his saddlebags. Once his ranch foreman was up, they stopped meandering and headed home.

Frank's phone vibrated about fifteen minutes later. He grabbed it. *A. Hollister* was calling him. Strange. "Marshall."

"Frank, I've been calling for hours, where the fuck you been?"

"Out riding fence. Why?"

"A plane, a Guardian plane, went down on my land. I have Zeke here working on the pilots."

"Went down?"

"According to the pilot, it was shot down. Surface-to-air missile."

"When?"

"About three. Can you find out what the fuck is going on?"

"I'll call you back."

John shot him a look. "What's going on?"

"Our transport plane was shot down on Hollister's land."

"What?"

John pulled out his phone while Frank dialed Amanda. The phone rang off the hook. He looked at John, and the man shook his head. "Call the Annex," Frank barked, and he dialed the switchboard for Guardian. The line blared a long squeal. Damn it. He looked at John.

"No answer."

"Let's go." Frank leaned forward. "Yah!" He spurred his mount, and it took off. Frank leaned low over the saddle. His gut clenched as his mind worked overtime.

"Frank!" John was beside him, their horses racing toward home. "We could be heading into trouble."

He knew it and hated it, but getting closer was the priority right now. They couldn't help anyone from out here.

Chief held up his hand. Both Drake and Dixon froze. Letting Chief lead them through the labyrinth of tunnels was fucking hard. Joy and Jillian were both at the big house. Drake was sick with worry, and Dixon was bordering on insane.

"She's pregnant," Dixon breathed in a whisper. Both he and Chief snapped their attention to his brother. "She's really sick. I didn't want her to go to the big house, but you know how she is. I don't know if she could protect them in her condition."

Chief nodded, and Drake placed a hand on Dixon's shoulder. "Let's go get them."

"Whatever it takes," Chief murmured.

"As long as it takes," both Drake and Dixon finished.

"The second tunnel from the right," Drake reminded Chief of the system that took them to the main house and the barn beyond.

Chief nodded, and as one, they ghosted around the corner of the underground passage. Drake slipped back into a life he hadn't lived in a long time. He carried his M4A1 as an extension of his body and moved in synchrony with his team. The caution they used moving through the tunnels was essential. They could have been compromised. Anubis would work on setting up a sentry at the place where the tunnels converged, but that would be a last-stand situation. The protocol was to shut the doors as you passed through them and lock each. The doors were of tempered steel, and nothing less than an acetylene torch and three hours of steady work would get through them.

Chief's hand went up again. **Listen**. Chief used American Sign Language to communicate.

Drake stopped breathing and listened. Footsteps. From the sound of the footfalls, there were numerous people. Chief made eye contact with him and nodded to the other side of the Y where the tunnels would join. He crossed the tunnel access point soundlessly and assumed a kneeling position, his M4A1 propped on his knee and in position to take out as many as he could. Carefully, he flicked his selector switch to 'Auto.' The two clicks echoed. The metal-encased tunnel acted like a sound amplifier, and those clicks sounded like cymbals clanging. The footsteps halted. Dixon leaned out from behind Chief and mirrored his position. Chief leaned forward, bracing his hand in a Y at the corner of the wall. If some motherfucker had found their way down into the tunnels, they would be dead.

The sounds of footfalls had stilled. Drake strained to hear anything. A slight scuff was his only warning before Shae and Joy rounded the corner, guns drawn and ready to blow shit to Hell and back.

"Stand down!"

"Don't shoot!"

Both he and Shae had called out at the same time.

Dixon jumped from his position and sprinted to his wife. The woman literally swooned, à la Scarlett O'Hara, as he reached her. Dixon caught her and lifted her into his arms.

"I'm okay." Joy's harsh rasp revealed that lie for what it was.

"Go. Get her to Doc," Drake said, and Mike

nodded. Dixon's eyes slid over to Amanda as she emerged from the tunnel. She nodded and made a shooing sign with her hands. Dixon spun and took off down the tunnel.

"Who else is with you, Mom?" Drake lifted from his stance slowly. He prayed that--

"Drake!" At Jillian's shout, he launched. He grabbed her and pulled her into him. He buried his face in her hair and whispered stupid words that meant nothing except that he loved her. She started to cry, and that's when the rest of the women came forward. He rocked his wife back and forth and ticked off each of the women and girls as they came into view. "Thank God." He kept Jillian against him as he scanned the crowd. "Where are Frank and John? The hands?"

"The hands left first thing this morning, fixing water tanks, and they'll be gone for at least two days. John and Frank rode out, checking fence to the northeast. They're out of cell reception and might not have heard the siren or explosions." Shae ran her hand through her hair. "I don't know how to reach them."

"They are both cautious and careful men." Chief hugged Amanda but spoke to Shae. Everyone knew not to touch Shae; she still had issues from her captivity, but Chief gave her what comfort he could.

"I know," she acknowledged. "It doesn't stop the worry, though."

"They'll make it back. There are ways to get here without being seen. Both John and Frank know them."

Amanda nodded and stepped back from Chief's hug. She drew a breath and squared her shoulders. "What's happening? What are we doing, and what do you need from us?"

And that was why everyone loved Amanda. She wasn't a wilting flower. Hell, none of the women were. Except Joy, which was cause for major concern. That woman was hard as nails and vicious. She'd gutted out taking point with Shae while sicker than a dog.

"We can discuss that back at the Pit." Drake looked over at Keelee. "Adam wanted to come, but he had to relocate his patients. One wasn't handling the evacuation well."

The tenseness of the woman's features melted, and she hugged her daughter to her.

"Isaac and Kaeden?" Sky asked while holding both Lyric and Kadey's hands.

"Both safe and working to figure out what is happening. We'll take you to them."

"Mom, what about the animals?" Lizzy asked.

"Baby, we'll take care of them as soon as we can, but for now, it's a matter of making sure *we're* safe." Keelee glanced over at him, and he nodded.

Survival.

That was where they were now. But soon… soon, they'd turn the tide and go on the offensive. At sunrise. He and Dixon had designed the Pit, the tunnels, and the ranch's defensive measures. Come sunrise, the bastards that had dared to take them on would wish they'd never been born.

CHAPTER 10

Frank's horse faltered, and even though he didn't want to, he eased up. That's what saved his life: the snap of the bullet blew his cowboy hat off his head.

"Shooter!" He screamed the word and kicked his left leg out of the stirrup, grabbed the saddle horn, and moved from the saddle, letting his right leg and hand keep him from falling off his mount. He pulled his rifle from its boot and extended it in front of the horse's chest, firing back in the direction he thought the bullet had come from.

John rode low over the saddle, his horse a bit smaller than Frank's, giving him some cover. "The culvert!"

He hadn't wanted to use the culvert. He'd

wanted to get to the ranch, but getting there alive was the key. John's horse turned, forcing his mount to veer. He couldn't hear shit over the pounding of their horses' hooves. If someone shot back, he didn't know. John jolted in his saddle and dropped to the side of his mount. "Leg!"

Fuck. They had to be surrounded. Frank could see the small valley the culvert ran through. "We get to the washout, drop down, and unsaddle and unbridle. We'll turn them loose." The horses would be safe if they were off, and those bastards wouldn't be able to follow them through the culvert's access point.

The ground dropped, and Frank stopped his mount at the bottom, damn near tumbling onto the hard South Dakota soil. He uncinched and dropped his horse's bridle, grabbed up his rifle, and looked back at his foreman. John was slower. As the man unsaddled, Frank grabbed his rifle and unbridled his horse. The tack was left on the ground and the horses pranced away, confused. He grabbed John and snugged up under his foreman's arm, helping him run. The man was game, and they moved. He pushed John into the culvert, their rifles held out of the standing water in the damn thing. It was a death trap if those shooters moved in before they got into the access point, but it was their only chance.

John's labored breathing mixed with his as they crawled through the muck, heading to the center of the cement tube. Once there, Frank grabbed the lever and put all his weight into it. The thing squealed like a stuck pig, but it moved. As soon as it was open, he shoved John through, ignoring the man's instructions for him to go first, and then poked through both weapons. After he was in, Frank took one more look to where his horse had stopped. The animal's ears were up, and he was tracking something, which meant whoever was shooting at them was closing in. *Fuck.* What the hell was happening? He dipped into the small accessway and scurried through, dropping over the ledge. John pulled the door shut and locked it from the inside. Frank straightened and winced. He was too fucking old to be running from fucking gunmen.

John slithered down the wall and sat hard on his ass. Frank moved over and got a good look at what was going on with him: a bullet had burned a furrow on the outside of his leg. It was bleeding a good amount, his jeans dark blue from where the shit had soaked through the denim. Frank grabbed his bandana from his pocket. It wasn't going to fit around the man's leg. "Give me your bandana." John squirmed and pulled it from his back pocket. Frank tied the two together and then tied the bandage over his leg. "You'll live," Frank declared. "Let's get going."

John nodded and Frank helped him stand. "What the fuck is going on?" John muttered.

"Going to find out. Let's go." Frank set a bruising pace, but John kept up. They both had loved ones that were in danger. Stopping or taking their time wasn't in either of their characters.

Jeremiah grabbed his phone. "Wheeler."

"Open your clinic. We have operatives converging. It will be a long night for you." Joseph's voice scratched against his nerves. He'd never learned to like the man.

"I'm at the clinic. I couldn't stay at home. It's closer to the ranch here." He stared out of his building to the nearly deserted street that defined Hollister.

"Reaper will be there within minutes. I told him to wait for you."

"Are we driving out?"

Joseph answered, "No. We are waiting for reinforcements and sunrise."

"What in God's green Earth would possess you to wait? We could help."

"You will get dead. Period. This is an operation that will require more than just us. We have two teams, a lot of borrowed SEALs, Reaper, and me inbound. Ember will stay with you until we know the extent of injuries or deaths."

Jeremiah closed his eyes. "Tell me they had a plan in place in case something like this happened."

"We do, which is why we are going to be in position at sunrise. Stock up on coffee, Doc. We'll need it."

"When will you be here?"

"Getting on a plane to Rapid City now," Joseph growled.

"I never thought I'd say this, but hurry the fuck up and get here." He watched as an SUV he didn't recognize pulled off the highway into town. "I think your man may be here."

"Good. He knows to stand by." The phone disconnected without warning.

"Goodbye to you, too, asshole." He shoved the phone into his pocket and stepped out onto the wooden porch that wrapped around his medical building. He recognized Reaper and lifted a hand. The man pulled up in front of the building and got out of his vehicle.

"Doc."

Jeremiah extended his hand. "You know what's going down?"

Reaper grabbed his hand and shook it. "Not in detail, but enough to know it's bad." The assassin looked around and dipped his head toward the door. "Let's go inside."

Jeremiah led him back to his office. Zeke wasn't in, which was unusual. If someone came by, he'd call the man. If he had to, he'd call in his wife, Eden, who was a nurse practitioner. But right now, not having Zeke at the clinic was better for everyone.

Reaper followed him into the office, shut the door, and unhooked the landline from the telephone socket in the wall. Jeremiah watched as he checked the handset and the underside of the phone before he unplugged the computer from its power source.

"What the hell is going on?"

Reaper held up a hand. He pulled a device from his pocket and walked the entire office while looking at the machine. He then passed it over the computer and the phone. "Good. No bugs."

"Excuse me? Who would want to bug my office?"

"The same person who blew up Guardian's headquarters and has assumedly attacked the Annex." Reaper sat down on the leather couch patients never sat on and kicked his feet up on the sofa.

Jeremiah dropped into the chair. "What?"

"You don't get the national news out here?" Reaper narrowed his eyes and cocked his head.

Dear God. Jeremiah's hands shook so violently, he clasped them together. "I... we do, not here. I have satellite at home."

"The Washington building was destroyed."

"Survivors?"

"Unknown. It's a zoo. I don't know any more than that."

"What do we do?"

Reaper pulled out his phone. "Now, I tell my pregnant wife I made it safely, pretend everything is normal, and wait for backup. Once those tough bastards show up, well, then we go in and take out the motherfuckers who dared to mess with ours."

"Is there any danger to anyone not on the

Marshall Ranch?" Jeremiah shifted his gaze out the window to his little town.

"Not going to lie to you, Doc. I don't have a fucking clue. If shit happens, we'll deal with it. Until then, we wait. Help is on the way."

"What if they need help now?"

Reaper put his phone in his pocket and turned his head to stare at Jeremiah. "Let me put this in basic terms. There are deadly men and women on that ranch. People *I* wouldn't want to go after. The men and women who work for Guardian know what we will do, and more importantly, we know what *they* will do and when they'll do it. *That* is our advantage. The stupid son of a bitch who is trying to attack us is going to die. The only concern I have is whether or not I'll be able to take the shot. Because, Doc, I want to take it." The assassin leaned back and closed his eyes. "Time to rest. It's going to be a long-ass night."

Jeremiah leaned back in his chair and assessed the massive man resting on his couch. What the fuck could he say to that? Nothing. Damn, he wished that asshole Joseph and this backup that was coming would hurry up and get here.

CHAPTER 11

Andrew Hollister jogged from the barn to the house. He'd met the town's doc once since he'd been back, and if he remembered correctly, the guy's name was Zeke. There was a truck with a camper shell and medical equipment parked out front of the main house, so he figured the doc had arrived. He trotted up the stairs and entered the house. The front room had been transformed into a triage center. The two men his ranch hands had brought in were sprawled out on single mattresses, probably brought over from the bunkhouse.

"Any chance of a fire?" His father, Senior, as he was called by everyone who worked on the ranch, barked the question as soon as he saw Andrew walk in the door.

"No, sir. I put out the flames that hadn't burned themselves out. We won't put cows in that pasture until we can clean it up, though. Did you get ahold of Mr. Marshall?"

"Just now. He didn't know shit and will call us back with information. I figured I'd call the aviation commission or maybe the cops." His father's hands found his hips and he rocked forward.

"Senior, I'm going to meet the ambulance at Hollister. Can I get some help loading these guys into my truck? The back is rigged with cots for situations like this."

"You got it. When?"

"Give me five minutes to make sure this compound fracture is immobilized." Zeke talked as he was heading back to the men.

"Sir, could I see you?" Andrew motioned to his father's office. His old man narrowed his eyes but nodded.

When they were in the office, Andrew closed the door. He drew a deep breath and started with a preemptive strike. "Please hear me out on this before you tell me I don't have a clue what I'm talking about. That plane was shot down by a surface-to-air missile. Whoever shot it down has declared war on Guardian. I've worked with their people overseas. They are the epitome of teams you want on your six. You know that Frank has ties to Guardian. Everyone in Hollister knows it, but nobody says a damn thing because of loyalty and what Guardian's presence has been able to provide for the town."

His father crossed his arms. "And?"

"And I think that this was a strike against Guardian. I'll follow the doctor into town when he gets these guys loaded. From there, I'll go to the Marshalls'. If there is something going on, I'll know it, and maybe I can help."

"Don't like it." Senior shook his head.

"Sir, you know I'm right." Damn it, the old man was so stuck in his ways.

"Don't like it. When you got injured overseas, it almost killed me. I couldn't make it through you getting hurt here."

Gobsmacked, Andrew blinked at his father. It was the first time he'd said anything resembling a caring sentence to him since he was... hell, six? He cleared his throat. His father looked anywhere but in his direction. My God, that had to have hurt the old man. Andrew spoke, his voice raspy, "I don't plan on getting hurt. I'm damn good at what I used to do even though I'm not much of a rancher."

His father's head snapped in his direction. "Who told you that?"

Andrew literally took a step back. "You. Over and over again, but now's not the time to get into that. I'm following Doc to Hollister, and then I'm going out to the Marshall Ranch to try to help." He spun on his heel and hit the door, his emotions all over the place.

"Zeke, I'm following you in."

"Good. Both of them are stable. I'll have Dusty drive, and I'll be in the back with them. You can give Dusty a ride back." Zeke was shoving items back into his kit.

"No. My boy's heading over to the Marshall Ranch. I'll send Ryan in to fetch Dusty," Senior's voice boomed in a commanding fashion.

"Whatever you need to do. I'm ready to move them. Andrew, grab the stretchers from my truck, please." Zeke continued to shove things back into his bag. "Dusty, we'll roll the sides of the blankets they are laying on and use that as a grip to move them from the mattresses to the stretcher."

"Got it, Doc." Dusty hustled to the side of the

mattress and started rolling the blankets to use as handles.

Andrew hustled outside, unstrapped the stretchers, and hurried back in. They had the men moved and strapped into the back of Zeke's truck ten minutes later. Andrew trotted to his truck and got in. The keys were in the ignition, as always. He turned it over and waited for Dusty to head out. His father came out, and as they started to pull away, the man pointed at him and mouthed 'be careful.' Andrew dipped his head in acknowledgement.

It took longer to get to Hollister than it should have, but he knew Dusty didn't have a clue about what could be going on at the Marshall Ranch and was being overly careful with his damaged cargo. They pulled off the highway and trundled down the main street to the medical building that had also been built while he was gone. The town had nearly doubled in size, and the houses built on the side of the hill were all new. People who worked in one way or another for Guardian.

"Status?"

Milton cleared his throat. "Hound is dead. There seem to be underground hiding places. No personnel have been acquired."

"Who is this?" The man's hiss sounded as deadly as a viper, but Milton wasn't afraid of a voice.

"Milton."

"Where is Casey?"

"Blowing shit up." Milton glanced over toward where Casey was working on the other side of the hill.

"Repeat that?"

Milton sighed and spoke slowly. The guy might be his boss, but he was a moron. "He's blowing shit up. Comms were taken out. He took out buildings, too."

"Milton, is it? How did Hound die?"

"Shot in the head, might have been one of ours or one of theirs. Ferguson is missing. One other casualty. He got himself blowed up." He watched as Kaiser and Aster walked into one of the outbuildings they'd cleared earlier.

The silence on the other end of the connection dragged on. Finally, the man's voice rasped, "Explain the underground situation."

Milton did, to the best of his ability. "Don't

know if the spaces are interconnected or if they are holed up underground in like shelters or something."

There was a long pause. "No one was found anywhere?"

"No, but they *were* here. Cake in the oven, vehicles in front of buildings. Houses recently occupied. They just... ghosted. Like those villages overseas when they know the military is pushing through. Just gone."

"Hold the objective. We'll be landing within the hour. Meet both planes that will be landing at the airstrip and make sure Casey is with you."

An airplane. Of course, the money always traveled first class. "We have two teams on cordon. I have two men with me on the ranch side of the complex. Casey is on the business side. No one is getting in or out."

"Stand by for our arrival."

Milton disconnected the call. He turned and looked at the metal tube stuck into the ground. Aster's words still bounced around his head and had taken seed. Milton had that feeling too. A lot of people weren't going to get out of this alive.

Joseph King sat strapped into the C-17's cargo seat next to his wife. They were the only passengers, and he was okay with that. He had way too much on his mind to try to deal with people, too. His brothers' children were with his brother-in-law, Christian. Thank God. Tori and Faith were missing. His experience told him if they weren't dead, they would be. Bastards took them for a reason. His objectivity was skewed, and he'd be damned if he wasn't trying to second-guess his instinct on the matter.

The thing was, he had no idea who the enemy was or what they wanted as an endgame. That caused a fuckton of problems. He'd contact Charley as soon as they were on the road and get an update. His family was in that building and on the ranch. Whoever was fucking with them had made themselves an enemy. One who never quit. As soon as the plane leveled out, he unbuckled and stood up. "Stay here." He tossed the words to Ember and headed to the equipment that had been on the plane when they were picked up.

He opened the door to a blacked-out SUV that was strapped down in the cargo bay and popped the back hatch. Ember joined him at the open hatch. "Not listening." He growled the words.

"You are correct. I'm not. What do you need me to do?" Ember crossed her arms and stared at him. He knew his fiery red-headed wife; she was stubborn.

"Nothing. I'm checking to see what type of equipment we are working with." There were five SUVs and only two of them. "I need to know what is in each vehicle." He opened a watertight, hard-sided cargo box. Perfect.

Ember picked up a uniform shirt from the top. "Black and grey?"

"For night operations." Technically, they'd be moving in at sunrise, but the black and grey battle dress uniforms would blend in, making them shadows rather than targets. They also had an added benefit. Every Guardian scope and night vision device would instantly identify those uniforms as friendly. The technology worked miracles when a diverse group who'd never worked together were converging on a target. "How many are there?" He let her pull out the uniforms and count them while he searched through the rest of the equipment.

He was inspecting a cache of ammo in the vehicle when she finished. "Fifty sets. All but five are XXL. Why so many?"

He shrugged. Details he wasn't willing to share with her. They would upset her even more than she was now, so he hedged. "Big effort. Go to the front vehicle and open it up. We need to check and see what they have."

Ember paused after a step or two and looked back at him. "Do you want a detailed listing?"

"Exactly. All weapons, ammo, any scopes, NVGs, comm gear. I need to know everything."

"I sure as hell hope we don't get stopped by the police on the way north." Ember headed up to the front vehicle. He chuckled to himself. The woman was oblivious to the emergency lights in the grills and the fact that they had POTUS support and wouldn't be questioned. They were going to be flying on the highway and no one was going to stop them. The trip was going to take a fraction of the time it usually took, and the other drivers would need to stay tucked up to his ass as he traveled at over a hundred miles per hour.

He went to the third vehicle and opened the back. "Well, hello, beautiful." Joseph opened the metal case and actually smiled. Hands-free comm devices. He did a quick sum. Fifty sets. The next box contained heavy weapons. Two M-240's and three M-204 grenade launchers. The case below that had ammo for those weapons. Everything they needed to eradicate whatever the fuck was going on at the ranch. He glanced at his watch. Sierra and Alpha Teams would land about twenty minutes before they would. Each team would drive one of the vehicles. The SEALs that the President had sent were arriving about ten minutes after them. He spoke to himself, a bad habit he'd picked up recently, "Gabriel thought of everything."

"He didn't think that Guardian would be attacked," Ember snapped at him, suddenly by his side.

He moved to her and wrapped her in his arms. "He prepared for it, though. He designed that building in D.C. and the Annex to provide safety and a way out, should something happen. This isn't his fault."

She fell into him. "I know. It's just so damn hard not knowing. I'm worried and, yeah, afraid. How much longer are we on this damn plane?"

Joseph pulled her against him tightly and glanced at his watch. "Another two hours."

"Promise me we're going to come out of this together."

He ran his hands up and down her back and said nothing. He wouldn't lie to her, and she knew it. There was a real possibility that people would be injured or killed. It was part of the profession. He'd been away from the dangerous aspects of the job for too damn long. He practiced the basics, kept his skills honed, but nothing prepared you for being in the field like actually being in the field, doing the work.

"Joey, please." She lifted her face to him, and he read the desperation in her eyes. Emotion that she'd been holding in.

"I won't lie to you. But I will be careful." He was always careful. He lowered and dropped his lips onto hers. When he lifted, he spoke just loud enough so she could hear him over the drone of the engines. "I want to live. I want to be with you and our family. Nothing is more important to me than you and the kids."

She wrapped her arms around his neck and stared up at him. "Do those people come back here?"

He glanced up to the front of the plane. "No reason for them to come back." The loadmaster would be the only one who'd have reason to come back, and that wouldn't be until they started their approach. There were cameras, however. His eyes flicked to the small round eyes.

"Then make love to me, Joey. Make me forget. I want to feel you inside me when you and whoever is meeting us leaves me in Hollister."

He glanced at the bulkhead one more time before he pulled her hands from around his neck and grabbed one of them, tugging her to the back of the farthest SUV.

"Take your clothes off. All of them."

She stood completely still, her eyes wide and shocked. "What?"

"Do it." He sent his eyes down her scrub-clad body. There wasn't an angle for them to be seen here. He wanted to have his wife on his terms. He waited, knowing she was processing what he wanted. Her pupils grew larger and her neck and face flushed red. Yeah, his baby girl wanted him and wanted him to make her feel him. He was going to do that. They both needed the distraction right now.

He kept his eyes on her as she lifted the baby blue cotton material over her head. The utilitarian cotton bra held her full breasts, and her red hair pulled back in a single braid slid over her shoulder. "Keep going." She glanced toward the front of the aircraft. He grabbed her chin with his fingers. "Look at me. Only me." He wasn't going to let anyone else into this time. It was theirs, it was precious, and it could be the last time he made love to his woman. Nothing was going to come between them.

She toed off her tennis shoes and untied the drawstring of her scrub bottoms. After loosening them, she slid them over her hips. God, she had a perfect body. Soft, curvy, luscious, and all his. She glanced up at him and he lifted his eyebrows. "Don't test my patience."

Her breath caught at his words. Yeah, the forced nakedness with the chance of being caught had his woman hot. He could see the excitement and dread fighting. She reached behind her and released the clasp of her bra. "Joey," she whispered as a plea.

"Now." Her bra fell from her breasts, and she dropped it into the back of the truck. "Finish it." The blush traveled from her chest, up her neck, and into her cheeks. Her embarrassment turned him on, not that he needed to have it. She was the best aphrodisiac in the world. She slipped her white cotton panties off and placed them with the bra. Her rose-colored nipples were taut and pebbled. He bet if he palmed her sex right now, she'd be wet. He moved forward, cupping both breasts and rolling the nipples between his thumbs and fingers. Her head dropped back, her mouth open as she gasped. She loved the bite of pain and he loved inflicting it. He lowered his head and whispered, "I'm going to fuck you so you know who you belong to."

"I know. I belong to you. Only you." She gasped when he added pressure to her nipples.

"You're going to be with Wheeler."

"He's married."

"I don't care. I hate him." The man was a good shrink, but even after all these years, he would always hate the man who'd dared to kiss his woman. "And I'm going to show you how much I hate him."

He spun her around and bent her over. Her hands landed flat against the carpet of the rear end of the SUV. He bent over her and bit her shoulder. She shuddered as he scraped his teeth to the other shoulder and bit it as well, slowly adding pressure until she whimpered. He released her flesh and licked the spot, kissing the red mark before he repeated the process. He reached under her and found her nipples. As he consumed his woman, he pinched and rolled them between his fingers. Her soft mewling and whimpering added one hundred percent octane to his red-hot lust. He pushed her down so her shoulders were resting on the carpet. Keeping her there with one hand, he released himself from the jeans he was wearing. He stroked his cock, smearing the precum over the crown and down his shaft. Centering behind her, he slammed into her sex. Her sounds—fuck, they were everything. He relished in every cry even as she pushed back against him as he entered her. She wanted it harder, and he was going to oblige. Grabbing both of her shoulders, he demanded, "Pleasure yourself."

Her arm moved and her hand snuck under her. He felt it moving over her clit, and that's when he let loose. Fuck, they hadn't had sex like this in months. He moved his grip to her hips and pounded into that warm, wet slice of absolute heaven. Her cry and the clench of her body under him pulled him over, and he fucked her through his release. Hard, so his oversensitive cock ached, too. Finally, he slowed and dropped down over her. They stayed like that, coupled together and panting like they'd run a marathon. He lifted a bit and kissed her between the shoulder blades. "I love you, Ember. Never forget that."

She lifted onto her elbows and turned to look at him. "I will always love you, Joey. Only you." He held her eyes and moved in for a soft, tender kiss. That was the one they'd both remember because they didn't happen often. Her worried eyes held his as he stared at her when he pulled away.

"Stay here. I'll get you a uniform to wear." He dropped a soft kiss onto her cheek before he pulled out of her and stowed himself. He headed to the SUV to get her clothes to put on. He'd change with her. Change into a person he hadn't had to be in a long time. Once again, he'd bring forth the rage and the hatred that had almost consumed him. He would become one of the most feared assassins in the world. The man who'd died yet lived. He would once again become Fury, and he would rain hell on earth.

CHAPTER 12

Mike White Cloud stood next to Anubis in the Pit's war room. He looked at each man and woman standing around the table. Drake, Jillian, Shae, Asp, Billy, his wife Taty, and sitting at the end of the table, Joy, receiving an IV of fluids. Adam and Dixon stood next to her like twin sentinels. "We are operating under Sunrise Protocols. Have we made contact with the staff shelters?"

"I did," Anubis acknowledged. "Thanks to our underground systems, we reached them via the hardwired communications system. We have seventeen people in the tornado shelters. The facilities that were destroyed, the cafeteria, the gym, and rehab centers, have confirmed three personnel remained in the facilities and are unaccounted for."

Jillian raised her hand and asked, "Families are going to start wondering where they're at, won't they? I mean the staff that live in Hollister and commute to the ranch."

Shae leaned forward as she spoke. "We have two still here. Jenkins lives alone, and Thompkins' wife and kid are at her parents' this month, at least, according to the latest paperwork. No one else is supposed to report back to work until Monday morning."

"Where are our power levels?" Mike asked as he put the blueprints of the defensive functions of the Annex on the table and unfurled them. Asp caught the paper on the other side and held them open.

Jillian held up a small tablet. "We have enough power to run all systems for six months, seven days, eight hours, and twenty-two minutes. Give or take a second or two."

"I'm not staying down here six months. What are the assignments?" Joy snipped the comment, and Dixon put his hand on her shoulder. She sighed loudly. "I'm fucking fine. Just dehydrated. Ask him." She jerked her head in Adam's direction.

"You need to rest," both Dixon and Adam said at the same time.

Mike spoke as Joy opened her mouth to argue. "We have time and won't count you out unless you tap out or Adam medically disqualifies you." He had mad respect for the assassin and it would be her call, but he'd also make sure he didn't put her at any unnecessary medical risk. He stared at Dixon while he spoke. The man's jaw tightened. He didn't like it, but the man married an assassin; he knew what he was getting into.

"What about Frank and John?" Shae asked the question and glanced down at the blueprints. "They have to have figured out something was wrong by now. Where do you think they'd enter the system?"

Mike pointed to the prints. "There are three access points that they could get to from the direction they were riding. Here, here, and here." He pointed to each as he spoke.

"Then we need to send someone to the end of each and look for them." Anubis nodded.

Mike agreed, "Yes. With the families accounted for and given the amount of time we have before we need to go on the offensive, that is what I'm recommending. Dixon, I need you to stay here. I want you to go over each one of the hydraulic systems to make sure those damn things are working. I don't want them to malfunction and cost a life." It would also keep the guy busy and away from his wife who, if his instincts were correct, was suffocating under his hovering.

Mike continued, "Shae and Drake, you take that tunnel. I'll take this one with Taty. Billy, you and Asp take the last one. Take medical kits, just in case. Anubis will stay here with Jillian. It will be dark shortly. I want to activate the camera system after dark. Anubis, we need to get that ham radio antenna lifted. We need a way to contact the outside world."

"Jillian, do you have a battery pack I can hook up to power the antenna?" Anubis turned to find her to ask the question.

"I do, but that antenna is aboveground. Why can't we use the comms we have installed down here to contact the outside?"

"Because those fuckers got lucky. Somehow, they knew to blow the north side of the barn. It took out our backup comm nodes. The attack on the comm building took out the primary system."

"So, you'll have to go aboveground?" Joy asked.

"I will."

She shook her head. "No offense, you're too big, too slow, and you haven't had to be a Shadow in... in a hell of a long time. I'll go. I can slip out, ghost to the antenna, hook it up, and be back without anyone seeing me."

"No," Dixon barked.

"She's right," Asp agreed and crossed his arms. "As much as it sucks, she's the one to do this. She's tiny and a pocket ninja. Chances of anyone seeing her is next to nothing."

Dixon pointed to his wife. "She's pregnant."

Joy rolled her eyes. "Thanks for spilling the beans. Yes, I'm knocked up. Barely. I'm going to do this."

Mike interrupted the argument he saw coming, "Adam, is she medically cleared?"

Adam stared at Dixon and nodded at the IV pole. "I'm giving her fluids and anti-nausea meds. When this is done, she's cleared."

Dixon swore bitterly and glared at Adam. Mike cleared his throat. "Dixon, I appreciate the situation you're in, but you need to step back and see the big picture. She is our best shot at getting comms. We have a mission at sunrise, and we need to know what support we'll have. She goes."

Dixon snarled. "You don't know they'll check

for ham radio communications. It isn't in the protocol. I don't like it. I don't agree with it, but as everyone has pointed out, it isn't my call."

Mike left that comment alone. He turned his attention to other matters. "Jillian, can you cut all power to the above-ground buildings?"

"Yeah, of course." She nodded. "Why?"

"It gives Joy more cover, and if these aggressors are looking for us, they'll have one more obstacle to overcome," Anubis filled in the rationale.

"Wait, if you cut everything, there will be absolute silence. They'll hear the antenna go up when she powers it." Dixon looked from Mike to Anubis.

"No, because we are going to set a distraction," Mike corrected him.

"What kind of distraction?" Shae asked.

"Dixon, feel like blowing something up?" Mike asked.

"You have no fucking idea."

"Good. Go make me something that will send them scurrying." Anubis agreed.

"What about our cameras? Can't we see what's happening?" Taty asked.

Anubis sighed. "Only three survived whatever destruction happened above. One on top of the silo, but that has limited range of vision, one at the end of the flight line, which does us zero good, and the one at the main road. There has been no movement there."

Mike hated being blind, but that was why they had protocols in place. He looked at the people surrounding him. "Everyone has their assignments. Rally back here as soon as you finish your assignments and check in with Anubis or Adam. Are your patients tucked in?"

"They are. One is worse for the wear." Adam crossed his arms. "He shouldn't have been moved."

"All right. Doc, you've got the patients and the families until we start running the countdown to the Sunrise Protocol. We'll need you to arm up then. Everyone clear on their missions?"

He received head nods all the way around. "We are going to take back our home. Whatever it takes."

"As long as it takes." The response echoed around the table.

"It better not fucking take six months," Joy muttered.

Andrew pulled in behind Zeke's vehicle. The ambulance hadn't arrived yet. "Where is the rig?" he asked as he opened his door.

"They were coming up from Rapid, not Belle. They'd made a run. Help me get them inside." Zeke dropped the tailgate, and Dusty was there to help, too.

Two men exited the clinic. One Andrew knew from Ryan pointing him out one day, Doctor Wheeler, a shrink. Ryan had thought Andrew should talk to the man. *That would be the day.* He'd been shoved full of meds and talked in groups while in the military. It did nothing for him. He nodded at the man and let his eyes drift to the other. There was nothing in the guy's appearance that made him easy. He was big, hard, and had eyes that missed nothing.

"What do you have, Zeke?" The one who was the shrink jogged down the stairs. "A plane went down. Both—"

The other man was off the porch and leaning into the back of the truck within an instant. "Guardian 343?"

"Yes." The one with the fractured leg said, "Surface-to-air missile."

"We got your mayday. Armageddon Protocol. Copy?"

"Copy." The man nodded.

"We've got it now, man. Rest easy." He put his hand on the man's arm and glanced at the unconscious pilot. "We will make this right."

"Whatever it takes," the injured man said.

"As long as it takes, brother." The big man backed away.

Zeke moved back in with a huff. "If I can treat my patients now?"

Andrew helped carry one stretcher in with Dusty and Doctor Wheeler, and the other man carried the unconscious pilot in under Zeke's supervision.

When they were free, Andrew walked up to the big guy. "Can I talk to you? Out there?"

The man shook his head. "In here. Jeremiah, I'm using your office."

"It's all yours," Jeremiah answered as he helped Zeke get his patients situated.

Andrew followed the big guy and waited for him to shut the door. "My name is Andrew Hollister, recently Marine Recon."

"Thank you for your service. I'm Roman." The reply was polite but gave no other information.

"Right. I have a belief that the people on the Marshall Ranch may be in trouble. As you are Guardian, I am assuming you have the same understanding?"

The man narrowed his eyes and crossed his arms before he asked. "What are you basing your assumptions on?"

"An aircraft shot out of the sky belonging to Guardian. The fact that Guardian has a presence on the Marshall Ranch that everyone knows about and no one mentions. The fact that my father contacted Frank Marshall and he was unaware of the plane going down but said he'd get answers and hasn't called back."

"You've spoken to Frank Marshall?"

"My dad did."

"When?"

"I'm not sure of the exact time, but not more than forty-five minutes ago. Is that important?"

"Yes. Very."

"So, there is a situation?"

"There is." The man nodded.

"I want to help."

The man shook his head. "We have a response force coming."

Andrew drew a breath. He got it. The man

didn't know him. Didn't know his training or capabilities. "I'm thirty minutes north. The downed aircraft is on our ranch. We didn't see anyone else in the wreckage."

"There were only the two of them," the man confirmed.

"Good." Andrew nodded and turned to walk away.

"Hollister?"

He stopped and looked over his shoulder. "Yeah?"

"You were planning on going to the ranch, weren't you?"

"Damn straight."

Roman smiled, transforming his resting bitch face into something more socially acceptable. "You're either one of the bravest men I've ever met or the stupidest."

Andrew chuffed a laugh. "According to my old man, I'm the second."

Roman shook his head and he stared directly at Andrew. "Your old man is dead wrong, isn't he?"

Andrew shrugged. "I've had my moments."

The man's eyes narrowed, and he cocked his head. "*Captain* Andrew Hollister, United States

Marine Corps. You were in the news about a year back. Maybe more."

Andrew closed his eyes. The service had made a damn big thing of it. "Yeah, you have a good memory."

Roman moved to the desk. "Give me your cell phone number. If we need help, I'll call."

Andrew rattled off his six-oh-five area code and then the rest of his number. "I'd appreciate it if you didn't bring up the news coverage to anyone else."

"You got it, and for what it's worth, you can have my six any day." The man slipped Andrew's telephone number into his shirt pocket.

Andrew nodded. It was worth a lot, especially after everything that had happened.

CHAPTER 13

Joseph held Ember's hand as the hydraulic maw of the C-17 opened on the tarmac of Ellsworth Air Force Base, a few miles south and east of Rapid City, South Dakota. Standing outside the aircraft were eleven men. Sierra Team and Alpha Team. He walked down the ramp with his wife and strode over to Tempest. "Long time." He extended his hand and his brother clasped it tightly.

"Hate to meet back up this way." Tempest released his hand and then politely nodded to Ember. The man knew not to get too close. Joseph was a possessive bastard and a jealous one, too. He admitted it.

"Let me introduce you." Tempest turned to his team. "Sierra Team. My skipper, Travis. Ricco, comms and marksman, Scuba, entry and weapons specialist, Harley is demolitions, and Coach is our medic." Joseph shook each man's hand.

"I'm Rocker. Alpha Team skipper. This is Tech, he's our comms and entry specialist. That big guy is Bull, he's a heavy weapons and demolition expert. Strings is logistics and our marksman, and Nova, our medic and all-around smartass."

"Hey, I resemble that remark." Coach stuck out his hand to the other medic. The guys shook and stepped back.

"I'm Joseph King, this is my wife, Ember, and I run the Rose. I recognize a few of you from training. We have a thirteen-man SEAL team inbound. They will be here in less than twenty. Until they arrive, we need to unload and fuel up these SUVs."

Joseph stopped talking as a string of cars pulled up beside the aircraft. He tugged Ember behind him and casually crossed his arms.

"Who is in charge?"

The brusque question lifted Joseph's hackles. He was on a hair-trigger and this bastard just stomped on his one remaining nerve. "That would be me." He didn't move, didn't offer to introduce himself, or ask who wanted to know.

"Colonel Brasselton. I'm the Support Group Commander. We were asked to provide an escort to the main gate. The South Dakota Highway Patrol are at the gate, ready to escort you to your destination. Is there anything you need? We've been told to make it happen, and I'm here to make sure it does."

"We need these vehicles fueled." He pointed to the ass end of the aircraft.

"I'll get some drivers."

"No, sir. Nobody but my people touch the vehicles or equipment. They'll follow you to the fuel and follow you back."

"Good enough. How long before you unload?"

Joseph looked back to the loadmaster. "When?" He called out the question.

"Good to go!" The reply came back.

"Sierra Team, make it happen."

"Let's go." The team sprinted up the ramp and each one took a vehicle. Joseph and the others moved to the side as the SUVs fired to life.

"Get them to the pumps, use my vehicle's card, and fuel them all up," the colonel spoke to the man who was standing beside his staff car. The driver popped back into the car, and as the SUVs came off the plane, he did a wide U-turn and had a six-SUV procession following him.

"Anything else I can do for you?"

"ETA on the last plane?" Joseph glanced at his watch.

"They are on final. I heard the call over the radio as we were pulling up. Shouldn't be too much longer."

"We'll take it from here, Colonel. Thank you for your time and assistance." Joseph glanced at his watch. He needed to make contact with Charley or Gabriel and find out what the hell was happening, and he didn't need any non-Guardian personnel around when he did so.

The man nodded and turned away, heading to one of the many vehicles that had accompanied him.

"Alpha Team, I need a non-hostile cordon while I make this call."

"On it. Gentlemen, you heard the man." Rocker gave the word and the men dispersed, seemingly in a casual walkabout, but there was no way anyone was going to get close enough to listen. He pushed

Charley's number, praying she was on-scene and could give him an update.

"What?" Charley's voice snapped across the connection.

"Sitrep." His gut clenched. He needed information.

"We have a clusterfuck of biblical proportions. Besides that, Jade, Jared, and Nic are safe. Smoke, Smith, and Maliki are working to get whoever is in the exit tunnel from CCS out. They said they have signs of life, but we don't know who is in there. Jacob got word out that Jason is severely injured. His back. I have three teams securing the scene from above, and we are clearing the building that collapsed over the executive exit."

Fuck. Even though there was good news, Jewell and Zane were unaccounted for. Jason was injured. Fuck, fuck, fuck. He prowled back and forth. Just when he was about to speak, he heard Charley say, "Oh, shit. There's Jewell and Zane with Smoke and Maliki."

He stopped, and his world righted itself even more. Jewell could help more than anyone. He snapped out his command, "She needs to go to the mountain ASAP."

Charley snorted. "You want me to tell her that? Zane is injured. He's wearing a sling and he's limping."

What? Fuck that. "Is he breathing? If he is, he'll suck it up. Get an aircraft fueled and get her to the mountain." Joseph snapped the command.

"Hey, here's an idea, *Joey*. You call and get that done. I've got my hands full."

Joseph blinked and looked at the phone. She hung up on him.

"What happened?" Ember asked quietly.

"She fucking hung up on me and she called me Joey again."

"I don't care about that, *Joey*, give me a damn update, would you?"

He lifted his eyes to her. She was right, he'd fix his Charley problem later. "Jason is hurt. Badly. His back. I don't think he or Jacob are out, but Jacob made contact somehow. Jewell, Zane, Jade, Nic, and Jared are out."

Ember almost collapsed. Her hand went to her mouth. "Oh, thank God." Tears filled her eyes. "Jason is strong. He'll be okay. He has to be."

"Yeah." Joseph punched the number to the Rose on his phone. Thanatos answered after the third ring. "Are you on the ground?"

"Yes. Sitrep."

"Your brother Justin and his wife are in residence. A NY team is following the family to Mountain Protocol. Your sister is being escorted to the mountain by her husband's security team. We've just heard Jade, Nic, and Jared are out."

"Jewell and Bengal, too. I need a plane at the airport to take them to the mountain. Make it happen."

"On it. I'll call when it's done."

"Did Lycos get anything useful?"

"So far, only video of the attack. It's a professional hit. Several different vectors, staggered timing to ensure the most destruction. It's a miracle anyone survived."

"Jewell will get us information. Call back when you have the plane ready." He lifted his voice as a Navy C-20, otherwise known as a G-IV, whined its way down the taxiway to them.

He closed contact and whistled. Alpha Team closed in on him, and they waited together for the executive aircraft to come to a halt. When the engines shut down, the door was opened, and thirteen men walked down the steps. The first out he didn't recognize—but he recognized the second.

"I'm Lieutenant Evers. I'm looking for Joseph King."

"This is Joseph King." Ted "Bear" Black walked straight to him. "Dude, you realize I'm still in the Navy, right? Working for you isn't a bad idea, but I'm going to have to set limits."

Ted extended his hand and Joseph gripped it. "I wanted people I could trust. We have a situation on our hands. Lieutenant," Joseph acknowledged the squad's commanding officer. "I'm not going into anything until we reach our rally point." Joseph nodded to the SUVs that were flying back down the perimeter road. "We're going to be escorted by the Highway Patrol, but if they try to slow us down, I'm going around them. I need your best drivers behind the wheels. You have two of those vehicles for your team. Stow what gear you absolutely need. I have uniforms, comms, and weapons."

"Roger that." The lieutenant turned and rallied up his team.

Ember leaned into him. "It seemed surreal up to this point. Like it was all a bad dream."

He put his arm around his wife's waist. "Shit is about to get very real, baby girl." Life and death real.

Five minutes later, Joseph floored the gas pedal of his SUV and flew behind two South Dakota State Highway patrol vehicles. Two more traveled with their convoy at the ass end of the procession, and there were SDHP blocking major intersections. He glanced at the speedometer. One hundred and thirty miles an hour. It was damn near a straight shot north, but the HP would ensure all intersections were blocked and they would be unimpeded.

His phone rang and Ember answered it, putting it on speaker. "The plane will be ready to take off in twenty-five minutes."

"Got it. Anything else?"

"Negative. Status quo."

"On the road to Hollister. I'll contact you when we have everything set up."

"Understood."

"Call Charley. The number before the Rose."

Ember did as he asked, put the phone on speaker, and then grabbed the oh-shit bar. Her hand was going to be permanently molded into the grip by the time they made it to Hollister.

Charley answered, "What?"

"The aircraft will be ready to fly in twenty-five

minutes. Have them there," he snarled at the impertinent woman.

"I'll let them know. Where are you?"

Hell, he couldn't give her a mile marker, they were driving way too fast for that. So, he gave her what he could. "Driving to Hollister from Rapid City."

"Do you have an update on the ranch?"

God, he wished he did. Wished this was all a drill, but it wasn't. "No. We'll move in tomorrow morning."

"Do you have enough personnel to retake it?"

Charley's question was one he'd asked himself. 'It depends,' was his only answer. "The ranch has a few surprises of its own. We'll work in concert with those assigned to the Annex. We're doing this by the numbers. Mostly."

"Your part is the one that's off-script, I'm assuming."

He glanced at his wife and then had his eyes back on the road as he responded, "You know me so well."

A loud sound came from the speaker. Charley exclaimed, "They're through!"

"Where?" Joseph snapped the question.

"The executive tunnel. I'll call you back as soon

as we know anything." Then he was listening to nothing. She'd hung up on him again. He ground his teeth together and tightened his grip on the steering wheel. He needed to teach that little girl a lesson. Obviously, the last instructional session he'd given her hadn't lasted.

CHAPTER 14

Frank stopped and listened. John had been leaning on him more and more as they moved. "We're going to take a break." He leaned his foreman against the wall. John didn't argue, and in the incandescent lights, his washed-out complexion and profuse sweating were confusing as hell.

"What the hell did I miss?" Frank bent down and grabbed the rip the bullet had caused in John's jeans, pulling to extend the tear further. Blood, and not from the wound. He lifted the denim, and sure enough, a hole oozing blood. *Fuck.* "You were shot twice."

"Explains the pain," John grunted.

"And the blood." *Fuck.* He ripped the jeans

further and felt the other side of his leg. "Not a through and through."

"Go and get help. I'll be okay." John slid down the wall while extending his leg. The bandana he'd used to stop the bullet burn's blood flow was soaked and useless.

"Do you even know me?" Frank grumped and pulled his belt off.

John held up a hand. "Man, don't use a tourniquet. I'm partial to my leg."

"Wasn't planning on it." Frank unbuttoned his shirt and ripped off his T-shirt before folding it into a thick pad. He placed it on top of the bullet hole and then strapped it with his belt. "Compression, not a tourniquet." Frank put his shirt back on while looking down the tunnel. They'd closed two emergency doors behind them, locking both. They could rest, it was safe, and if he knew anything, he'd bet, sooner or later, whoever made it underground would come looking for them.

Frank leaned against the wall, making sure he had a grip on his rifle. John had placed his own weapon by his side. He'd seen the man shoot and was glad to have him, no matter how diminished he was at the moment.

"Seriously, go get Doc or a medic. A wheelchair

would be appreciated," John laughed.

"First, you'll live, and ain't no one going to push your ass when you can hobble. Didn't figure you for a lazy one." Frank pulled out a piece of taffy and handed it to John.

"Thanks." John took it but didn't open it. "Can't wrap my mind around who would do this. Thought those women were gone."

Frank grunted. The Fates. The organization was still around. Guardian was mopping up. "In the absence of power, a vacuum sucks all types to fill the void."

John blinked at him and then snorted. "You pretend to be a simple cowpoke, but these one-liners you toss out lead me to believe you're a hell of a lot more educated and traveled than you let on."

Frank grunted. Life had educated him, but yeah, he'd seen the world and decided he didn't much like it. "Been around a bit when I was younger."

"Well, that I believe, but who? The airplane was shot down. No answer at Guardian. No answer at the Annex. What the hell is going on?"

Frank shook his head. He and Gabriel talked daily. There was nothing on the scope. They were actually hitting their stride. Enough teams, training, recruitment, and investigations with solid closures. They weren't involved with any ongoing cases. Most were connected to humanitarian efforts or protection. He didn't know what was going on in the Shadow world; it wasn't necessary for him to know. It could only be something from that side of the house. Had someone figured out a Shadow's identity and tracked them to Guardian? Some of the bastards the Shadows took down were connected and plain evil. "I don't know. Seems to be coordinated. Takes money. Big money."

"That it would." John unwrapped his taffy and popped it into his mouth, shoving it to his cheek. "And weaponry. What would cut comms in D.C? Or for that matter, here? The comms are redundant as I learned when I wanted to extend the hayloft to hold more hay."

Frank grunted in acknowledgement. The secondary communications node was hidden in the hayloft. John's attempt to take down the wall had alarms going off and he'd ended up on the business end of Mike's automatic. "Should have told you. Out of sight, out of mind."

Someone would have had to know where the secondary comms were and deactivated them.

Or... he slammed that thought back into his mind and shut the door on it. He was worried sick about his family, his wife, the Annex. Pulling out negative thoughts wouldn't do anyone any good and would keep him from focusing on the task at hand.

"Damn glad Mike doesn't have an itchy trigger finger." John closed his eyes and sucked on the taffy. "Give me another minute and I'll be ready to go."

"I'll give you two."

The lights shut off. Frank lifted his rifle and swung it, activating the lights again.

"Do you think they're okay?"

Frank didn't have to ask who. He knew what John meant. "Not going to think any other way." He couldn't go there or he'd go over the edge, and that could get more people hurt or killed.

John sighed and folded the piece of wax paper that his taffy had been wrapped in. He put it in his pocket. "Give me a hand up."

Frank moved off the wall and reached down, anchoring himself as he pulled against John's weight, helping the man up. Once he was upright, Frank handed John his rifle, regripped his own and pulled John's arm over his shoulders. "We'll stop again."

John nodded, and together, they moved forward.

Frank closed another door about ten minutes later. John was struggling, but the bandage seemed to be stemming the flow of blood. He didn't reckon John had lost enough to pass out, but he was weak and hurting for sure.

He kept his eye on the black of the tunnel. Dark turned to light as they activated each sensor. It became a measurement and a goal. The next sensor. The next—

The lights at the other end of the tunnel lit. His rifle was up a second before John's.

"Whoa! Don't shoot."

The men in front of him had their guns leveled on them. John's entreaty lowered all four weapons.

"Damn it, John, what the hell did you do?" Asp strode forward.

"He got shot. Twice." Frank was damn grateful to see the big guys. Asp and Billy were twin bookends of the towering type.

"Twice? Dude, didn't you learn the first time?" Billy said as they stopped.

"Obviously not. What is going on?" Frank straightened when John leaned against the side of the tunnel.

"Attack on Washington, one of the supply planes for here was shot down, and we were attacked."

"Casualties?" Frank snapped the question.

"Unknown in D.C. or the plane. Three here. Staff members. All your family is safe in the Pit," Asp replied.

Some of the weight he was carrying was lifted but not enough. Not nearly enough. "Sunrise Protocol?"

"Yes, sir." Asp gave him a quick double-take. Probably surprised he knew of such a thing. Well, there was a lot he knew that others didn't.

"Let's get back." Frank grabbed John's weapon. "I've secured all the doors behind us."

"Good. We'll get you back to the Pit. I know there are a couple ladies who will be damn happy to see both of you. John, can you walk, or do you need me to give you a ride?"

"Dude, my leg is killing me, but I can make it."

"We can get you there. Come on, my man. Your wife is waiting." Asp rounded Frank as John stood, and Billy got under one of John's arms, Asp under the other. The men grabbed each other's arms and made a seat for John to sit on. Once they were settled, Frank led the procession and they moved, the men walking five times faster than he and John had fared. It took fifteen minutes to make it to the mouth of the Pit.

Adam met them at the doorway, quickly assessing John's leg. Shae ran up beside them as the men followed Adam. He could hear John trying to reassure Shae he was okay. In the light, the blood all over the man's leg looked bad.

The first person Frank saw was the one he needed to see the most.

Amanda jumped up from the couch and raced across the massive area. "Frank! Oh, thank you, Jesus!" his wife cried out as she collided against him. He pulled her tight and held on. The feel of her softness against him grounded him in ways that Asp and Billy's reassurances couldn't. She was safe.

"Dad!" Keelee's voice rang out, and he released Amanda with one arm and grabbed his daughter as she came to him.

It took several long moments before he was willing to release either of his girls. "Have we heard anything about what happened in D.C.? Are the kids okay?" Frank asked the question as he hugged the women. They both shook their heads.

Damn it. He released them after a final squeeze. "I need to talk to Mike."

"He's searching the tunnels. He'll be back. Shae just returned about a minute ago. I'm glad she was able to be here for John."

"Me too." He hated he'd missed that second wound.

"Kaeden is here." Amanda stuck close to his side.

"I'll need to go speak with him."

"I'll get you something to eat and drink," Amanda offered. "And a change of clothes."

Frank glanced down at his bloodstained jeans and shirt. There was mud and muck caked from the knee down where he'd crawled through the culvert water and mud to access the tunnel. He grunted and bent down to kiss his wife. "Thank you."

She smiled, wiped her tears away, and she and Keelee headed to gather him some things. He strode across the opening and headed straight for the conference room. Anubis got up and extended his hand. "Thank God. John?"

"Shot twice. He'll live."

"Can he still shoot?"

Frank nodded. "Should be able to. What do we

know?" He listened as Anubis outlined the little they'd been able to find out before being attacked. "How bad was the attack on D.C.?"

"If you're asking do I think everyone will get out, I don't know. I don't know if they had any warning or how long it took for the building to go down. We are going to send Joy out to run up the ham radio antenna. Ethan has a receiver. We're hoping we'll be able to communicate with them that way."

"We should have help in the morning." Frank nodded and looked at the map of the property that was spread across the table.

"We can't bank on it," Anubis sighed. "We have limited resources with just us. If this had happened last week? Four teams were here for refresher evidence-gathering training. This week? We're down to staff and those patients rehabbing."

"We lost three above?"

"Unaccounted for in the shelters, and we believe they would be eliminated by the forces that took the ranch. We also believe the big barn was taken out. No secondary radio communications."

Frank sighed and then nodded. "I'll go check in on John, but he can hold a gun, and that bullet didn't take out his eyesight."

"We'll rig something so he can sit and spin. We need our best shooters."

"Asp and Billy plus John. Who are you going to put on the fourth one?"

"If Blocker was better, I'd say him, but he's not doing well. The trip downstairs was too fast and too soon after his surgery. Adam is watching him close."

"Run through who we have and look at the marksman records. We need the best." Frank tapped the map. "When are we running through the protocols?"

"As soon as I get everyone back. Dixon is checking the hydraulics. Joy should be getting ready to sneak out now."

"Where is she exiting?"

"Her house. She said, and I'm quoting here, 'I'll kill any motherfucker who messes with my dog and that damn cat.'"

Frank grunted. He didn't doubt it. "She'll have good cover to make it to the silo."

"And we've turned off the power to the topside so it will be darker."

Frank rubbed his cheek. "Half-moon tonight and no clouds." His daughter-in-law was one of a kind, that was for sure, but damn it, he hated sending her out into the unknown. "Dixon?"

"Like I said, checking the systems. I think Mike separated them so he wouldn't hover and she wouldn't kill him. He's also building a distraction, should we need it to get Joy out of any tight spots. We have to get that antenna up and her back down here. I told him to make the distraction small. We can't mess with them too much or they'll be ready for us in the morning, and we're not sure of the makeup of the force up there."

Frank nodded and scraped the cement floor with the toe of his filthy work boots. "I'll talk to him. Amanda suspects Joy's pregnant."

"Oh, that was confirmed in no uncertain terms, but she's not going to let that stop her." Anubis shook his head. "I've never met a fiercer personality in my life."

"Yeah? Wait until she becomes a mom." Frank tapped the table. "I'm going to check on John and Dixon, then get cleaned up. Whistle when you're ready to do the brief."

"Yes, sir. And I'm seriously glad you made it in." Anubis stood and offered his hand again.

Frank took it again and nodded his head. "Yeah, I'm pretty excited about that, too."

CHAPTER 15

Joy headed down the corridor where Anubis had told her Dixon was working. The damn man was going to drive her crazy. He glanced up when she came in but went straight back to work. "Pouting?" She asked and crossed her arms.

Dixon didn't look up. "I'm soldering, you shouldn't be here."

"Then fucking stop and talk to me because I'm not leaving." She was going to set boundaries right here and right now.

He set the device he was holding down and turned to look at her. "So, now you want to talk?"

"No. I never want to fucking talk, but it's obvious *you* need to." She didn't blink as she held his stare.

"You're risking your life and the life of our baby."

"And if I don't go out there, we're pretty much going in blind tomorrow morning. How many are going to die then? You? Me? Frank? Drake? I know I can do this. What is more important is *you* know I can do this. Where is this macho bullshit coming from?"

"You're pregnant!" Dixon yelled at her.

"The baby is maybe the size of a fucking pea! Doc gave me anti-nausea meds and I'm fine. I will get that antenna up and do what I need to do up there. I refuse to change who and what I am because I'm pregnant, Dixon. You better digest that quickly, or we are going to have problems."

"Then I guess we have problems. That is my baby, too and I don't want you or her hurt."

She narrowed her eyes. "If I wasn't pregnant this wouldn't be an issue."

"Yes, it would!" Dixon threw his hands up in the air. "Don't you get it? It kills me when you leave on a mission! I go fucking insane every single time. I hate that you're still taking assignments."

Joy digested that bit of information. "We've talked about this."

"No, there was no discussion. You told me you

were continuing to work. You've never asked how I feel about it."

"Because it is *my* decision." She lowered her voice. "I'm married to you, that doesn't give you the right to change me or make decisions for me."

"And after the baby is born? Are you going to accept missions?"

"I don't know," she answered honestly. "I just found out I'm pregnant. I thought I had the flu. I haven't even thought about what I'll do tomorrow after we retake this land, so I can't answer you. But one thing I will tell you: I love you and I love my baby. I will not take unnecessary risks. I don't do that, and I haven't done that since we hooked up." She was damn careful ever since that mission where her target had almost killed her. Dixon had seen the bruises from that disaster. There hadn't been a close call since and there wouldn't be. She actually valued her life and wanted to have a family with the frustrating hunk of sex seething at her from across the room.

"Is that supposed to make me feel better?"

"Yes." She lifted her hands. "It is the best I can give you and more than I've ever given anyone else."

Dixon swallowed hard and looked up at the

ceiling. "I know." He dropped his eyes to her. "I know."

They stood silent for several long seconds. She had no more words to give him on the subject, and it seemed he didn't, either. She looked behind him. "Are you going to deploy that?"

He glanced at the device he was making. "Someone will if it is needed."

"What is it going to do?" She needed to know so she wouldn't be taken by surprise.

"Lot of pop and bang, not much damage."

Joy nodded. "I want your cell phone."

He cocked his head. "Why?"

"Because I'm texting everybody we know, Ethan, Logan, all the Kings. You have all their numbers programmed. I don't. As soon as I'm aboveground, I'll push send on all the texts and then head over to the antenna. If I'm in the clear, I'll see if I have any responses and gather what intelligence I can. If not, well, maybe the texts get out so they know our status."

"If that was us up there, we'd be jamming transmissions."

"If that was us up there, I wouldn't have volunteered to go out. We are the best-trained, best-funded, and best-managed force in the world. You know that." Joy stepped closer to him. "You also know I wouldn't do this if I didn't think I could do it."

Dixon pulled her into him. "I know."

She breathed in the wonderful scent of the only person she'd ever loved. She'd changed so much to be with him. Hopefully, he saw that. She *was* trying.

"I love you," Dixon said as he held her.

She sighed, and the weight of the world slid off her shoulders. "I know."

"Guess I don't have to mend fences?" Frank's voice from behind them startled her, which pissed her off.

Dixon released her. "Thank God." He walked over and hugged Frank. The man slapped his back a couple times after returning the embrace. "Do Mom and Drake know you're here?"

"Yes. Drake had just come back as I left John with Adam," Frank said and pulled away. "Congratulations." He spoke directly to her.

"Thank you. What is wrong with John?"

"Shot. Twice. One is minor. Doc is fishing out the second one from his leg now. You going up?"

"I am." She nodded.

"Good. We need information on what's

happening and you're the best fit for that mission." Frank leveled his gaze at Dixon. "You know that, right?"

"Yes, I do." Her husband glanced over at her. "She's careful."

"I am. Frank, do you have your cell phone with you?"

The man frowned. "I do. Can't use it down here."

"I know, but you have all the bigwigs programmed in your phone, right? Gabriel, his wife, all the Kings." He nodded, still frowning. "Good, I need it. I'm going to send out texts to everyone once I'm clear of the shielding."

"They could be jamming."

"Yeah, we thought about that, but if they aren't, we can get information out and back in."

Frank reached into his pocket and handed the phone to her as he told her the numerical lock combination to unlock the screen. "Reception will be iffy. The cell tower booster was in the barn. With no backup comms, seems the barn is gone."

"Everything might be. I'll work on the why's and what's when I get aboveground." She glanced at her watch. "Which is soon." She turned to her husband. "I'll come find you when I get back."

"I'll be waiting at the tunnel entrance at the house. You need me, you make noise. I'll be there."

Joy smiled. "Do you think I need backup, Quick Draw?"

"No, but I'll be there regardless of need." Dixon dropped a kiss on her lips.

She spun out of his arms and headed down the corridor. With her husband back in line, she could focus on the mission at hand. She would copy and paste one text. Anubis and she had crafted it earlier. As she walked down the long walkway, she opened Frank's phone, found Gabriel's number, and typed:

SRS P 5:13

T- 15

She copied and pasted the information to each person. Sunrise Protocol. They were using the actual sunrise at 5:13 minus fifteen minutes. They'd launch their offensive at 4:58 a.m. She hoped someone would get the message and that Ethan would be monitoring his ham radio. That kid was damn sharp.

Milton made his way to the airstrip. Damn, the money put into this place was evident. Everything was well-maintained. Well, except for the shit Casey and Hound had blown to hell. It was dark now, and they'd been ordered to put flares alongside the airstrip so the planes could land. *Planes.* Two. What the fuck, were they bringing in more troops? He sighed. The teams on the perimeter had failed to track down two men on horses. They'd followed them to an old gravel path between a stock pond and pasture. The horses were grazing near the saddles, but there was no trace of the men. Yeah, he didn't want to be the one to tell the money that bit of news.

He kept clear of the glow spewing from the emergency flares that now lined the concrete flight line. Stupid to take the damn place and then light it up with flares. If there was anyone left out here, they'd be targets.

He watched the heavens, looking for the flashing lights of a jet. As of yet, he hadn't seen any. Other than the flight line, the compound was dark and quiet. Something Casey did had taken out the power grid. The asshole. He'd had men posted and watching while Casey had ransacked all the houses — allegedly looking for people. What he'd taken was a small arsenal of weapons, jewelry, and money.

Milton leaned against the wall of a small building by the flight line. There were no computers. None. He lifted his eyes to the heavens. The medical facility had two small laptop computers, but as far as he could see, no internet connections. Who didn't own computers? What was this place, a cult? He blinked at that thought. Man, that would explain a lot. Underground shelters. Doomsday preppers maybe? The slow blink of a wingtip light on an aircraft turning caught his eye.

He stayed where he was and watched as the plane lined up for a landing.

Joy opened the tunnel door and listened. She was in the basement of their home. The downstairs was Dixon and Drake's man cave. A massive screen and projection TV for their stupid games lined one wall. An overstuffed, U-shaped pit group was to her left, facing the television. She stepped out into the closet and narrowed her eyes. Someone had tossed the place. Fuckers.

She waited and let her eyes adjust, listening for

any sounds. A smile crossed her face when she heard the tick-tick-tick of Sasha's nails dancing across the floor above her. Carefully, she made her way through the trashed room and up the stairs. She stepped over the fourth and seventh stairs. They squeaked when any weight was applied to the riser. At the top of the stairs, she stopped in a crouch. The door was open a crack.

The cat was curled up on the only kitchen chair that was still standing upright. Sasha pranced somewhere to her right. There was no light except for what moonlight was coming through the windows. Joy listened for several long moments before she pushed the door open. The cat's meow sent Sasha's toenails scrambling. She swiped up her old puff of a dog and put her hand around its yappy muzzle. "Shhh." She moved back down the stairs and into the closet. Cat trotted right behind her. Joy opened the trap door and set Sasha in, grabbed Cat, and dropped her in, too. She shut the door and winced as Sasha barked. It could barely be heard, but still. Hopefully, Dixon would be at the tunnel access point soon. The dog would settle down when he got there.

She retraced her steps back to the kitchen. Once on the main floor, her anger pegged into the red zone. Someone had ransacked the entire house. She slipped out the kitchen door, making sure to hold the screen door so it wouldn't slam against the wooden frame. Three steps across the porch and she landed in the soft earth beside Jillian's rose bush. Staying down, she moved her eyes in short, measured distances, scanning for things that should not be... *Holy fuck*. Half the barn was gone. She glanced to her right and then to her left, and only after making sure she hadn't been spotted did she focus on the barn. *Son of a bitch.* Carefully, she moved along the porch until she could peek up the hill. With a sigh of relief she didn't know she was holding, her shoulders fell. The main house looked to be intact. She glanced at her watch. *Enough sightseeing.*

She pulled out Frank's phone, hiding the light activating the face had caused under her black shirt. She pushed 'Send' and scrolled through every contact that was associated with Guardian, hitting send on each. Once it was done, she pushed that phone into her ass pocket and studied the area again.

Joy crouched low and moved silently from their house to the drover's cottage. The small shack split the distance between her and Shae's homes. At the back of the small structure, she pressed into the wall and stopped to gauge her next route.

A cough. At a distance and to her right. Joy carefully swiveled on the toes of her shoes and worked her eyes through the darkness until she saw the man. He was leaning against the outside of one of the smaller outbuildings. A flick lit up the darkness, and she memorized the profile of the man's face as he lit his cigarette. Slipping further along the shadowed back of the drover's cottage, she examined the route to the barn. She'd need to get past it to the grain silo. The easiest way to the silo was through the barn, but Shae had evacuated that way, and they weren't re-using tunnels, just in case someone had followed them down.

She made sure there were no other sentries and moved. Halfway to the burned-out barn, her ass started vibrating. *Fucking great. I'll get right back to you, my BFF Jill.* The vibrating of Frank's phone was a literal jolt in the ass to get her moving. She rounded the destroyed portion of the barn, keeping herself as low to the ground as possible. At the back, she shimmied down the side of the barn. Her ass lit up again. *Seriously?* She crouched down and waited for the vibrating to stop before she scanned the last leg of her journey.

A man strolled from the pasture where the girls kept their calves. Her eyes narrowed, and she slipped her gaze to the fucker's right. There. Ethel was blonde, and she could clearly see the light-colored calf standing beside a darker shadow. Lucy. Thank God. She felt like killing someone already; if that bastard had hurt those girls' pet cows, she would have had to slit the bastard's throat before she put the damn... *What the hell?*

She pushed back into the wall as a red glow filled the sky behind the main house. Joy glanced around her and then back at the glow. Not a fire, the reddish hue got brighter. Is that what Dixon had built? She glanced at her watch. No, damn it, she had six minutes left before that was supposed to be deployed.

A scuff to her right dropped her into the shadows. Another man crested the side of the little cow barn where she was waiting.

"Kaiser, what the fuck is that?"

"Flares to light up the flight line."

"Fucking stupid," the man muttered. Honestly, she agreed with him. These weren't tactical geniuses. Joy waited in the darkness. The man was standing directly in front of her now. He patted his pocket and pulled out a pack of cigarettes. He put one in his mouth and lit it. The obnoxious odor of cigarette drifted toward her as he blew a lungful of the shit in her direction. Her stomach lurched, then rolled, doing a double barrel half-pike straight into 'God, I have to puke' land. She stopped breathing and willed the bastard away from her.

"You got a light, man?" Kaiser called out to him. "Mine died on the last butt."

The man in front of her grunted something and ambled off. She swallowed hard and prayed her stomach would behave. As the two men met up, she made her way to the silo and slid behind it. The great metal cylinder rose into the air and contained grain or some shit like that. *Whatever.* She found the ladder and started up the side of the structure. At the small platform about thirty feet off the ground, she knelt and pulled the battery Jillian had given her out of her back pocket—the pocket that wasn't vibrating—and disconnected the wires for the antenna at a small junction box. She'd practiced with a mock-up in the tunnel, so hooking the battery up took less than a minute.

Her head snapped up at the sound of an

airplane. *Fuck*. Her eyes swung to where the distraction was supposed to be deployed. From her vantage point, she could see over the hill to the Guardian side of the complex. *One, two, three...* She kept counting as the men from that side of the facility put themselves into silhouette against the glow of the emergency flares. Six men total? The aircraft coming in would probably have more men. *Shit.*

The aircraft's whine was enough to cover the sound of the antenna going up. *Fuck the distraction.* She hit the button, and the smooth, electrical whirr of the antenna lifting into the air sounded for almost a minute. She taped the battery to the side of the metal tube and glanced at the flight line. The plane had landed and was taxiing. She glanced at her watch. The distraction didn't go, which would have pissed her off if she was counting on it. But it made sense. Deploying it was useless now that everyone's attention was on the flight line.

She turned and looked straight up. A camera. The small red light blinked on and off, and it was pointed straight at her. She lifted her hands and signed:

Six men I can see. Barn destroyed. Houses ransacked.

She hoped they were able to see. After glancing to see what the assholes she'd gone through to reach the silo were doing, she took a chance and pulled Frank's phone from her back pocket.

Rdv pt HLSTR

t-15 ackngd

Fury

Fury's acknowledgement of her message meant they had backup, which was gathering at Hollister.

She closed her eyes and drew a deep breath, regretting it immediately. The faint smell of cigarette smoke that lingered on her clothes was enough to make her gag. She concentrated on shallow breaths through her mouth and worked her way to the edge of the platform, checking to make sure the two idiots she'd seen on this side of the complex were still occupied with whatever conversation they were engrossed in. They were. Thank God.

Joy pocketed the phone and used sign language to relay the text to the camera still pointed directly at her. She shoved the phone into her back pocket and started down the ladder only to stop about three steps down.

From where she was, she could see the aircraft clearly as it pulled to a stop. The G-6's door opened and ... *Damn.* She counted as men stepped onto the tarmac. Fifteen, three teams. *Wait...*

Joy watched as two people were taken from the plane. *Taken?* Yes, they were being manhandled, forced to move forward. The two people were surrounded by five more men. She stared at the two people being pushed around. Females. That was all she could see from here. *Fuck.* None of this made sense. None.

She glanced at the fuckwads watching this side of the ranch. They'd separated. Her eyes darted around until she found both. Carefully, she made her way down the ladder, one foot down, pause, one hand down. She wasn't going to call any attention to herself. The assholes might not be very good sentries but that didn't mean they weren't good shots, and damn it, she promised Dixon she'd be careful.

Once down, she retraced her steps, diverting at the last minute to go to the front of the small barn where the girls kept their pet cows because one of the sentries was taking a whiz behind it. She stopped and listened, waiting for the man to shake it off and get the hell away from her, when she heard a soft whine.

What the fuck?

The barn door was open; getting inside didn't take a second. She squatted by the door and listened. *There.* Moving to the stall, she peeked in. Lady. Frank's dog. How had she gotten locked in a stall? She opened the pen door, and Lady toddled out to her. She pet the old woman's head. *How in the hell am I going to get you out of here?* With the load of men getting off the plane, it would only be a few minutes before whoever was in charge sent them out to secure the area, and tomorrow morning at sunrise, lead was going to be flying.

She moved to the barn door with Lady right beside her. She whispered, "Sit." The dog immediately plunked her butt down. It was going to be impossible to get the white and brown collie to her house without being seen. *What to do?*

Lady perked up and her head snapped toward the complex side of the ranch. Seconds later, Joy heard the whine of another jet coming in for a landing. She glanced out the door, and sure enough, whiz-boy was heading back to where the other guard was. A shout from the other side of the big house echoed and then gunfire. Both men reacted and ran toward the hill that separated the complex from the ranch.

"Come." Joy sprinted across the expanse, not trying to conceal herself or the dog. Lady ran by her side as she flew across the open area. The sound of gunfire from the other side of the hill lit a fire under both of their asses, and she and Lady launched up the steps of her house. She didn't give a flying fuck who heard the screen door slam when they ran inside. As soon as her hand was on the door, Dixon was there. Lady shot past them.

As Dixon pushed Joy into the house, she spat out her new information. "Gunfire on the other side. At least twenty men arrived on the first aircraft. Two prisoners, I think they're women. A second plane just landed."

"I heard the gunfire and the second plane land. Did you get a response to the text?" Dixon moved her toward the stairs to the basement.

"Yes, Fury acknowledged fifteen minutes prior to sunrise." She pulled out the phone.

Dixon took the phone and glanced out the windows. He typed a message and hit send.

"What did you tell him?"

"Reinforcements, two hostages, probably

women, and another plane landing, unknown personnel."

Joy nodded. She and her husband flew down the stairs and reopened the tunnel. She called to Lady, who was hesitant to go in. Dixon picked up the dog and they stepped through, sealing the door as Sasha pranced around them, yipping like a maniac.

"You had to rescue the yapper, didn't you?" Dixon put Lady down.

Joy picked up her poof, which silenced her immediately. "She counts on me to take care of her."

Dixon put his arm around Joy and pulled her into him. "And Cat? Lady?"

"Listen, if you're going to make a big deal of this, I'm leaving." She pulled away.

"You're just an old softy, aren't you?" Dixon rocked a bit as he pulled her back to him.

"Tell anyone and I'll break your joystick," she murmured.

He chuckled, "Not a soul. I promise."

CHAPTER 16

"What does it say?" Joseph asked as he flew over the asphalt. They were about five minutes outside of Hollister.

"You've got two new ones," Ember said. "Jacob, Jade, and Jared are flying out. They need a drop zone cleared."

"Fuck, okay, we'll get that sorted when we get to Hollister," Joseph growled. "Text back, 'Copy all and stand by.'" He waited for her to text.

She shook her head a moment after she stopped typing. "I don't know what this means, but I'll read it exactly. It's from Frank's phone. It says, '*2xac, +20insurg, 2ncbt-f, hrdio.'* What does that mean?"

"Two aircraft at or coming to the ranch.

Twenty or more enemy insurgents and two noncombatants. Ham radio, they are telling us we can reach them via ham radio," Joseph deciphered the code for her.

"Tori and Faith? Could they be the noncombatants?"

"They could be, but we aren't jumping to conclusions." He didn't tell her the 'f' at the end of that message meant female, but his wife was damn smart. If it was Tori and Faith, the bastards better pray those women were unhurt. Death for anyone who hurt his family would be slow coming and painful.

He pumped his brakes a couple times, letting the convoy sucking up to his tailpipe know he was going to be slowing down. Taking a ninety-degree corner from the highway into Hollister meant they had to slow down. He let his foot off the gas.

When they reached the turnoff, he had to brake a little harder than he wanted. Ember's hand shot to the oh-shit bar, and she gasped loudly. "Sorry, sorry." She breathed the apology. He got it. She wasn't a thrill-seeker and, as a doctor, was safety-first oriented.

They barreled through the small town. It hadn't changed since the last time he was here. He pulled up behind the clinic. The SDHP turned around and headed out of town as the other SUVs pulled in beside him.

Reaper opened the door and stood watching as Joseph exited the vehicle. Reaper's eyes narrowed. "Took you long enough."

"Fuck you," Joseph growled and extended his hand. Reaper grabbed it and shook it.

"We have a place to talk."

"Good. Wheeler, can you get my wife some food and coffee?" He swung his gaze to the shrink he hated for no good reason other than he'd kissed his wife. Bastard.

"Is that code for get lost so you can talk?"

"No, it's code for my wife needs food and coffee. I'll brief you on what you need to be briefed on."

"Joey, I can speak for myself. Remi, I could use a drink, not coffee, something with alcohol, and I don't think anyone here has eaten."

"We can fix that. Gen will hook us up." Jeremiah extended his elbow and Ember slipped her hand through it. She glanced at Joseph. "Don't you dare leave without telling me you're going."

He lifted an eyebrow at her and nodded. Nothing like being whipped in front of the troops, but fuck it. She'd earned the right to know when he slid into the shadows.

"Let's go."

Reaper led the way, and they filed into Wheeler's building. "The pilots were here earlier. An ambulance made it here about an hour ago to take them down to Rapid City. Both were alive. The town doctor went with them. The copilot confirmed it was a surface-to-air rocket. The pilot hasn't regained consciousness."

Joseph nodded and laid down the tube he'd grabbed from the SUV. He pulled the top off and unfurled the contents across what appeared to be an exam table. "I know we can't all see this at once, so team leaders, rally up, everyone else, tune in. Guardian has been attacked at Washington, D.C. and here at the complex on the Marshall Ranch."

Lieutenant Evers' head snapped up. "Complex as in…"

"As in rehab and training facilities along with communications and overseas operations planning and execution." Joseph pointed to the map of the ranch. "This hill separates the complex from the ranch. These are houses holding staff and family. This path leads to the complex. The flight line, here. Here is the communications building, believed to be gone as well as the barn over here. If they were still standing, we would have communications with the underground facility where our people have taken refuge."

Evers glanced around the table. "I'm the only one here shocked as shit that there is an underground facility, aren't I?"

Rocker chuckled, "Welcome to Guardian, Lieutenant. We have the best toys."

"Obviously." The man looked at Joseph. "Sorry, go ahead."

Joseph nodded. "We have received two text messages from the complex. Obviously, someone slipped out to send the information. First, we will be conducting the operation in coordination with the personnel assigned to the complex exactly fifteen minutes before sunrise. Which gives us too few hours to work the plan and deploy. Second, I need a clear drop zone for three personnel inbound. Somewhere close but not close enough for the plane to be seen or heard at the ranch."

Reaper lifted from his position at the far end of the table. "The Hollister Ranch. They can come in from the north."

"Why that location?" Joseph asked.

Reaper crossed his arms and said, "Captain Andrew Hollister, USMC."

"Why is that name familiar?" Rocker, Alpha Team's skipper, spoke up.

"He was a Congressional Medal of Honor recipient last year. He's also the one who brought the pilots in, and he was heading to the Marshall Ranch on his own because he knew something was off. We drop on his land, and he'll get them to us."

"Call him. Find out where would be the best drop zone. We'll need horses. We can get close, but horseback is the quickest and quietest way to get to where we need to be." Joseph turned back to the map and stared at it. "I need comms here. Secure."

Travis turned. "Ricco, get a secure phone line up."

"On it, Skipper." One of the men darted out of the room.

"Alpha Team, you'll come up from the south, Sierra Team, you enter from the south also and work your way to the ranch with the rest of us. Once at the ranch, you're to circle the boundaries silently and post up on the north side in a one-hundred-and-eighty-degree arc. Alpha Team, you'll do the same from the south. Four of us will go inside and bring out the two women.

"Lieutenant, I need your team to cover the outer perimeter. We need your squads to circle the ranch buildings and the complex. Maintain a three-sixty. Take out anyone posted watching the ranch and anyone trying to leave."

"Got it." Evers nodded.

"When we deploy, Alpha and Sierra teams, you'll need to take positions no closer than here, here, here, and here." Joseph pointed to four boundaries on the map.

"Why not let us get closer? If we can get closer, we'd have a better field of fire," Travis asked.

Joseph chuckled. "Trust me, you don't want to be closer. I'll get into specifics after I make a few phone calls. Right now, each of you make sure your team members know what the assignment is and what the boundaries are."

"Question." Lieutenant Evers crossed his arms. "How are we going to tell friendlies from foe when shit starts? We don't know your people. They don't know us."

A chuckle spread around the room. "What's so funny?" Bear, the man Joseph had asked for specifically, asked.

Joseph nodded at Travis, and the team leader explained, "We will provide you uniforms and weapons. Our uniforms emit a radio frequency. When you look through our scopes and NVGs, you'll see green if the person you're concentrating on is a Guardian. Red for bogies."

Joseph continued, "The complex knows where we will set up. If you are within this area when Sunrise Protocol starts, you're fair game. So, stay out of this area and wear our uniforms. Other than that, if someone is shooting at you, shoot back."

"No one from the complex will be behind us?" Bear asked.

"No. Again, we don't know if there is an outer cordon for the area, that's why the SEALs are on the perimeter. They'll tighten in and take out anyone posted. They are trained to not be seen. The Guardian teams will clear in through one point and then deploy. We have POTUS authority to take out anyone trying to stop us from taking this facility back."

"Skipper, comms are up," Ricco called from the other room.

"Gentlemen, the uniforms are in the SUV outside along with an arsenal of weapons, scopes, comms, and NVGs. Bring the cases in here, please. We don't need to put a show on for the citizens of Hollister."

"All twelve of them," one of the SEALs said.

Joseph left the map on the table. "Ten minutes. Brief your teams and unload the equipment." He exited as the men shifted behind him.

"This way, sir." Ricco nodded down the hall. "Do you want me to stand by?"

"No. I've got it,"

He waited for the door to close and picked up the phone. He pulled out his cell phone, unlocked it, and scrolled through numbers until he reached the right set because he didn't bother memorizing telephone numbers any longer. He punched in the numbers and listened as the phone connected and then rang through.

"Go." Bengal's voice was a sound he was happy to hear.

"How is she?" His sister took the weight of the world on her shoulders.

"In the zone. She's working with Ethan. Where are you?"

"Hollister. Setting up and starting the ops brief for Sunrise Protocol." He glanced out the window to the darkness that enfolded the small town.

"She's captured four images of our trigger men for the rocket launchers in D.C. We have the CIA doing facial recognition on them. She's tracking weapons purchases and running intel through the FBI, but we haven't found a signal that a domestic terrorist event was being planned. No chatter, so not a terrorist organization."

Joseph narrowed his eyes and stared out the window into nothing. "Privately funded?"

"It is our assumption at this time," Zane agreed. "She's running through the list of personnel that have been prosecuted via investigations. That isn't looking like it will pan out with anything."

"What about the Shadows' targets? Retaliation?"

"Who would be able to track that type of information? None of our operatives have reported anything amiss."

"Who is at the Annex for rehab?"

"Hold on. Jewell pulled the ranch information earlier." He waited as Zane retrieved the information. "The last report that she had access to via her secure email server, and thank God for that backup, we have three patients. Two team members recovering from injuries overseas, and then Blocker."

"Blocker. I don't know that name."

Zane grunted. "His real name is Mitchell Bridges. He's an undercover investigator we've had in Boston for almost four years. He was the one who went undercover and blew apart the O'Hara family's hold on the city. During the takedown, he was shot twice in the gut. Four operations so far."

Joseph remembered now. The mafia family had been escaping justice for almost a decade. The New York-centered branch of the Irish mafia had suffered a huge loss when the upper echelon of the Boston branch of the family was indicted and kept in jail without the possibility of parole until their trial. Whenever that was. "He could have been tracked."

Zane was quiet for a moment. Joseph heard Zane moving and then a door shut. His fellow assassin spoke quietly, "I'll have her look into it. Other than that, we have nothing. She's doing what she can. The computers are adequate, but she's stressed and worrying."

"We need to know who funded the purchase of the rockets. Keep her focused on that. Everything else is secondary. Have her follow the money." He closed his eyes. "She's not responsible."

"And yet, that is exactly what she thinks. Her mom and Frank, plus the rest of the family at the ranch, are in jeopardy. Jason is hurt and she didn't get to see him. You know she doesn't know how to process this without finding herself at fault," Zane replied dryly.

"There is nothing I can do from here." He felt as helpless as a fucking child. "We are in this together. All of us. Find the weapons sales, follow the money. We'll handle the ranch, and we might have a location on Tori and Faith."

"What?" Zane's sharp question damn near popped an eardrum.

"Lower your voice, asshole. I got a text from the ranch. Someone went topside to send it. They have at least twenty more men at the ranch. Two planes landed or are landing. There are two female noncombatants and something about communications with a ham radio."

"Ham radio? Ethan has one in the computer room." He could hear Zane walking and the door opened again. "Ethan, turn on the ham radio, the ranch is up."

"Fucking right." Joseph heard Ethan's exclamation.

"We'll get them. I'll call you back when we know what's going on." The line went dead.

Joseph cocked his head and dropped the phone onto the cradle. A muscle beside his eye twitched. If one more person hung up on his ass today, he was going to slit someone's throat. He didn't care whose at this point, but someone was going to die.

He picked up his cell and dialed again.

"Blue."

"Sitrep."

Maliki sighed deeply. "We've been helicoptered to the best spinal care facility on the east coast. They're doing tests now. Nic is getting us a change of clothes and something to eat and drink while we wait for an update on Jason. Poet is checking on Tippy and Tommy and grabbing a shower at Jason's. I'm still in shock. I can't believe what I saw."

"You'll process it. You're strong. What do you know about Jason's status?"

"He couldn't feel his legs, which, all things considered, was a good thing."

"What are you saying? How in the fuck is that a good thing?" Not feeling his legs wasn't a good thing at all.

"He was in excruciating pain in that tunnel. After getting him out, the leg that was causing so much pain numbed out on him."

"Did something happen during transport to make him lose sensation?" Fuck, his brother had so much on his plate; he didn't need this, too.

"Honestly, I don't know. Maybe? It could have been the move, or swelling around the damaged area, or any number of things. We moved him by the numbers."

"How long until we know the prognosis?"

"Later is all I know. What I have is just bits and pieces, which I refuse to assign to a diagnosis unless I have the rest of the information. We have the best medical minds here. Gabriel made sure of it."

"He's my next call. I won't have my phone with me later. Call Zane and give him updates, will you? I'll check in as I can, and if you get in to see him, tell him I have his six. We'll get these fuckers."

"Will do. You watch your back, my friend."

"Always. Whatever it takes."

"As long as it takes."

Joseph hung up and dialed the one number he did have memorized and not written down anywhere.

"Tell me you have good news."

Fuck, Gabriel sounded old and damn tired. "Someone went topside and sent two texts. They are working via Sunrise Protocol. T-minus fifteen minutes. I have the SEAL Squad, Alpha Team, Sierra Team, Reaper, and Tempest here with me.

I'm going to pull Tempest from Sierra team to infiltrate with me. I know that ranch like the back of my hand. The three of us are going to take out as many inside the camp as we can before the complex springs the trap."

"I saw the texts. I doubt it would do any good for me to tell you not to move in before the coordinated time."

"It would not. There are two female noncombatants on the ranch. If Tori and Faith are there, I'm going to get them out. Alive. Where are you?"

"Jacob will want to be with you."

"No doubt." He would make sure his brother's head was screwed on straight first. "You're driving?" The connection sounded like he was in a vehicle.

"Yes. Driving to the building. Or where the building used to be." Gabriel's voice was low when he admitted where he was going.

"Why?"

"I have to see it. In person. Charley has it locked down."

Joseph dropped his chin and sighed, "You are too important to be out in the open."

There was a long pause. "My life exploded tonight. With the exception of the Rose, what I've spent a lifetime building has crumbled. After I go through the rubble, I'm flying to South Dakota. When—and I repeat, *when*—we have those bastards in hand, I will ruin whoever did this. Absolutely ruin them and anyone connected to them."

Joseph heard the quiet rage in his mentor's voice. "You'll have to get in line, my friend."

There was a short pause. "Jason's doctor called me about ten minutes ago. It's not looking good."

"I just talked to Maliki. He said you had the best docs available with him." Even if his friend wasn't jumping to a diagnosis, it seemed the other doctors didn't have that worry.

"Too damn little," Gabriel sighed.

"This isn't your fault," Joseph spoke again.

"I understand that, but tell me, what did we miss?"

"You know as well as I do it could be one of a million suspects we've incarcerated or family of people we've removed. Hell, it could have been the mafia that Blocker took down. I asked that Jewell look into that end, too."

"That only happened last week. This was a planned mission executed against us."

"I know. I'm grasping at straws like everyone else."

"I'm here." Gabriel's words were a mere whisper.

"I'll let you go. We'll find out who's responsible. Whatever it takes."

"As long as it takes," Gabriel said before he disconnected the call.

"Shit." Joseph ran his hands through his hair. A knock on his door snapped his head up. "Enter!"

Ember slipped through the door carrying a medium-sized white box. "Food." She set the box down and pulled a thermos out from under her arm. "Coffee. Carry on with what you were doing. I'm going back across the street to help Remi's sister heat up enough food for the crew in here." She bent down and kissed him. "The weight of this does not rest on your shoulders, Joey. You are not responsible."

He leaned up and kissed her one more time before she ghosted out his door. He stared at it for a moment before he spoke. "But if I don't get everyone out, it will be my fault."

He unscrewed the top of the thermos and used it as a cup to pour the coffee. Fuck, it smelled delicious. He picked up the phone and dialed the Rose. Taking a peek into the box, he damn near drooled.

The sandwich was stacked high with meat and cheese.

Thanatos answered just as Joseph was about to take a bite. He sighed and put the damn thing down. "Where is the plane holding my siblings?"

"About an hour out," Thanatos answered quickly.

"I'll have drop coordinates shortly. Anything else you need from me?"

"I have the branch chiefs from the domestic side calling in every twelve hours. They have everything handled. The Shadows were never recalled. Anubis must not have had enough time."

"Put a message out with my authorization staying all missions no matter what phase they are in."

"I have. Gabriel told me to do that about thirty minutes ago. Just filling you in. The teams that are overseas are problematic. When Jacob gets to comms, he needs to authenticate the recall. Obviously, there was a step I wasn't aware of. Ever have people from three different continents tell you to fuck off?"

Joseph chuckled. "Not lately, but it's happened."

"We've got a loose grip on this. The branch chiefs will keep the Domestic Ops sections going."

Thanatos stopped talking. "Is this the end for us? For Guardian?"

"No." He could fucking guarantee that fact. Guardian was down, but they weren't out.

"The death toll in Washington has hit seventy-five. Civilian casualties are holding at eighteen. That's including the two teams that were killed at Jacob's house. The men working nights have checked in. Lima Team's leader had switched with one of his men so his man could have the night off. He's pretty fucked up."

"I can only imagine the shit that this is putting on people. I'll let Doctor Wheeler know and see if he can set up virtual sessions. If you can't reach me, get ahold of Gabriel. I'll be in touch with the coordinates."

"Hey, Fury?"

"Yeah?"

"Don't get dead." Thanatos cleared his throat. "Don't get dead, man."

"Getting dead is not on my agenda." He hung up the phone and stared at the sandwich that had seemed so damn appealing less than three minutes ago. Seventy-five Guardians dead. Almost a hundred total. Whoever did this was going to pay.

CHAPTER 17

Gabriel took a single step forward and stopped. He swallowed hard and stared at the pile of debris where Guardian used to be. The sounds of doors shutting behind him didn't turn his head. His security team would deploy even though Charlotte had the areas secured. The flashing red lights of fire vehicles, blue lights of police, and yellow flashing lights of utilities vehicles danced in a muddled, multicolored swirl on the far wall of what was left of the building. Powder coated everything, giving the area a muted, grey aura. Death and destruction hung heavy in the air. People plodded, determined as they worked. Small pockets of activity punctuated the vast expanse of rubble. Artificial lighting highlighted areas where people moved with purpose. He'd driven down this street too many times to count, and yet it was completely unrecognizable.

"Dad."

He turned. "Charley. Dan." He acknowledged the presence of his youngest and then nodded to her husband. The man was covered in grey dust, streaked with sweat and blood.

"We found three more survivors," Charley spoke quietly as she closed in on where he was standing.

"Good." He turned back to the devastation. "I'd like you two to continue as point for this." He sighed and looked at his daughter, expecting a fight.

She nodded. "We've got it, but we want to be in on the rebuild."

"I'm not sure we will rebuild. At least, not here." He couldn't imagine putting his people in jeopardy again.

"If the tunnels weren't constructed, we would have lost so many more," Dan spoke for the first time.

"We lost too many. That's why I'm thinking of decentralized control."

Charley snapped her head in his direction. "We need control of HR and comms."

"But they don't need to be in the same location," Dan said the words he was thinking.

"CCS?"

"Could be in South Dakota. It doesn't need to be here." *Or overseas, for that matter.* Having a node on each continent made sense. They had access to the Genesis satellite array so there would never be downtime.

"Do you have any news or updates? We're in the dark here," Charley asked after a minute.

He put his hands in his pockets and made sure they were out of earshot of anyone. His team was milling close by, but that was it. "The response force is at Hollister. Two texts from the ranch. Over twenty combatants. Two female noncombatants."

Charley whirled. "Tori and Faith?"

"That is the assumption." His mind spun with questions he hadn't processed because of what was in front of him. What connection did Tori and Faith have to who did this? Why take them back to the ranch? What was the reason to take *them*? He turned. "I need to call Jewell."

"What?" Charley called after him.

He stopped and turned, speaking clearly. "Take care of this, Charley, you two are in charge." With that, he jogged to the privacy of his car and his phone.

Jewell flicked her eyes to the corner of the room where Zane waited for Ethan to do whatever he was doing to get his radio to line up with the ranch's. Ethan spoke as he spun a dial. "It doesn't always work. It depends on the bounce of the signal." Ethan sat down and pushed the button on the bottom of the standing mic. "GDNMNT1 calling GDNRCH1"

"GDNRCH1 copy."

Ethan pumped a fist through the air. "We have them."

"Let me talk." Zane asked for the mic and Ethan un-assed the chair in a heartbeat. "Sitrep."

"All family secured in Pit. Three staff missing. Multiple buildings destroyed. Rocket-launched missiles. Two AC. First plane twenty-plus men, two noncombatant females. Three IR cameras up. No information is available on the passengers or cargo of the second AC. Sunrise Protocol T-minus 15. Status?"

Zane scribbled on the pad and hit the mic button. "Family at ground zero safe. One critical at medical. Missing two females. ID possible?"

Jewell stopped typing and stared at the radio as if her concentration could make Anubis respond the way she wanted him to respond. "Negative. Cameras limited."

Zane said the cuss word she was thinking and then keyed the mic. "What do you need from us?"

"Contact Fury, advise we are a go."

"Roger. Will continue to monitor."

"Standing down until go. GDNRCH1 clear."

"T-minus 15, that means they will go fifteen minutes before sunrise, right?" Jewell looked at the clock and calculated the time difference.

"Correct." Zane got up. "I'm going to call Fury."

"Tell him we have seven known buyers in the last year." Jewell went back to work.

"Where are we on finding out who the real buyers are?" Ethan asked as he resumed his seat.

"We are playing the shell game."

"The what?"

"Shell game. Watch and learn. See, this company purchased fifteen shoulder-launched cruise missiles. The company is a shell. You can see here the managers' names. Most legal ones in the United States are registered through the SEC. This is an overseas company. You can tell by the website information." She switched screens and pulled a list of information. "Built ten years ago in Nigeria. It could be a legit entity, but odds are they are masking purchases. This is one we will track."

Ethan leaned over. "How?"

"Oh, that is the fun part. We start with the information about the web page. See the IP address? That's where we start." She walked Ethan through the process twice and then sent the files to his computer. She'd done this enough to see that the entity behind that purchase would end up somewhere in Africa. All the markers were there. She pulled the next entity and started working.

The phone beside her rang and she stopped. "Is that for you or me?" She pointed at the landline.

"No one calls here unless Dad is going on a recruiting trip, so odds are it's for you." Ethan continued typing as he looked at her.

Damn, she respected the hell out of his abilities. Now he just needed an education. One she could provide him if he wanted it. The phone rang again, and she picked it up. "Ah, hello?"

"Jewell, Gabriel."

"Hey, how did you know to call——"

"Jewell, first, you know you have permission to go dark, and second, why would someone take Tori and Faith back to the ranch? Who would know of both of their connections to it?"

Her mind screeched to a halt. "First, I went dark without permission, and second... I don't know, maybe someone that knows the family."

"Right. Scrub everyone, Guardian or not. Someone knows that one or both of them have a connection to the ranch. Someone with a huge ax to grind."

"Okay, but how far back do I go? Where do I start?" She shoved a pencil into her mouth and bit down. Her mind raced. It was an impossible task.

"They were taken at Tori's. Concentrate on her and Jacob first, but don't neglect any tie to Jason and Faith. What about Reece's dad?"

All the wheels in her mind screeched to a halt at once. Shit, she couldn't even remember the guy's name. "Man, he's dead? Or in jail? I can't remember. But he was a biker, right?" It had been years since she'd researched that information. Normally, she'd pull the research up, but her files were gone.

"Is Reece there yet?" Gabriel's tone lowered.

"Yeah, they settled in about an hour ago." Jewell looked at the clock. She had so little time. Less than three hours. "Friends of family, Gabriel, that is an impossible task. I don't know who Tori and Faith see, where they go. I don't know who they've opened up to. How am I going to track this?" Her gut dropped. "I can't do it. There are too many variables. Too much data and no logical path to determine who would be a suspect and who wouldn't, and that's assuming I knew everyone and everything about every conversation those two families had with the people they interacted with."

Gabriel was silent, but her mind wasn't. She was useless. She ran her hand through her hair and pulled out a pencil from her messy bun. She snapped it between her fingers and closed her eyes tight. *Damn it, what good are you if you can't find out who did this to your family?*

A set of big, strong hands gently touched her shoulders and then started to rub them. Zane. God, what would she do without him?

"Jewell?" Gabriel's voice pulled her back to the conversation.

"Sorry, I was thinking." *Yeah, of what an absolute waste I was.* Zane's hands gripped a bit harder as if he knew what she was thinking, and he probably did. He knew her better than anyone else in the world.

"What if you ran the people you narrow the sales down to against people we know about? When Reece wakes up, get the name of his bio dad from him. I know they've told him everything."

"Yeah, I could do that. Gabriel, I'm sorry—"

"Stop right there. You have nothing to be sorry about. This isn't on you. I know you and Ethan are doing everything you can to get to the bottom of this. Just keep the connection between Tori and Faith in the back of your mind. It is just another data point."

"Another data point." She nodded. She understood that.

"I'll let you get back to work. I'm heading for the airport."

"Why?"

"I'm going to the ranch." His voice sounded determined.

"You won't get there before sunrise." She glanced at the clocks. He had to land in Rapid or Ellsworth and then drive up.

"I'll be there," Gabriel answered. "Get us some information."

"I'll do my best." Her deflated words dropped across their connection.

"Your best is all I ask. Whatever it takes, Jewell."

"As long as it takes, boss." She hung up the phone and glanced at the clock. As long as it didn't take longer than two hours and twenty-seven minutes.

Zane leaned down and whispered, "You've got this."

"I don't know where to focus." She stared at her computer and then lifted her eyes to meet his.

"Who bought the firearms?"

"But Gabriel wanted me to run people associated with Tori and Faith."

"And you will once you find out who bought the weapons. If there is a connection between any of them and a case Guardian has worked, a junction where the two connect, you've got your target. I'll go wake up Reece and find out his sperm donor's name. We'll take it back to grandparents, too. That old man of Faith's was a complete asshole. He might have had old debts and enemies."

Jewell nodded. Grandparents and parents. That was twenty-four points. Maternal and paternal grandparents for Faith and Jason and maternal and paternal grandparents for Tori and Jacob.

"Twenty-four data points to form an interrelatedness or association. Wait, don't wake up Reece. I can get the information from the security clearance paperwork." She leaned forward and drilled through her ghosted hard drive. "Yes, I still have that information."

"Cross-reference what you find through twenty-four points of data. You can do that in your sleep." Zane squeezed her shoulders.

"I can." She nodded and glanced up at him. "I can," she said with more confidence.

"I know." He bent down and kissed her. "What can I do to help?"

"Just be here." She smiled up at him and then turned back to her computer. "Ethan, where are you with that shell company? Has it landed in Djibouti yet?"

"Somalia, how did you know?"

"I've done literally thousands of these traces. We are jumping into hyperspeed. I need a database of every name you research. Here. Everyone connected with that search and the next ones." She pulled up an Access database and configured it quickly. "Use this."

"Got it, but how are you going to find a connection between names?"

She smiled. "We're going to use everything in our power to scrape as much information as possible about these twenty-four points of information and the names we uncover and put it into this database. If two names ever cross, we'll have our answer."

"Then tell me how to speed up this process." Ethan looked at her. "The method you showed me is too cumbersome. How do I take the short route?"

Jewell smiled. "Watch." She grabbed a pencil out of her messy bun and bit down on it. Her hands flew across the keyboard as she worked.

"Damn, that's excellent. Hold on." Ethan grabbed a file and mimicked her actions. They worked in quiet for fifteen or twenty minutes.

"Wait, this one is U.S. and it has an SEC registration." Ethan looked over at her.

"All U.S. shell companies are supposed to register with the SEC. Send that to me. I have to get into their firewall and get the information without being seen. You take the next file. Don't forget to copy and paste the names."

"I've been doing that as I go." Ethan continued to type as he spoke. She glanced at the database. It had grown to over a hundred names so far.

"Good. That is the second-to-last purchase. Take that one and the last one. I'll get this cracked and information traced, then we'll start the cross-reference."

"On it."

Jewell jumped when Zane popped the top of an energy drink and set it beside her. He put a cup of coffee beside Ethan. "Dang, I could get used to the service," Ethan quipped. "Thank you."

"You can't keep him, he's mine." Jewell took her eyes off the computer long enough to send a smile to her husband. He winked at her and went back to his chair. She took a long gulp of the drink, typing with one hand.

She glanced at the clock. God, she hoped she could get all the names processed.

CHAPTER 18

Jacob King sat motionless in the cargo seat of the C-130 that was flying him, Jared, and Jade to South Dakota. To say he was in a dark place mentally would be the fucking understatement of the century. He held his phone in his hand, waiting for information. Jewell would find something. She always did. Then... Well, then he'd track down the motherfucking bastards that had Tori and Faith.

He occupied the time by thinking of ways to torture the bastards. He'd been around the Shadows long enough to know some of their methods. Phoenix burned his victims alive. He shrugged his shoulders. No, that would be too fast. If someone hurt his wife or Faith, he'd tie the bastards up and skin them alive. Strip by strip.

Jared leaned forward as much as his safety harness would allow. "Where are you at? You just growled."

"Thinking about what I'm going to do to the people who took Tori and Faith."

"Shouldn't you be fixated on getting them the hell away from those bastards first?"

Jacob slowly panned his eyes to his brother. "If they are alive, yes."

"They are," Jade said from his other side. "Tori is as tough as nails, and Faith, too." Jacob returned his gaze to the other side of the aircraft. Jade continued, "Jewell will find something."

Jacob sneered, his mind going back to exactly what he would do to the son of a bitch that had them.

"Jacob, you can't go on a one-man killing spree."

"Really?" He turned and looked at his brother. "Tell me you'd do anything less if someone had taken Christian from you."

He turned his head just as Jade opened her mouth. "Or Nic. Don't come after me with judgement."

"Not judgement. Just saying it doesn't need to be a one-person show. No matter what it takes, I'll be beside you. You know that." Jared's matter-of-fact tone caught his attention.

"I'll castrate them for you before you do whatever you want to do. I watched during the round-up last year. Slice the ball sack, push out the nuts, and pull them off. Easy peasy." Jade nodded and crossed her arms. "Yep, I'd take pleasure in castrating them for you."

Both he and Jared stirred a bit in their seats. Fucking Jade. She was one of a kind, that was for sure.

His phone lit up. He almost dropped it in the rush to unlock it. "What is it?" Jade leaned over. He read the words and then read them again. *Fuck*. He stared at his phone. Two women being held at the ranch. No ID. He swallowed hard and passed the text notification to Jared.

Jared read the text before he commented, "It could be Tori and Faith."

"What? Who? Where?" Jade demanded. Jared handed the phone to her and let her read the messages. "Okay, so we go in before they launch the Sunrise Protocol and get them." Jade lifted a shoulder as if the feat would be no big deal.

"*We* aren't going to do that." Jacob pointed to her and Jared. "You are going to be in Hollister until we call for you to come out and process any of the motherfuckers on that ranch that make it through the morning."

"Excuse me?" both of his siblings said at the same time, stereo objections with emphasis.

"How many active operations have you been on in the last five years?" he point-blank asked his brother and then turned to stare at his sister.

Jared answered, "None, but I could say the same about you."

"Not true. While you both have been working in the strictly corporate world, I have been on missions." There were two that he'd gone out on in a supervisory role to coordinate with high-level governmental representatives. Plus, he still worked out with the teams as they processed through Washington. There was always a team at the gym and always a young buck that thought they could outdo the old man. It was harder to keep up, true, but they weren't talking about gym challenges here, they were talking about his wife. And Jason's wife. *Fuck.* He was going to be the point of that fucking spear.

"Jacob, I'm jumping out of an airplane. I better

get to kick some fucking ass." Jade crossed her arms and stared at him.

"If Joseph allows you to go in with the teams, I won't stop you, but I need you safe and I need you to process anyone we manage to capture at the ranch. You'll do the interrogations." He spoke to Jared on the last point. His brother was the best damn interrogator he'd ever seen. He took his phone and punched in a text to Maliki asking about Jason.

"Twenty additional men. What the hell is going on?" Jared rubbed his face. They'd all been through hell and they were all running on fumes, or, at least, he was until he got that message. Now, he'd power through the deepest trenches of Hell to reach Tori and Faith.

"I wish I knew. The good thing is Tori knows that ranch like the back of her hand. If they get free, she can hide until we get there." Jade offered him a small smile as she spoke.

"Why take them to the ranch? Why Faith and Tori? What connection do they have to this mess?" Jared said, obviously trying to process the information the same way Jacob was.

"I've no idea. There is nothing there. We don't take risks, we don't talk about the ranch, and just in case someone slips, all of the people we hang out with are vetted. Hell, even the kids' friends are checked out."

"What about Faith's family?"

Jacob shook his head. "We ended that." Jason had made damn sure she wouldn't have any issues with that motorcycle club. "And it's been years since any whiff of what was left of that club has made it to us." Jacob leaned forward. "But Tori worked for the CIA. You know how I found her. Her agency set her up and left her in the wind. I made sure the supervisor who permitted it... went away. Forever. That entire section was shut down once Gabriel submitted his report. That's the only thing I can think of that could raise its head again."

Jared narrowed his eyes. "Anyone specific?"

"Yeah, two people come to mind. Doctor Amari, he was a particularly vile participant after the situation happened. His job was to get information from her, not treat her. She suffered because of his actions. He was terminated based on videos they found of his sessions with Tori. Those digital files led to the removal of the section supervisor, the one above the one I... handled. While he had plausible deniability, Senior Supervisory Agent Champlain was demoted and eventually terminated by the CIA for gross misconduct."

"So, two names for Jewell to check into." Jared pulled out his new phone but stopped. "Does she have a cell phone?"

"I don't know. Call the Rose and have them relay the information to her." Jacob closed his eyes, and the image of his wife appeared. *God, Tori, hold on, babe, I'm coming.*

He drew a deep breath and focused on the fact that his boys were safe, and if Tori was at the ranch, he would get to her. He *had* to get to her. She was his life.

Andrew Hollister glanced at his watch. Another couple of minutes. He'd double-checked the GPS coordinates he'd given Roman, his new Guardian point of contact, before he'd sent the text. He shifted on the seat of his ATV. He'd had the hands drive out the other three, and Ryan, the ranch foreman, had driven the hands back to the bunkhouse. He was pretty sure his hands thought he'd lost it, but the only one he'd explained things to was Senior.

He saw the lights of the plane coming in from the north before he heard the engine. The plane flew overhead and banked, flying north again. By the silhouette in the sky and the sound of the engines, the plane was a C-130. The Air Force used them for transport. Smaller profile, they were a workhorse, and he'd spent too many hours in transit in the jump seats of those airplanes. The bird he'd flown home on was Air Force, too. He didn't remember the medevac flight, but he remembered waking up at Walter Reed.

Andrew picked out three chutes. He clicked his key over and flashed his lights three times, letting the people know where to aim their landing. It was as level as it got around here. No trees and no fence line for them to get tangled up in. He watched the parachutists circle lower and lower. The first hit the ground, landed on his feet, and was gathering his chute as the second landed. Not as graceful or practiced, the second man moved a bit slower but went after his chute. The third one landed, somersaulted, and popped back up immediately. Smaller but tall. He couldn't say why, but from this distance, he'd bet the third person down was a woman.

He started his ATV and the others. The first

man walked his way, the chute bulging under his arm. He extended his hand. "Jacob King."

Andrew nodded. "Andrew Hollister. Strap your chutes to the back platform. I'm taking you cross-country to town, it will save us about thirty minutes, but don't get in front of me and stay in a line unless you want to become Swiss cheese from the barbed wire."

"Oh, man, I'd love some cheese about now," a woman's voice confirmed his assumption. He turned as she came into view.

"How far?" the other man asked as he went to an ATV and started strapping his chute down.

"About twenty miles as the crow flies." Andrew pointed south. He waited for the people to mount the ATVs and pulled out. He didn't ride stupidly, but he did push the envelope, looking back every now and then, making sure his charges were keeping up. They were, so he pushed it faster. The only time he slowed down was to get them over a cattle grate or through a gate. The stopping and starting cost them time, but it was minimal.

As he crested the last hill before Hollister, he came in a bit too hot and flew about five feet before he hit ground. The ATVs behind him copied his speed and, assumedly, his jump. He heard the woman whoop and laugh. *Lord above, she must be a handful.*

He led them straight to the back door of Doctor Wheeler's office. A couple lights turned on as they passed by, but hopefully, the inhabitants of Hollister would go back to sleep. He cut the motor and dismounted.

He moved to the side as his three charges greeted another man at the back door. Big hugs, hushed words. He understood the intensity if not the actual situation. "You got them here in a hurry."

Andrew jerked. Roman spoke from where he was standing just behind him. "Fuck, let's not do that again, okay?"

The man chuckled. "Sorry, a byproduct of the profession."

Andrew wondered what type of profession that was, but asking was out of the question. He could guess. Instead, he let it go and asked, "The horses made it?"

"Yes, about fifteen minutes before you did. Where did you get twenty-six horses and saddles?"

"Twenty are ours. Six come from a neighboring ranch. Some of those saddles are older than sin, but the cinches and straps are new, and we did what we could to make sure they wouldn't have issues."

Roman cocked his head. "The neighbors and the hands didn't ask questions?"

Andrew shook his head. "We wouldn't ask for help if we weren't in need. It's a code out here. If you're asked and you can provide, you do. Someday, you might be the one asking. Hands have an idea of what's going on, but nobody asked, and I didn't say."

"Good people."

"The best. Too bad it took a trip around the world for me to figure that out." Andrew motioned to the porch. "Anything I can do to help?"

"Not right now. Why don't you head over to the café and grab a cup of coffee?"

Andrew shook his head. "I don't think so." Roman gave him a quizzical look so he explained. "I don't spend much time away from the ranch. I'll head back. Use those ATVs as you need them. I'll have someone pick them up tomorrow afternoon. I'm assuming things will be settled by then?"

The man looked at his watch. "Things will be settled in the next couple hours."

Andrew turned and looked at Roman. "At sunrise, then? Watch out for highlighting yourself on the hills. Don't crest high. Follow washouts or go around them when you're on horseback. If you don't, you'll silhouette yourself and be a perfect target."

"Sounds like you know what you're talking about."

Andrew shifted his gaze to the man who'd met his charges on the porch. "Joseph King. Thank you for your help." The man extended his hand and Andrew shook it.

"Andrew Hollister. Not a problem. I'll head back and let you get on with your pre-departure brief."

The man gave a low, evil-sounding laugh. "I like you."

Andrew swung his leg over his ATV. "You say that like it's important."

The man shook his head. "Not really."

Andrew fired up his ATV and put it in gear. He left without looking back. It didn't matter if he was liked. As a matter of fact, he'd prefer if nobody in this town saw his face ever again. He made his way back to his father's ranch, to the soil where he'd spend the rest of his life and then be buried. If he never left again, it would be too soon.

Joseph watched the man leave over the high swell of land to the north. Once it was quiet, he spoke. "He's our type of man."

"He is," Roman agreed.

Tempest's voice came from the darkness. "Read the write-up on him. He lived through hell."

"I think he's still there," Joseph mused quietly. "Tempest, we need four horses. Dark brown or black. As soon as Jacob gets changed, we're heading out. Have that SEAL team load up as well as both Alpha and Sierra Teams. We'll drive out to the points we discussed earlier. The SEALs will deploy and secure the area. Sierra and Alpha Teams will move to the interior kill zone boundaries. We'll do our thing once they are set, and we have distance to cover."

"On it." Joseph didn't hear his friend leave, but then again, he didn't expect to.

"I'm briefing Jared on the plan. He'll run the op from here. Make sure all comms are working."

"You got it." Reaper went up the stairs into the medical building that they'd taken over. Ember walked out as Reaper went in.

"You sent someone to come get me?" She moved up to him and he wrapped her in his arms.

"I did. I'm leaving in about ten minutes. Jared and Jade will be running the operation from here. When we're done, you'll be needed at the ranch. Jared will bring you out."

"But there is still time before sunup." Ember put her head on his shoulder.

"We have to move into position." He pulled her closer. "I promised I'd let you know before I left."

She lifted her eyes to him. He could see the tears in the light from the porch. "Don't you dare leave me." She whispered the words, but they were loud and clear.

"It is not my plan to leave you." His plan was to kill the motherfuckers who dared take on Guardian, find Tori and Faith, and then get to Washington to check on Jason. From there... Well, from there, they'd start rebuilding the finest organization on the fucking planet.

But right now, he was going to hold the woman who'd given him a reason to choose life all those years ago.

CHAPTER 19

Amanda King sat down on the king-size bed. The rooms in the Pit were functional and comfortable, but the reason for her being down in them was utterly unfathomable. She listened to the shower running as her husband washed his close encounter with death from his body. She'd left John and Shae about a half-hour ago. John was going to be fine, according to Adam, but knowing that John and Frank were shot at had rattled her to the point of tears. It had been a long time since she'd cried. The last time was when Frank had told them he was cancer-free.

Her eyes traveled upward and, as was her custom, she said a prayer of thanks and a prayer of protection, this time not just for her children but for her husband. She knew the man. If his ranch was attacked, he was going to be part of the solution, which meant he would be aboveground when they launched the counter... attack? Offensive? She'd heard both terms.

Dropping her eyes to her clasped hands, she studied the veins that ran over the back of her hand. When had she aged? She looked up, seeing her reflection in the mirror. Her hair had more grey in it now than it did black. Her skin no longer had the youthful firmness, and wrinkles now etched deep lines through her skin that bruised far too easily. Strange, really. In her mind, she was still the person she'd been years ago. The mirror reflected a hard life, but she wouldn't change a day of it. Well, except for Chance dying. But if the march of time hadn't happened exactly the way it had, she wouldn't have met or fallen in love with Frank.

The water shut off in the adjoining bathroom. Her heart ached, and she was terrified. She knew the risks her family took. That was nothing new. She'd sat beside hospital beds as they healed, held them as they cried, dried the tears, and gave them encouragement, but she'd never been in the crosshairs. How did they do it? How did they manage under the fear and the unknown? How did they let their husbands and wives walk away when it might be the last time they ever saw each other?

A tear slipped over the edge of her bottom lid. How was she going to face the next few hours?

The door to the bathroom opened and Frank walked out, a white towel wrapped around his narrow hips. He was closer to seventy than sixty, but his body was firm and tight. The grey hairs that ran through his chest hair matched the ones that had nearly taken over his darker hair. The girls had taken after their mother's coloring, not Frank's darker complexion and hair. He wore his hair longer now that he was done with his treatments, his little 'screw you' to cancer. The close-shaven beard was another new acquisition, but she loved it.

"What's this?" He walked up to her. The scent of a different soap floated around her. His thumb traced the track of the tear that she'd let escape.

Her voice cracked as she spoke, "I'm afraid." She looked up at him as her eyes filled with tears, and his image wavered under her observation.

He sat down beside her and pulled her into him. "We all are."

"Then why am I the only one crying? None of the other ladies are. Shae accepted what happened without any hysterics. My God, if that had been you? I would have been a mess. Someone shot him, Frank. Not once but twice."

"It happens."

Amanda pulled back. "Not here! Not here it doesn't! This place is our home!" Her shrill words almost echoed in the confines of the room.

Frank reached for her hands and grabbed them in his. He lifted one and then the other, kissing the backs of them. "I opened this place to Guardian. It is their home now, too."

She sobbed and fell against him. "I know. I'm so worried. It's all just…"

"A lot to take in."

"Yes, why aren't you freaking out?" She slipped one of her hands from his and wiped at the tears in her eyes.

"Well, I've been in these types of situations before. I had those memories to draw from." Frank stood up and walked to the other side of the bed. He laid down on the top of the blankets and patted the covers. Amanda wiped her tears again, toed off her boots, and got into bed with him.

"Was that before Elizabeth?"

He sighed. "There was a short period of time after she and I hooked up that we didn't know she was pregnant. During that time, I worked for Guardian. It was short-lived but pretty intense."

Amanda rolled, extending her jean-clad leg over Frank's bare legs. Her hand found that springy patch of chest hair that had grown back after his treatments and she wound her fingers in it. "I'm a mess."

"You aren't. You're in a new situation." He kissed the top of her head.

"Do you have to be part of this?" She didn't want him to be. God, she'd give anything to keep him belowground with her.

"I'm not going aboveground."

Amanda popped up on her elbow. "You're not?"

"No. This is a Guardian operation. Do I want these bastards off my ranch? Yes, but I also know our family, the ones by blood, marriage, and association, know what needs to be done. I won't be the reason someone else is hurt, and if I go up there not knowing the tactics, or if I'm not fast enough, well, then I could be that reason." Amanda stared down at him. He held her eyes and lifted his palm, cupping her cheek. "By my calculations, we have a while before we need to worry about what's been going through your mind."

"A long time. I'm not letting you get out of this arrangement for a long, long time." She dropped down and kissed him.

"I'm game." He lifted off the bed and moved over her, deepening the kiss. She gripped his strong shoulders as he kissed her. When he lifted, she pushed his longer hair off his brow. "Do we have time for this? For us?"

His eyes didn't leave hers to check the time. "I'll always have time for us." He lowered again, and she closed her eyes. He undressed her with soft kisses that followed his fingers. Those teasing kisses were interspersed with long, searching ones that left them breathless and panting. He entered her slowly, moving into her with a languid, unrushed determination. His body and hers may have been older, but when they were together, she was in heaven and, for a time, ageless. The crest of their lovemaking swamped her with the same fierce intensity as the first time they'd made love.

She held him as he chased his release and accepted his weight when he lowered on top of her. It was her time to hold him, these moments after he released. Her time to wrap him in the protective love that he gave so freely. She stroked his back and wrapped her legs around his. He was the center of her world. He grounded her, treated her like a treasure, and gave her anything and everything she could ever want. Frank Marshall was her protector, her lover, and her husband. She was truly blessed.

Victoria Marshall blinked at the familiar terrain. They'd brought her home. She shot a look toward Faith before some asshole pushed her forward. The guards shoved them toward the side of the tarmac. She stepped on a rock, feeling it under her thin-soled, flat sandal. She waited for the bastard behind her to shove her again and staggered, then fell. The tarmac tore at her hands and knees. The denim of her jeans ripped, and the flop hurt like hell, but she needed it to look authentic. As she was yanked off the ground, she held onto a small rock that she'd found on the ground. The zip ties on her wrists she could defeat, but having a weapon was a necessity.

"Where in the hell can we keep these two?"

"I'll take care of them." Tori looked at the guy just in time to watch him grab his crotch and make an obscene gesture.

The man who held her lowered his rifle so it was pointing at the jerk. "Hands and everything else off. Where is your command post?"

"What fucking command post? We were told to take the ranch. We did."

The man holding her mumbled some choice words under his breath. "Where the hell is Hound?"

"Dead," another man answered. He stepped out of the shadows. "I was the one who called the number on his phone and let the guy know."

They didn't know who they were working for? Tori blinked at that revelation.

"I need a place to hold these women."

"The main house. It has interior rooms that can be locked," the one who had stepped forward spoke.

"Put them in the fucking shed." Mr. Obscene spat on the ground. "I'll keep guard." A leer formed over that ugly face.

"I wouldn't trust you with a female dog." Her captor tugged her toward the other man. "Team

One, secure the flight line for arrival. Team Two, search the compound. Team Three, establish an outer cordon and set up firing solutions. Team Four, with me." Tori watched as the men he commanded scattered.

"How the hell did they take this place?" the man Tori believed to be her captor's second in command asked as they walked into the darkness toward her childhood home.

"Not all of us are idiots like Casey," the one who'd suggested the main house replied. "He is a loose cannon. Those women aren't safe around him."

Tori glanced at Faith. Her sister-in-law shot her a questioning look. She shook her head a bit before she returned her concentration to the path in front of her. She had no idea why they were here.

"He touches either of them, he's dead," her captor mumbled. "What is your name?"

"Milton. I have two others on this side that are—"

Tori saw Faith pull away and trip the man that was holding her. Tori jerked free, too, and sprinted the opposite direction. A shout from one of the men sounded right before gunfire rang out.

"Cease fire!"

She sprinted toward the path that would take her to the houses. The sound of boots coming after her made her leap from the path and bolt to the left, then zigzag to the right. She flew down the hill and jumped the gulley at the bottom. Her sandal slipped on the grass, and she went to her knees. Hands grabbed her hair and her arm. She was swung by both into the ground, her face pushed into the hard dirt.

"Give me a needle. Now!"

Tori struck out with her rock. Her hand hit paydirt, and the man released her.

"Motherfucker."

She kicked as she rolled, her foot connected, and someone cussed. A heavy body landed on top of her. Her neck screamed with pain and felt like it was going to break, but she wasn't going to stop. Another set of hands grabbed her legs and a third sat on her feet. She felt the stab of a hypodermic needle.

"Where is the other one?"

"She fucking disappeared. We're looking for her."

Tori fought to stay conscious. *Hide, Faith. Hide.*

Faith flew over the ground. Her tennis shoes barely made a sound. She knew where she was going and how she was going to get there. Her black T-shirt, black jeans, and dark hair were going to help her hide. She ran down the path she'd jogged over a hundred times. Her goal was in sight. She saw the small bridge that spanned the washout at the bottom of the hill. She zigged left and shot off the path, squeezed between two lilac bushes, and jumped with her feet out in front of her. The hay bales that the boys had stacked at the bottom when they were building a fort cushioned her landing. She rolled off them and flew down the washout away from the Annex. The moonlight didn't reach the washout, and she fell twice but got up and ran as fast as she could.

At the end, there was a small, open space to her right and a larger one to her left. She ran to the right, to the back of the machine shop. Stopping with her back to the shop, she searched for anyone following her. Flashlights pierced the darkness, moving slower than she was, but they were following her. *Shit.* She searched for… *Perfect.*

Faith ran past the barn and across the open field. She slowed long enough to make sure she could make it up the steps and into the main house. She flew up the stairs and down the hallway to the right, into Frank and Amanda's room. The rifle rack that always held his guns was empty. *Damn it.* She pulled the drawer under it open and moved the fake bottom. A locked case holding Frank's antique handgun was sitting at the bottom. Faith pulled it out and grabbed a small box of shells that was beside it. She made her way into the bathroom, grabbed a pair of scissors, and dashed out again. If they were going to bring Tori here, she'd need help.

They wouldn't think that she'd run to the place they were going to be. She moved down the hall to the closet where Amanda stored the laundry hampers. Royce had hidden from everyone here for over three hours. Only she wasn't going to come out and say 'surprise' after her nap. She opened the door, moved the hampers out, and squeezed into the small space behind them, pulling the hampers in after her. She put the case down carefully and then the bullets. The scissors she used to cut her zip tied wrists. It was awkward and dark, so she moved slowly.

The thump of the front door hitting the wall froze her actions.

"Where?"

"This way. You can dump her in here."

Faith recognized the voices. *Dump her? Shit, Tori.*

"The boss is on the ground. He said to keep looking for the other one. We have to finish getting the surprise off the plane and wired."

"What the fuck is he going to do, sit on the plane?"

"If he wants to, yes. You. You're now responsible for that woman. If she escapes, you pay." The men's voices trailed away.

Faith sawed at the zip tie and almost cried when it snapped off. She rubbed her wrists and patted around in the dark for the case and ammunition. She thanked God that Jason had taught her about revolvers and automatics. She found the lever that opened the cylinder and placed the weapon in her lap. She pulled out one bullet, found the gun, and inserted the shell. She repeated the process five more times and then filled her front pocket with the rest of the shells, careful to make sure they were securely tucked into the denim. Once that was done, she moved the case and the box out of the way so she wouldn't accidentally kick it. Placing the gun in her lap, she dropped back against the wall and drew a deep breath.

What did she do now? How many men were in the house? Was Tori unconscious or tied up? Both? Her hand shook as she thought, *Jason, where are you? Come get me, baby. Please. If I ever needed a superhero, it's now.*

CHAPTER 20

"**W**hat's happening?" Jason pushed the words out. He tried to wake up. Tried to push past the feeling of... *Oh, God, no!* He was drugged. That terror of his past addiction lifted its head and his heart started to race; he felt the panic rising. He tried to pull the IV from his arm. Why was he in a hospital? What was happening?

He felt hands on his shoulders. "Settle down, Jason. It's okay. You're going into surgery. They need to relieve the pressure on your spine."

He knew that voice. Maliki. "Faith?" *He needed her beside him. Where was she?*

"They still haven't found her."

"What?" He tried to move to get to the drugs that were threatening his sobriety.

"Whoa, stop, big guy. The good stuff they gave you will kick in soon."

"Where's Faith?" He opened his eyes and blinked. Everything was blurry. *Fuck.* "What's happening?" He hated feeling like this. Where was Faith?

He grabbed at the hands that held him and squeezed.

"Jason, stop! You're going to break my wrist. You were in the Guardian building when it exploded," Maliki's voice snapped like a whip.

He stopped fighting. "Faith? Where is she?"

"Missing. With Tori. Your family is on it. Your job is to make it through this surgery."

He blinked again; the brightness dimmed. "I need her."

"I know you do, big guy. They'll find her. You just make sure you're here when she gets back."

He nodded, or, at least, he tried to move his head. Instead, he let the wave of nothingness take him away.

"Hello?" Jewell's voice was a godsend.

"Button, it's Jared. We're in Hollister. What do you have?"

"Nothing yet." She blew out a breath. "We have over five hundred names associated with the shell companies and we're running them against twenty-four data points. The two names the Rose gave us are muddled at best. Doctor Amari is working for some security contractor as lead investigator. His last known location was Egypt."

"How recent was that information?"

"Three days."

"He could be stateside by now." Jared looked at the map of the ranch. "What about Champlain?"

"He is accounted for. He was in a car accident three days after being terminated by the CIA. He's been in an assisted living center since he was released. He is a paraplegic."

Jared narrowed his eyes. "So, a definite ax to grind."

"Not sure how much he could do," Jewell mused. "I can have an investigative team from the area pay him a visit."

"Do that. No stone unturned. Also, track Amari. See if he's come into the United States." Jared nodded to Jade, who came back into the room.

"I've already asked the FBI to run it down. They are being helpful for once."

"Hey, girl. How you holding up?" Jade asked as she sat down.

"I'm waiting on my program to scrape information and cross-reference these data points. What are you two doing?"

"Trying to figure out how to manage an operation without direct comms."

"What do you mean?"

"We have teams going into the ranch as we speak and they have comms with each other, but I don't have comms with them. We're in the dark."

"No, you're not. Do you have a laptop?"

Jared stood up and pointed at the desk. "Yes, Jade, grab that, would you?"

The woman was out of her chair and snatched the laptop.

"What is the IP address?"

"How do I find that?" Jade looked at the phone in the middle of the desk.

Jewell sighed. "Seriously?"

"Well, yeah? I don't do this shit, you do!"

Jared could imagine Jewell rolling her eyes. "Fine. First, tell me, is it hooked up to Wi-Fi?"

Jared pointed to the icon at the top. "Yes."

"Okay, type exactly what I tell you."

Jewell rattled off instructions to Jade and the woman typed. "Slow down, Jewell, I only have two fingers here."

"Oh, my God. You're henpecking?"

"Don't judge, I'm tired and I don't want to make a mistake." Jade's pointer fingers tapped out the required letters and symbols. "Okay. Now what?"

"Nothing. Now I take over," Jewell said, and Jared watched as the computer went crazy with different screens, command prompts, and execution files opening like crazy.

"How the fuck does she do that?" Jade pointed to the screen.

"The same way you piss off people. It comes naturally."

Jade frowned at him. "I'll have you know I've had to work at that skill."

"You've made terrific progress," Jared drawled as he watched his other sister's work.

"There. You have the same software as we had at Guardian. Each team can switch to their own frequency so they don't talk over each other. You'll have command frequency and can hear them all. The patch is the same, just use your mouse to toggle between the frequencies to talk. Watch."

The mouse moved on their laptop. It clicked Channel One. "CCS to Fury."

"Fury. Good to have you aboard, CCS. Do you have news for us?"

"Comms can be segregated, allowing each team operational autonomy and command oversight. Other than that, I have nothing. Still grinding. Jared has mission control." Jewell signed off.

"Dom Ops, correction, Hollister to all units, comm check." Jared went down the list of personnel. "SEAL Team, switch to freq 2, Sierra Team, freq 3, and Alpha Team, freq 4. Hollister has command and control. CCS, I'll need you to monitor in case we need to get word to the Pit." Jared wanted everyone connected during this operation. His family was involved and his brothers were in a rage; he needed open comms.

"I'm here," Jewell said over the computer. The phone was silent. Jared reached out and pocketed it.

"Fury, advise when you are at ready position. All units, we have mission go in one hour on my mark." Jared watched the clock tick down. "Mark."

A clock appeared on the laptop's screen, correct to the second. He sighed and realized how much of

Guardian's technology he'd taken for granted. Never again.

His phone vibrated in his pocket. He lifted it and glanced at the text. "Jason is in surgery." Jade closed her eyes and shook her head.

He tapped on the icon to freq one and informed his brothers, "Archangel is in surgery. I'll update when I have more." *Or when the mission is over.* He glanced at the clock. God, he hoped it was a simple procedure. Jason had already been through hell and back.

His phone vibrated again. He glanced at Jade. "Gabriel is inbound. He's landing at the ranch." He glanced at the clock and sent the time hack to his boss.

"How does he think he won't be shot out of the sky?"

Jared lifted his eyebrows as he read the text that just landed on his phone. "Like this." He showed the screen to Jade.

The woman's eyes popped open. "Well, that would work."

"Indeed." Jared dropped the phone back into his pocket. "All right, we don't have a visual on this, so we need something to use..." He glanced at the desk. "Look for colored tacks or something we can put in the map when they report in. I want their positions and positions of hostile units."

He keyed the mic. "CCS, contact the Pit. Have all comm units for Sunrise Protocol tuned to this frequency."

"Already done," Jewell answered. Damn, the woman was good. He glanced at the clock. Fifty-seven minutes until all hell busted loose. Of course, that was if Fury, Alpha, and those two assassins didn't rip the ranch apart first.

Jared dropped into the chair and stared at the map. Where were the women? Who the fuck was running this show, and where would he be?

Ferguson stuck his thumb out as the semi approached. He heard the engine power down and jogged after the truck that had stopped for him. He looked up into the cab. A middle-aged man peered down at him. "Where you heading?"

"East." Hell, he'd go anywhere he could catch a ride.

"I'm going to Minneapolis. Hop in, I can use the conversation."

Ferguson nodded and headed to the passenger

side door. Conversation. He could do that. Not much of a price to pay for a ride. He glanced back in the direction of the ranch he'd left. Those stupid fuckers had no idea the hell that was heading their way.

CHAPTER 21

Joseph acknowledged Jared's comment about Jason's surgery and eased off his horse. He handed the reins to Jacob and signaled for his brother to stay because he'd be right back. Jacob glared at him but kept his ass in the saddle, which was about all Joseph could hope for.

He crouched as he crested the rise where he met up with Lt. Evers and Bear. He lowered his NVGs and scanned the landscape.

"Three bogies. Red." Evers pointed in evenly-spaced distances.

"Take them out." He gave the order.

Bear nodded. "Those three aren't the only ones out there, I'd bet a month's wages on it. L.T., you go west, I'll go east. We'll meet at twelve o'clock."

"Time is of the essence," Joseph growled. They had to be at the ranch in time to breach the inner perimeter and find the women.

Evers grunted, sliding down the hill until he couldn't be seen. Joseph followed the SEAL. Evers stood and lifted his NVGs. "Wait for us to take out these three, then move forward. We've got your three, nine, and, eventually, your twelve. Your six is flagging in the wind, so keep it down."

"You've got ten minutes."

"I need eight," Bear replied as he and the lieutenant swung up into their saddles. The men trotted back to their squad and dispersed in a matter of moments. He'd known he fucking liked that man.

"Hollister and lead team, this is CCS. We have confirmation of identity on three of the four rocket triggermen in Washington, D.C." Bengal's voice broke through the comms.

Joseph got into his saddle and took his reins back from Jacob.

Jared responded and asked, "Who are they?"

"All three are known mercenaries. Last confirmed location for all three was Egypt."

"Let me guess, three days ago," Jared said.

Joseph glanced at Jacob. His brother lifted his

shoulders, his eyebrows buried in deep furrows. "I didn't get that intel."

"Neither did I," Joseph said.

"Briefed before comms were set up," Jared batted away their comments.

"Yep," Jewell confirmed. "The FBI tracked the plane that brought them back. The manifest states twenty-one souls. Customs cleared them. The scan of the passports gave us photos of the men, including a positive confirmation of one of them being Dr. Amari. The names used are obviously false identities. The FBI is doing facial recognition scans on all the others. I'm sending the photo file to your laptop."

"Affirmative. Fury, Alpha, did you hear?" Jared inquired.

"Copy all." Jacob leaned forward, his forearm resting on the saddle horn.

"Amari?" Joseph snapped the question.

Jared spoke before Jacob could. "He is now a lead interrogator with a known mercenary coalition. The type you buy for dirty deeds you don't want traced back to you."

Jacob swore bitterly. "He's also the fucking psychiatrist I told you about that interrogated Tori after we returned her to the CIA."

"So, this has roots in her past," Joseph mused. "But why would they bring her out here? Why go after Guardian? What could that fucker have to gain by charging up that hill?" Joseph asked.

Tempest spoke for the first time. "He shouldn't have the resources to do this. No matter how well-paid the man was, he wouldn't be able to coordinate the attacks. That takes big money. Fate-type money."

"And connections. Mercs could get the weaponry if they were well-funded, but getting the hardware into the U.S. and through, or rather, *around* customs would take someone with black market logistical experience," Reaper agreed.

Jacob swore bitterly. "Or someone who could pay others to get the hardware into the States. It all comes back to money. Who is bankrolling this?"

Jewell's voice came through the comms. "I'm running the names we harvested from the shell companies tracked through the hardware purchases. My guess is we'll find that over half of the people on that list could have funded this."

"Keep working, Button," Joseph growled and glanced at his watch. He reined his horse over to his brother. "Where is your head?"

Jacob glared at him. "Right fucking here."

"Make sure you keep it here. You don't go rogue on me, you understand?"

"Keeping that trick for yourself?" Sarcasm dripped from Jacob's question.

"Maybe, but if I do go rogue, you'll know it." He glared at his brother. He needed Jacob to focus on the mission and not get himself killed.

"I want the son of a bitch that took her. If she's hurt, he's dead."

Joseph stared at Jacob for a solid minute before he nodded. "I don't know of anyone who deserves that shot more than you at the moment."

"Except maybe Jason," Jared's voice interrupted their moment.

Jacob swallowed hard and nodded. "I'm here. I'm not going rogue."

They sat quietly on their horses until Jared's voice came over the comms. "Evers just reported in. Four bogies down, not three."

"We're on our way." Joseph tickled the ribs of his mount and they moved forward. His horse pranced as they made their way toward the ranch. He glanced at his watch. Once they were past the SEALs, he let his horse have its head and they galloped straight north. He knew the SEALs would circle them and take out any sentries on the periphery. They weren't close enough to the ranch to be heard, and they needed to move. He leaned down and let his horse run.

Tori woke slowly. The drug they'd injected her with was a bitch. Fast-acting, and just like in the jet, waking up was taking forever. One thing that registered was she was in the half-bath off the living room in her old family home. She willed the fog that encroached around her away, but things were still thick and slow, her mind with them. She concentrated on the towel hanging off the brass hook by the sink and tried to breathe deeply. In and out. With every breath in, she counted to four, with every breath out, she counted to six, filling her lungs with fresh air, praying the steady beat of her heart would dissipate the sludge running through her veins.

"The boss man is going to make his way over. Is she awake?" She recognized the voice. The one who was in charge of the teams.

Tori closed her eyes and let her chin drop. She listened to the door open and the scuff of boots on the hardwood floor. "No."

"Whatever. Pick her up and bring her."

She kept her eyes closed and her body limp. The man hefted her, unceremoniously shoved a shoulder into her gut, and lifted her. His hand grabbed her ass. He rubbed it and squeezed it through her jeans. She managed not to react, thanking the drugs for the first time for delaying her reactions. How long had she been out? She opened her lids and peered through her lashes. Was it still dark? An hour? Maybe more? Where was Faith? Had they caught her? Dear God, what was happening? Jacob would be searching for her, that she knew, but would he ever think to come to the ranch? She let her eyes close again. He'd know. Someone at the Annex would let him know. But... how did they land? Where were all the people? God, had they been killed? Her dad? Amanda? Keelee? Lizzy? Everyone?

Her heart slammed faster with each unanswered question. "Put her over there in the corner. I don't want her trying to run again. Did anyone catch the other one?"

"No, the bitch obviously knew the area. She can't have gone far. The men on the outer perimeter were alerted and watching for her. We'll get her as soon as it's daylight. Set the electric lanterns over there and there and turn them on. You sure she's out?"

Tori's skin prickled. Thank God. Faith knew the ranch from playing with the kids. She'd know to hide. Tori swallowed hard. *Where would she hide? Where would she go?*

The man who was carrying her answered, "Yeah, felt her up good and not even a twitch. What's the boss doing? Holding court or something?"

"I don't ask, and neither should you. Your name is Milton, right?"

Tori flopped when the man carrying her set her down. The back of her head hit the logs of the wall. She slid to the floor, and her hair covered her face. Slowly, she opened the eye that was closest to the floor. Her ride's size twenty-something boots were right in front of her, but she could also see three other sets of combat boots in the room, black pants tucked into the top. One had a knife sheath inserted in the top of his boot as well.

"Yeah. Milton."

"Tell me about Casey."

"Not much to tell. He's insane. Shouldn't be allowed to breathe, but he gets the job done. He's obsessed with what he does to women to the point

Hound ordered him not to touch any women on the ranch."

"Then go find him. Tell him if he can find the other one, he can have her after the boss gets done with her."

"You got any idea what he's going to do to her?"

"No, and frankly, I don't give a fuck. Go." She watched as the man hesitated for a moment and then headed out the door.

"Get a couple more lights," the leader barked, and one of the men left. She watched the door. She was in her dad's study. The fireplace was to her left, her mom's portrait above it. To the right were two huge leather chairs facing the fireplace, a small table, and a lamp between the chairs. The bear skin was a grizzly her father's father had killed years ago when grizzlies still lived in South Dakota. Just up from that was the small bar, and then her father's desk. The lights were placed on the tables. Flanking the walls were photos of her, her sister, their families, and other loved ones on display.

She stared out the door and watched as a pair of patent leather shoes appeared. Black slacks. Not combat gear. *Was this the boss?* She closed her eye to the point that she could still see through her lashes.

The man walked in, and she heard a snap of someone's fingers. The three combat boots walked out of the office. One on one, she could do. How she'd make it through the guards outside the room was another question, but she could—

"I know you're awake. Sit up or I'll pump you full of adrenaline. Enough to make your heart explode."

Her gut rolled. She knew that voice. It was what she'd heard in her nightmares for years. Her arm was grabbed, and she was yanked off the floor. Her eyes flew open. *Amari*. The fact that he held a gun on her was the only thing that stopped her from lashing out. "For this, you're going to die," Tori growled.

He laughed and stood up, still pointing the weapon at her. "For this, I'm being paid more than you can possibly imagine. How wonderful it is to be paid to do what you've dreamed of doing for over a decade."

"Guardian will stop you."

"Guardian does not exist any longer, my dear. The building was destroyed and all the occupants inside were killed."

Her world crashed to a stop. No, there was no way. "Liar."

"No." He dropped several pictures in front of her. She blinked, trying to register what she was looking at. When it sank in, she shook her head. No, no. "Anyone can modify pictures. You're lying."

"I'm not. Your children are dead. I took joy in slitting each one of their throats. By the way, the oldest, he fought valiantly. The youngest, well, he cried and begged for you."

"Liar! They were—"

"Safe? No. They were not. They *are* dead. Would you like to see photographs?" He pulled out his phone with his free hand and thumbed the screen.

Tori closed her eyes and shook her head. No, no, he was lying. He was fucking with her mind again. They weren't dead. Jacob and the boys weren't dead. They couldn't be. She wouldn't believe it.

"Oh, dear Victoria, you still haven't learned that I don't lie. Think back to our time together. Did I ever lie? Tell you any falsehoods? No. I did not."

He hadn't, but that didn't mean anything. He was manipulating her; it was what he did. Still, tendrils of icy doubt and red-hot stabs of fear sliced through her, her mind and body fighting a war for dominance. Her body reacted to the fear and her mind rejected it. Her hands shook. The end of the zip tie fluttered from her movements. She slammed her head from the left to the right, forcing the denial from her lips. "I don't believe you, you *bastard*."

Amari shrugged his shoulders. "Language, Victoria. And I don't care if you believe me now or not. You will. Soon. I was able to destroy everything you hold dear, just as you destroyed everything I once had. A fair exchange. But..." A smile split the man's face. "I win, my dear. My employer wants you alive. For now. He'll be here shortly. Once he's done with you, he has promised me that I could have you. If you thought what you went through before was difficult, well, I've refined my skills."

"My children are alive, and these pictures are doctored." She kicked at the photos on the floor.

Amari shrugged and manipulated his phone again. The sound of a reporter's tinny voice was clear. "The death toll at the Washington, D.C. headquarters of Guardian Security continues to grow." Tori snapped her eyes to the phone Amari was holding. On the screen was a helicopter view of the block where Guardian was located. She recognized the logo on the footage and the face of the reporter that flashed onto the screen.

"No," she whispered, not believing what she was seeing. Amari muted the video, but the footage was held in front of her. Oh, dear God, how could anyone live through that?

Her eyes filled with tears, and she closed them tight against the images. A sob broke from her. *God, no. No. Jacob. Her family. Her babies. No.*

"Now, about your boys. I can show you the pictures now, or we can wait until we're alone. Yes, alone. I think I'd rather enjoy your suffering and I'd like to keep it to myself."

"No." Her heart shattered.

"Oh, yes, I have videos, too. I wanted you to see everything. The oldest, he tried to be strong, as I said. The twins and the youngest went before he did. They cried for you. Begged for you and their father. It was a pleasure to tell them he was dead and that you gave them up so you could live. Poor little ones. Their hearts broke before they died."

"No!" Tori screamed the word. She screamed it over and over until she couldn't scream any longer as if the word would counteract Amari's deeds. She curled into a ball on the floor, her heart, her life, her will to survive fractured and obliterated.

CHAPTER 22

F aith jerked at the sound of Tori's scream. God, someone or something was hurting her! She pushed the laundry baskets out of the way and cracked the closet door open. Tori's screams were heart-wrenching. Dear God, what were they doing to her? She pushed the door open further and waited. Tori's screams continued. She had to help. She had to!

Inching out of the closet, she tiptoed down the long hall to the stairs. She got on her hands and knees and crawled along the banister to the far set of steps. Now Tori's cries were muted, but she was in pain. Faith put her back to the wall and slowly stepped down the stairs. She could see one… no, two men at the door to Frank's study. She took another step down and pointed the revolver at the closest man as she stepped down another stair. As one of the two men looked up at her, their guns lifted and she squeezed the trigger, two bullets into the chest of each man. When they fell, she ran to the study, her gun lifted and pointing at the man standing over her sister-in-law. He pointed a gun at Tori and lifted an eyebrow. "Put the gun down or she—"

Faith pulled the trigger. The man spun, and his gun discharged. She raced over to Tori and grabbed her. "Come on! We have to go!"

At the sound of scraping, Faith turned. The fist that slammed into her face sent her flying into the log wall. She bounced off the pine log and fell into a slump.

"You fucking cunt."

Faith coughed, choking on the blood she was swallowing. She rolled to her side and spat out a mouthful of blood and a couple of teeth. She saw her gun and lunged for it. A boot slammed against her ribs. She screamed, grabbing her side, rolling away from the boot and protecting her abdomen. She sensed more than saw when Tori pounced on the person who'd kicked her. Faith opened her eyes and watched as Tori moved like a woman possessed, raking his eyes with her zip tied hands. When he threw up his arm and backed away, Tori slammed her knee into the man's crotch.

Faith's brain engaged and she scrambled for her gun but froze when the barrel of a weapon pushed against the back of her head. "She's dead if you kill him."

Faith froze. Her eyes darted over to Tori, who was on top of the man, her hands around his throat. She was using the zip ties and the grip she had on the back of the man's head to strangle him. His face was purple, and he flailed ineffectively, trying to knock Tori from him.

The man holding a gun on Faith flicked the weapon from 'Safe.' Faith knew the sound and so did Tori. "Now!"

Tori sobbed and let go. The man gasped and shoved Tori off. He rolled and gasped for air while another son of a bitch pulled Tori by her hair back to the corner. He reached back and slapped her hard. Tori's head bounced off the wall.

"Leave her alone, you bastard!" Faith screamed as Tori tried to crawl back into a sitting position.

The leader, the one in charge at the plane, yelled orders. "You. Go find Casey. He can take care of *this* hellcat. Hurry up, the boss is going to be here soon. Get those bodies out of his sight. You, go check on the doc."

"I will survive. However, it appears as if I am in need of a bandage if you would be so kind." Faith heard the accented voice before she saw the patent leather shoes step in front of her. A large drop of blood hit the hardwood floor and spattered. So, she'd hit the man. Good. She didn't regret a single squeeze of the trigger.

"What do we have here?" Faith didn't move and neither did the barrel from the back of her skull. Mr. Shoes bent down and put his hand under her chin, lifting her face. A skinny, mousy man, balding, with strands of hair combed over the top of his shiny head. He wore thick, black-framed glasses. The bastard smirked at her and then licked his lips. His leer made her stomach roll with disgust. "You are the sister-in-law." He rose and sighed. "This one is not necessary to our plans. However, she may be of use to keep that one compliant, so don't let her die. Not yet."

Faith spat out blood that had pooled in her mouth. It landed on the man's silk trousers. "Go to hell, you son of a bitch." She tried to move toward her gun, but the barrel at the back of her head pushed her to the floor.

Another sigh from that mouse of a man. "I've changed my mind. Let your person do what he will with her."

"Lead team, this is Hollister Control, I'll go by Hollister. SEALs have secured the perimeter. Twelve bogies neutralized. Alpha and Sierra team are in position behind boundaries. Sunrise Protocol in twelve minutes." Jared announced his presence, identified himself and confirmed what Jacob knew was supposed to happen. Their teams wouldn't advance inside the kill zone, but he, Fury, Tempest, and Reaper were already inside the boundaries and moving quickly through outbuildings, clearing each to ensure the women weren't being held in one of them.

"Lights in the main house." Tempest's voice in his ear swung his head toward the house. Tempest had shimmied up the silo's ladder and had a bird's-eye view of both the ranch side and most of the Annex. "Movement at the flight line. A team forming at aircraft."

Fury nudged him. When he looked, his brother signed:

Main house. You and me. Reaper lookout.

Jacob nodded, and he and his brother worked toward their objective. They both dropped at the sound of gunfire.

"Shots fired. Five. Men running to the main house." Tempest's voice narrated exactly what he was seeing and had heard. He moved up to see around the corner of the small barn that was closest to the house. From this angle, he could see the front porch, but his view was obscured by Frank's swing. Joseph slid up next to him.

They watched as two men were carried out of the house and a team of men walked around the corner. There was a man in the middle wearing a suit. As he was walking up the stairs, someone pushed Faith out onto the porch. She fell and both he and Joseph started to rise.

"Hold. Incoming." Tempest's voice stilled them. Another team rounded the corner. The man in the suit bent down and extended his hand toward Faith.

Jacob watched as Faith spat at the suit-wearing son of a bitch. Faith was picked up and thrown toward a man. He grabbed her arm and laughed, pulling her away from the main house straight toward them. Two other men accompanied him.

305

Fury tapped his arm and whispered. "Four minutes. We get Faith, and then we take the house after sunrise."

He shook his head. "What if Tori is in there?"

"What if she's not? She could be anywhere," Fury countered. "Faith will have intel."

The bastard that had his sister-in-law marched her not more than ten feet from them. He winced as he looked at Faith's face, bloodied and swollen.

"Three minutes." Jared's voice gave them the countdown.

"Let's go." Jacob moved forward.

"Reaper, on our six," Joseph whispered as he followed.

Jacob cleared the corner and followed behind the men who'd pushed the barn door open further and shoved Faith into the building. He heard Faith scream and the sound of clothes tearing. *The fuckers*. He moved into the building. Faith's shirt had been torn from her and the bastard had her bent over a feed bin, her jeans pulled down, and he was grabbing his cock from his pants.

He brought up his 911 interceptor at the same time as Joseph. In almost perfect unison, they threw their knives. The blades nailed the fucker between the shoulder blades. Jacob took the bastard on his right and Joseph leapt at the other. He knocked the weapon out of his target's hand and levied all his pent-up rage at the fucker. He blocked an uppercut and grabbed the son of a bitch's head. One step sideways and twist and torque snapped the fucker's neck. He let the body drop, spinning to get to Faith. He reached her as she pulled her jeans up over her hips. She jerked away when he stepped up. "Faith, it's me. Jacob."

She flipped her hair out of her face, and he winced at the damage that had been inflicted.

"Where is Tori?"

"Two minutes." Jared's voice

Faith grabbed him. Her lips were swollen, and he saw several teeth missing, one broken. Her words were babble, but she was talking a mile a minute, "In the main house. They want her for some reason. They... God, Jacob? Where's Jason? You've got to help Tori! Are the boys okay? She's hurt. I heard her screaming."

Jacob tried to make sense of her babbling, but the words spilled into each other, and the damage done to her mouth made the words almost impossible to understand.

"Faith, slow down. Where is Tori?"

"The main house." She pointed as she said the words.

"In Frank's house?" Joseph asked. Jacob waited for her reply.

She nodded. "Tuddy."

"In the study?" Jacob asked to clarify.

"Yeth!" Frantically, Faith grabbed him and shook him. "Jathon? Boyths?" Her eyes filled with tears.

"He's alive. The boys are safe. Reaper, come here, please." The assassin ghosted inside the barn. "Get her to safety."

"Two minutes." Jared echoed Jacob's command.

Reaper took off his shirt, wrapped it around Faith's shoulders, and offered her his hand. She looked from Jacob to Joseph and then took it. "Go," Jacob encouraged her and watched as his sister-in-law and the assassin bolted out of the barn.

"Reaper, sharp left." Tempest gave directions to the assassin.

Jacob pulled his knife out of the back of the fucker that they'd skewered. "We need to make it to the house." Joseph reached down and withdrew his, too, wiping the blood on the man's filthy shirt.

"There is no time. You have incoming. Two

more men want to party." Tempest gave them the warning.

"One minute." Jared counted down.

Jacob ground his teeth, forcing back the scream of frustration that threatened to escape. Instead, he pushed back against the wall and waited. He'd kill every bastard on this ranch to reach her. *Hold on, babe. I'm coming.*

CHAPTER 23

Frank stood at the table and the plans Anubis and Mike had drawn up. He shook his head. "There has to be another alternative."

"There isn't," Dixon assured him, and Drake echoed his brother's words.

"You're experienced with the weapon," Mike added.

"I've messed around with it, true." He felt Amanda's hand on his shoulder. "But I gave my word that I'd stay down here." No matter which way he cut it, he was going to let someone down.

"We need you for cover fire," Anubis said and looked from him to Amanda. "He will lay down suppression fire while the marksmen do what they are trained to do. John is going up."

He felt his wife's hand tighten on his shoulder and reached up to cover it with his. "I gave my word." He wouldn't go back on it.

"But you didn't know about this then, did you?" Amanda asked.

"No," he admitted.

She drew a deep breath. "Then do what they need you to do. But I swear to God, Frank Marshall, if you get yourself hurt, I'm going to throttle you."

He stood and took her face in his hands. "Are you sure?"

She nodded and he saw the fear there. The fear she was trying to hide.

"I'll be back for you and then we'll go home." Amanda tried to smile.

"Mom, let's go into the kitchen and help the other ladies whip up something for these guys for afterward. What do you say?" Keelee spoke from Adam's side.

"Yeah, okay," Amanda agreed. She toed up and kissed him. "Do not get hurt."

"I'll do my best." He kissed her again and then watched her as his daughter put her arm around Amanda and led her out of the room, only then realizing it was the first time he'd ever heard

Keelee call Amanda 'Mom.'

Anubis continued as soon as the women were out of the room. "The sixty has been function-checked, it is locked and loaded. Frank, this is your position, and this is where we need you to focus."

Mike pointed to the map and continued, "John and Shae will be here. She will have his six because he's not mobile with that leg, but we need him at this location. Asp, this is your position, and Billy is here. When everything activates, you, Frank, are first to fire. I'll be below you, Anubis will be under John, Dixon under Asp, and Drake under Billy. Taty and Joy, you're handling comms."

The woman's head snapped up. "Wait a fucking minute."

Anubis lifted a hand. "No arguments. You are damn good in close quarters, but you are shit with a long gun."

Joy grunted. "Yeah, well, nobody's perfect."

"Taty's arm won't let her fire a rifle. You two will be our link to the mountain. Everyone make sure to check your comms on the way out of the room. Joy, the PA system is operational. Count down our arrival from sixty seconds out. I don't want anyone surprised when we activate. Well, except for those fuckers above us." Anubis stood and looked at Adam. "Doc, no need to tell you what you need to do."

"Arm up and protect the Pit, our families, and my patients." Adam crossed his arms. "Consider it done."

Mike straightened and looked at each of them in turn. "We have seven minutes. Get to your positions. At go, we are lighting up the ranch. Anything that moves is fair game. Use your NVGs until daylight compromises them just in case one of ours is inside the perimeter. They shouldn't be, but if they believe the two women Joy saw are Tori and Faith, I have no doubt someone is inside trying to find them. The good news is they know when we're activating. They'll take cover."

I hope, Frank mentally added to the end of that statement. That machine gun wasn't discriminating. It would level anything in front of it.

"Jillian, is everything powered and ready to go?" Anubis sent her a look.

"Yes, I've triple-checked each position. They will activate at the same time, and it will only take four seconds for it to happen, so hold on, you're in for a ride."

"Let's go, then. Remember, our people have our

six. We are reclaiming our home. Whatever it takes."

"For as long as it takes," Frank finished, and everyone else nodded their heads. He motioned to Mike, and they headed to their position.

"You all right?" Mike asked when they reached their objective.

Frank nodded. "Hope those boys keep their heads down."

"You know they will." Mike clasped him on the shoulder. "I have your six while you're out there, but take this. Slip it into your boot. The holster will clip to the top."

Frank took the nine mil, lifted his borrowed uniform pants, and clipped it to the top of his boots. Damned if he was going to wear combat boots.

Frank stood and stared straight at Mike. "Come on, son. We're burning daylight."

Mike chuckled. "How long have you wanted to say that Duke line?"

Frank grunted. "Longer than you've been alive."

Mike laughed and went downstairs. Frank opened the gate and closed it after himself. He hooked on the safety belt and checked his machine gun. The belt was the longest he'd ever seen, looped into a massive tray. The barrel of the weapon would melt before he ran through all those rounds.

"Sixty seconds. Buckle up," Joy's voice echoed through the tunnel system.

Frank gave a whistle. "You tight?"

"Good to go," Mike called up to him.

"Forty seconds. Jillian says to sit down or be on your knees."

Frank looked at the metal sheeting and then considered his old knees. Nope. He'd ride this bronc just like this. The belt would keep him from being bucked off.

"Twenty."

Frank wiped his hands on the uniform he'd borrowed. He rolled his shoulders and drew a deep breath, grasping the handles of the mounted sixty.

"Ten, nine, eight…"

Frank's mind echoed Joy's voice as she counted down. "One."

Holy shit!

The tower under him catapulted upward. As soon as he cleared dirt, he opened fire. The smell of sulphur hit his nose and the jerk of the machine gun fought his grip as he directed the line of fire. He swept left, gritting his teeth as men who were out in the open were mowed down. He couldn't hear anything else, but he knew the other three towers were up and the snipers on top of them were picking off the fuckers who dared to threaten his family and his friends. The men below each tower were protecting the higher positions. Chief circled below him, making sure Frank was unimpeded, maneuvering in a way that, due to his age, he couldn't.

An explosion to his right didn't distract him from his purpose. He swept right, keeping the weapon firing. The belt fed at a phenomenal rate, and brass flew from the weapon, littering the platform he was standing on.

"One minute." Jared's voice counted down the seconds. Jacob twisted, slapping his hand over the mouth of the man he'd engaged. A step, spin, and twist was all it took to bury his knife in the man's throat. He pulled back and slid that razor-sharp edge through the man's neck. A release of air from the windpipe was the only sound the bastard made when he met his maker.

He glanced over at Joseph just as he broke his opponent's neck. Dead weight dropped to the ground in an unnatural heap. "Five, four."

"Wait, wait! I have a name. I know who the money behind this is," Jewell's voice rang out. Jacob glanced at Joseph.

A loud popping noise, like the sound of a potato cannon exploding, reverberated around him. Jacob hit the ground and low-crawled over to where Joseph was tucked up behind the feed bin. Almost immediately, the sound of a sixty started bleating into the air. Jacob tucked his feet as a line of bullets sprayed past the little barn they were in. "What did Jewell say?" Jacob lifted a bit and yelled the question at his brother.

Joseph glared at him like he had two heads, and they both tucked again as the spray of machine gun fire flew past again. *Fuck.* Jacob got up close and personal with his brother and stayed there.

Tori clung to the wall and watched as Amari bandaged his arm. "Ah, he's here." Amari stood. "All is as you requested. May I introduce Victoria Marshall."

Tori stared at the man who entered the study. He, too, was wearing a bespoke suit. His hair was silver, and he was artificially tan, the orange tint obvious and horrendous. He studied her for a moment before he spoke. "Put her in a chair, please."

"Sir, she's a bit combative."

"I would imagine." A forty-five automatic appeared from his suit jacket. "She'll be no problem."

Tori watched as Amari bit back his retort and motioned for one of the others to put her in a chair. One of the two chairs facing the fireplace was moved, and she was grabbed, picked up, and roughly shoved into the chair.

Tori kicked the bastard who manhandled her, connecting with the side of his knee.

"Bitch!" He pulled back his hand to hit her. Tori ducked down, trying to avoid the contact.

"Hold."

The quiet command was heeded, and the guard limped toward the door.

She turned her attention to the newcomer. "What do you want?"

"From you? Nothing." The man shrugged and looked at Amari, lifting his eyebrows. "My chair?"

Amari moved the other chair and waited for his boss to sit down, taking up his place behind and to the right.

"I've accomplished almost everything I wanted to accomplish with the exception of one last act. Where is Frank Marshall?"

"What?" Tori's mind reeled. What did her father have to do with any of this?

"He is your father, correct?" The man crossed his legs and aimed the weapon at her.

"What do you want with him?" Tori heard the echoing pop and smiled. When it registered that an M-60 was firing, she threw herself to the ground. The men around her bolted out the doors—except for Amari and his boss. They didn't move, and the weapon on her never faltered.

"Do get up, will you?" Amari asked from his position behind his employer.

Tori pushed up, staying on the floor, and listened as the sixty rattled on. There were other sounds of rifle fire, people yelling, and then silence as the sixty stopped. Gunfire continued. Smaller caliber, intense bursts, moments of silence, and then the report of a large-caliber rifle. Marksmen. She leaned back against the wall. "They're coming for you."

The man holding the gun on her smiled.

Amari's face pulled into a frown. "Who?"

"Guardian."

"Guardian doesn't exist any longer." Amari waved off her words. Another burst of automatic gunfire. "The weaponry you heard would be our men."

Tori shook her head. "I didn't see a sixty-caliber with your men. They had M4A1's." Another echoing shot of a sniper's rifle sounded before a spray of bullets from a smaller-caliber machine gun. "And that was a Kate, an extremely accurate version of the M40. A sniper's rifle." She watched Amari's brow crease in concern. He turned and looked out the window. Tori blinked and then laughed, a bitter, heartless sound.

A helicopter. The deep thrum of the huge blades whopped the air. A gunship. Gabriel had sent backup. The distinct sound of fifty-caliber rounds thudding emanated before a massive explosion rattled the windows. It was followed by a second. "There goes your escape. They are coming for you."

Amari sprinted to the window and peeked out. "The airplanes. Sir, the airplanes have been destroyed."

Tori stared at Amari's boss. He held her gaze and asked, "Will Frank Marshall be with them?"

She spat at the man. *That's your fucking answer.* The only thing she had left in this world was her father, sister, and Amanda. He could torture her, and she wouldn't tell him a thing to help whatever perverted cause he thought he had. This bastard had empowered Amari, who'd taken her husband and her children. If she could, she'd kill him slowly and watch the life fade out of his eyes. She snarled at the son of a bitch and ground her reply through clenched teeth, "Fuck. You."

The man turned and looked at the portrait of her mom. "She was beautiful."

Tori's eyes darted around the room as she looked for a weapon. Anything she could use. *Kill him. Kill Amari.* She had to find a way. *Kill them before they hurt anyone else.*

"And so much better than... this." The man turned back to her.

Tori narrowed her gaze and flicked her eyes to her mother's portrait. How in the fuck would he know? The wheels turned and the gears in her mind shifted, slotting the bits of information together. Her eyes widened as she realized who this was. "You're—"

CHAPTER 24

"Cease fire!" The call came from Tempest. Jared repeated the command. A single rifle report echoed as Jacob rolled and hit his feet. "Alpha and Fury heading to the main house. That's where Tori is!"

Jared announced their movement through the comms as they bolted out of the small barn.

"Wait, I know who is funding this," Jewell exclaimed.

Jacob was running as he demanded, "Who?"

"Richard Berkley," she replied like that solved everything.

"Who?" Jared asked over the comms. Thank God he wasn't the only one who had no clue who the bastard was.

"Alpha Team, sweep in from the south. Sierra, in from the north." Jacob couldn't worry about who the fuck was bankrolling this now. "Tempest, any movement from the big house?"

"Negative, but I can't see the west side."

"Jared, west side tower?" Joseph snapped the command.

"Asp has the west side covered. Lower defenses are closing in," Jared relayed.

Jacob scanned the ranch as he watched Mike, Dixon, and Drake move in. Anubis rolled a person on the ground and zip tied their hands together. The process was repeated as each man advanced. Dead or alive, the enemy was immobilized.

"Hurry up," Jacob cussed under his breath.

"You want to be shot in the back, or do you want to survive this to get her out of there?" Joseph whispered next to him.

Jacob didn't respond. He couldn't. The time it was taking could be Tori's last moments.

"In position."

"Dixon, Drake, kitchen. Anubis, Chief, back patio into the grand room. Tempest, there is a door on the east side."

"In my scope."

"On three. Jared, you count it down."

"Let me put everyone on one freq," Jewell interrupted. "Okay, everyone can hear each other now."

"On three. One. Two," Jared began.

"Hold." Jacob spat the word out. Tori, blindfolded and zip tied, stepped out onto the porch, a gun barrel shoved at her back. She shook her head violently. He couldn't hear what was said. Tori shook her head again. The muzzle disappeared and the stock of the weapon struck the back of her head. She dropped to the porch in a heap.

"Motherfucker!" Jacob lunged forward, but Joseph stopped him.

"It's a trap."

"For who?" Jacob raged.

"Frank Marshall! Frank Marshall, show yourself if you want your daughter to live another day."

"Alpha, I have three in the great room," Chief reported.

"Skipper, we can see one in the hall," Drake spoke in a whisper.

"Who is this bastard?" Jacob moved a bit to see clearer. "Does anyone have line of sight in the front door?"

"I do," Asp reported in. "Two rifles on Tori."

"What is he doing?" Tempest swore bitterly after the question.

"Who?" Jacob leaned out.

Frank stood with his hands in the air at the edge of the pathway about four hundred feet from the house.

"Frank, no!"

The man ignored him and continued walking forward.

"Motherfuck. This isn't helping," Jacob growled, and he and Joseph scrambled to get closer, using Frank's movement as a distraction. They sprinted to the side of the house. Jacob rolled and leaned out around the corner where he could see Tori clearly. Her shirt was torn and smeared with blood. She lay motionless on the porch. He couldn't see her face, but he'd seen what they'd done to Faith. *Hold on, babe. Hold on.* The fuckers were going to pay.

"You wanted me. I'm here," Frank spoke clearly.

"Inside."

"Do you know who Richard Berkley is?" Joy asked Amanda as soon as Taty brought her into the comms room.

"What? Who?" Amanda stared at Joy and turned to look at Taty.

"Richard Berkley. Do you know who that is?"

"Yes, I think that's the name of the man Elizabeth was going to leave Frank and the girls for."

"Is my mom there yet?" Jewell asked across the ham radio.

"Yes," Joy acknowledged.

"Mom, this guy has amassed a fortune and has systematically poured the vast majority of it into funding a paramilitary organization. He only has a portion of the people he controls at the ranch. I've been trying to track movements through the FBI and CIA, but they are all stateside. They could be waiting for a second wave attack."

"Click that thing," Amanda snapped at Joy. Joy blinked and made a show of pushing the button on the microphone.

"Tell Gabriel and get word to Jared. We'll figure out a way to let the guys here know."

"I'm working on it," Jewell cussed low. "Bullets are louder than words. I'm calling Jared now. Stand by."

Amanda shook her head. "A second attack. That's insane! Do you think he'll do it?"

"He has money, and he wants revenge. Is he

mentally imbalanced? Seriously, what other motive does he need? People are vicious." Taty shrugged as if it were just another daily occurrence.

"No, no. I can't let Frank or anyone else be trapped. What can we do to help? What can we do that isn't being done?"

"The tunnel." Taty shot a look at Joy.

"Fucking right. I'm done sitting it out." Joy got up and looked at Amanda. "Can you use a weapon?"

"Damn straight." Amanda nodded. She sure as hell could and she was a damn good shot.

"Can you keep your shit together? No freaking out or crying when this gets tough?"

"Watch me." Amanda leveled a gaze at her daughter-in-law. "Or get the hell out of my way."

"There you go, Grandma. I believe you. Get her a gun, Taty." Joy moved to follow them but stopped. "Shit." She ran back to the fucking ham radio she'd been babysitting and keyed the mic. "Yo, Jewell, we're heading to the house through the tunnel. Let them know."

"Wait, what? Who's we? Joy? Joy! Who is *we*?" Jewell's voice echoed in the empty room.

~

"Through the window." Joseph pointed to the window above them.

Jacob looked up and then spoke. "Tempest. We're going in through the window. Watch our six."

"On it. You're clear."

"Asp, the second they move their attention from her, get her and get her to safety," Jacob spoke as he stood and pushed up on the casement window. Locked shut. *Fuck.* The only thing on the ranch or in South Dakota that was ever fucking locked.

"Billy and I are on it. Moving closer," Asp responded.

Jacob didn't acknowledge the comment. There was no need. He withdrew his bloodstained knife from its sheath and slid it between the window and the wood frame, jimmying the lock open. He returned the knife as Joseph pushed the glass open.

"Inside!"

The yell was clear as he dropped down into the laundry room. He moved to the door as Joseph entered soundlessly. "Alpha and Fury inside. Double D, Chief, move in as close as you can. Stay clear of the great room." He didn't need to tell them; they knew the house as well as he did. Joseph and he moved down the hall. They ghosted to the closed door at the end, providing them access they shouldn't have.

"Alpha, Moriah, and Taty at a minimum are entering through the tunnel." Jared clipped the words. "Also, Jewell thinks there could be a second wave heading your way."

"What?" Jacob ground his teeth tighter. *Damn it.*

"The man is the backer of the Domen Bridge Coalition. Only a fraction of the personnel employed are at the ranch."

"SEAL One, Alpha, and Sierra Teams, push back out."

"Affirm."

"Roger."

"Copy."

The acknowledgements came rapidly.

"You wanted me? I'm here." Frank's voice was too damn close. "I'm here."

"Step over her and get in here."

"Not until I make sure she's okay."

"Get inside or she will die."

"Then kill me now," Frank said.

Jacob held his breath. There was a rushed,

muted conversation from inside the house before one of the voices said, "Make it fast."

Frank Marshall bent down and then went to his knees. He palmed the small revolver Chief had passed him when he'd un-assed the tower and put it at Tori's abdomen as he moved her long hair to check for a pulse. Her hand covered his. He drew a deep breath. *Good girl.* He let her hair fall again, covering her hand and the weapon before he stood.

"Raise your hands. Turn around. Three-sixty." Frank did as he was told. "Step inside."

He moved forward and entered his home. The hallway doors to the right and to the left were shut. He glanced up at the massive chandelier made of antlers and took another step. "Move to your right." Another uniformed person waved his rifle in the direction of the study. Frank walked slowly. Each second he could gain the men outside was more time they had to rescue Tori. Frank strolled into the study and stopped at the doorway. Sitting in the chair he'd always sat in while talking to his late wife was a stranger wearing a bespoke suit. His hair was perfectly combed. His fingers, long and tapered, had shiny nails like he'd had them polished. His skin tone was off like he was trying to hide a sickness with makeup. Frank stared at him while the man returned his observation.

"Do you know who I am?"

Frank lowered his arms. "I can guess."

When the hired meat behind him poked him with the rifle, the man in front of him lifted a hand. "Let him be."

Frank walked into the room and headed over to the small cart he called his study bar. His shadow with the weapon followed closely. He grabbed a bottle of the good stuff and poured two drinks. Frank walked back, his shadow right behind him while he passed two guards at the door. He made eye contact with a third person standing to the side, a mousy little thing with beady eyes. The man was sweating his ass off and it wasn't hot. Reminded him of a rattlesnake for some reason. He was one to watch. Frank handed Richard a drink before he grabbed the chair from the corner and sat down beside the man that had orchestrated this mess.

"Why?" Frank took a drink and stared at the

portrait of Elizabeth. She'd been so sad in this picture. Would the man beside him have made her happy?

"You took her from me." Richard lifted the drink to his lips.

"No. You left her for money. You leaving her was the only reason she was with me." Frank lifted his scotch and swirled it a bit. He cocked his head at a slight sound outside the door, a scuffing sound right before the air conditioner kicked on.

He tuned back into Richard's words. "She would have waited. I had to orchestrate a demise for my parents."

Amanda watched as Joy jumped on the back of the man and... She winced and covered her mouth with her hand as the man's neck twisted violently. Joy landed on her feet and caught his weight, lowering him to the ground.

A blur of movement to her right drew both her and Taty's weapons. Dixon appeared where the other guard used to be, Drake right behind him.

A flurry of hand signals between Dixon and Joy ended in Joy rolling her eyes.

"What?" Amanda whispered.

"Lover's spat," Taty whispered back. "Come."

Amanda moved behind Taty, and as they approached the study, she could hear talking.

Frank. She could hear Frank.

Amanda glanced out the door as Asp picked up Tori. The weapon under her daughter's hand scraped. Everyone froze. Jacob and Joseph appeared in the doorway as Asp lifted Tori and the weapon, spun, and carried her away. Her son's eyes when they saw her would have been comical, but there was no room for levity.

"Ah, that's right. She wasn't good enough for them. She came from substandard stock, as we would say out here," Frank spoke slowly and clearly. Amanda shifted behind Taty when the woman nudged her back.

"Her bloodlines weren't deemed acceptable, true. But she was a rare beauty. She never told me your last name. I looked for her for years. Years. Of course, once you supplied your name, killing you seemed like a simple thing."

"Not so much." Frank sounded bored. She watched as Mike motioned to his wife and they slipped out the back door. *The window.* Yes, they'd have a shot at whoever was in the room.

"Guardian was an obstacle. A formidable one. But patience and discretion provided me with the information I needed. Doctor Amari here was useful on filling in the blanks about Elizabeth's children." The man nodded to himself and took another sip. "With enough money, obstacles can be moved."

"Why did you attack them? Why not just come after me?"

"Then how would you suffer?"

"That's the point to this? To the destruction and the deaths? To make me suffer?"

"It was in the beginning." The man nodded.

"And now?"

"And now it is my final opus, if you will. I'm dying, so orchestrating a magnificent salvo to destroy you has become an obsession, it would seem."

"That opus started with bombing Guardian."

"Then attacking your daughter's residence. Killing her spawn and taking her hostage." The man smiled and closed his eyes. A sigh of contentment fell from his lungs.

Frank leaned forward. "Yeah, about that. My family is fine, and the grandkids are probably playing on a mountain where you'll never find them about now."

Richard made a humming noise. "Not according to my aide-de-camp. The children were killed. His men killed them. Amari, show him the pictures."

Frank cocked his head as the weaselly son of a bitch with glasses cleared his throat. "I seem to have lost my phone, sir. But rest assured, they are gone."

Frank chuckled. "Now I know why you're sweating. You lied to your boss. I know for a fact all my grandchildren drove out of D.C. yesterday. My family made it out of the building, too. Some are here, waiting for you to make your move so they can end you for what you've done."

Richard didn't move. He stared at the painting for several long minutes. "When she didn't meet me, I believed she'd chosen you."

Frank stared hard at the man. Was he even listening? Did Berkley hear anything he'd said?

"I lived in mourning for the love you should have never had. Then, I received a call out of the blue. Do you know that I was going to kill myself? That Christmas when you called, I couldn't stand the thought of being without her any longer. After your call, it struck me. I wasn't the one that needed to die. It was you. You were the one who caused all of my pain, all of *her* pain. If you hadn't taken her away from me, I would have been happy."

"Again, you drove her away. I didn't take her from you. She turned to me for comfort."

"Comfort? How did she end up here?"

"She was pregnant. I stood by her and did the right thing."

"She loved me!" Spittle flew from Richard's lips as he shouted the words.

"True. I tried, but she wasn't happy here. She wanted to be with you. But we told you that." Frank finished his drink and held the empty glass in his hand. "You won't leave here alive."

Berkley chuffed and finished his drink. "It is strange that you think I didn't plan for this precise possibility." He put down the glass and stood, drawing a forty-five from under his suit jacket.

"What?" Amari lunged forward. "You said—"

Berkley lifted the weapon, and an echoing shot filled the room.

Time, space, and life coalesced into a millisecond of circumstances. Frank lunged to his right. The sound of gunfire exploded around him and screams filled the air.

Frank rolled to his feet, readying for...

Amari screamed again, a sharp, feminine sound that stopped everyone in their tracks. Frank snapped his head around, looking for Richard. Joseph was on that bastard, the guards were down, and Dixon, Drake, and Joy were zip tying their hands behind their backs although it was evident they were dead. Mike extended a hand to Taty and helped her into the room through the window.

Whimpering from the corner pulled his attention back to the room.

Jacob had the tip of his knife under the man's chin. There were rivulets of blood running down the man's throat.

Frank glanced to his left as Amanda walked into the room. He held out a hand, and she ran to him. He pulled her into him.

"I've got something." Joseph pulled a small, garage door opener-sized item from Richard's suit jacket. He tossed it to Dixon and Drake. Joy walked over and looked at the thing.

Joseph spoke as he zip tied Richard, "Jewell, do you have satellite?"

"I can, hold on. What do you need?"

"See if we have incoming."

The whopping thrum of the gunship that had landed earlier started again. It would be good to have that on patrol. For a second, he wondered who was piloting the thing. Jewell's voice came through their earbuds. "It will take a couple minutes."

Jacob's prisoner whined again as Jacob lifted him off the ground with one hand and growled something to him. He shoved the man against the wall. Jacob swore and stepped back, his arm still holding the man to the wall. Frank looked down at the pool of urine growing on the ground.

Dixon's voice rang through the aftermath happening around him. "This is a transmitter. It's been activated."

Richard coughed; blood flowed from his lips. "Your entire family in one spot. Your wife, your adopted children. Their wives." He laughed. "Those who live will suffer like I did. And you think I didn't win."

"Get out!" Jacob screamed the words.

"Go! Go!" Joseph lifted and helped Frank rush Amanda out the door. "Go!"

Frank looked back, praying the others got out. He felt the concussive wave throw him from his feet. He tried to keep Amanda's hand in his.

The ground rose, and he slammed down.

CHAPTER 25

"Amanda?" Frank lifted and grabbed for his wife. She moved and groaned. "Are you all right?"

"Yes, I think so. The boys? Joy? Taty?" Amanda sat up and shoved her hair off her face.

"Joseph?" Frank stood up, heading in Joseph's direction. "Joseph, are you all right?" He tossed several splinters of honed logs off Joseph and rolled Amanda's oldest over. "Amanda, come over here. Joseph has an open fracture."

"Jared, if you can hear me, get us medical, stat." Frank couldn't hear shit; his ears were still ringing. He shoved his fingers onto Joseph's neck to find his pulse. Joseph's eyes opened, and his good arm came up holding a knife. "Whoa there, son. It's just me." Frank moved as Amanda came over.

"I need to find out…"

"What you need, young man, is to stay still." Amanda's sharp tone caused Joseph to blink. "Frank will find out about everyone else. We're getting this covered before there is more risk of infection."

Frank stood up. He turned and faced Jacob. "Go find your wife. I'll get this." Jacob swung his head toward the house. Frank swore softly, "Damn it, go see if Tori is all right. I have to know she's okay."

Jacob nodded and headed away from the disaster. Frank moved carefully around the shattered logs and debris. His home, built like a fort, had survived the explosion. Somewhat. He picked his way through and found Dixon, Drake, and Joy with Mike and Taty. "Are you okay?"

"Yes," Dixon answered for all of them just before the sound of the helicopter flying overhead wiped out all possibility of conversation.

Frank turned to watch Ember, Doc Wheeler, his wife Eden, and Doc Johnson running toward them from the flight line. He met Ember and pointed to where Joseph and Amanda were. "Doc." He grabbed Zeke. "The women." He pointed to where Jacob had gone. Zeke sprinted that direction.

"You need someone to look at that cut," Eden said to him.

Frank frowned. "What?"

Eden pointed to his arm. Damn, he hadn't even noticed. "I'm fine. My daughter-in-law is pregnant. Could you check on her?" He pointed her toward where Joy was standing.

"Jeremiah, the rest are in the Pit. They've been through hell, but they're okay. Can you go talk to them about what to expect, the emotions and whatnot?"

"Not a problem." Jeremiah stared at the area in front of him. "How about we keep them down there until we have these bodies removed?"

"Solid plan." Gabriel's voice cranked Frank around.

"You piloting that thing?" Frank extended his hand, and when Gabriel grabbed him and pulled him in for a hug, he went willingly. Frank slapped his friend on the back. "Hell of a twenty-four hours."

Gabriel released him. "Ugliest I've had."

"Yeah. Jason?"

"Still in surgery. Berkley?"

"He was in the house when it blew." Frank looked at his home, the middle missing like a bite had been taken out of it.

Gabriel and he started walking toward the house. "That one was in the house, too." He pointed to half a body. One wearing patent leather shoes. Well, shoe. "Not sure who he was. Jacob seemed to know. Berkley called him his aide-de-camp."

"I have Jewell putting everything together for us. POTUS is demanding an update."

They stepped over a section of the house. Frank bent over and picked up a piece of the framing from Elizabeth's portrait. "I thought I'd seen the end of that tragedy when I called Berkley to tell him about what happened. What the hell did he stand to gain?"

"Nothing," Jeremiah said from near them. Frank hadn't even realized the man was walking with them. Showed how tired he was. "He had nothing to gain and nothing to lose. Berkley was obsessed with Elizabeth; rather, he was obsessed with her ideal. He didn't love her. He loved what he'd built her up to be in his mind."

Gabriel cocked his head. "Your spur-of-the-moment profile?"

Jeremiah nodded. "Nothing but speculation. It's what we're left with unless he left a letter or video or something. He destroyed Guardian because it was important to Frank's family. He kidnapped Tori to torture you. He would have gone after Keelee if everyone hadn't followed protocol. He wanted nothing more than to take from you what he believed you took from him."

"So, I'm the reason." Frank put his hands on his hips and stared at the devastation.

"No. Berkley is. This isn't on you, it isn't on me. It is on that man and only that man." Gabriel crossed his arms over his chest. "But Jeremiah was wrong about one thing." Both Frank and Jeremiah looked back at Gabriel. "He didn't destroy Guardian. He may have knocked us to our knees, but we aren't done. We'll rebuild and become more efficient, decentralized, and streamlined."

"Sounds like you have plans." Jeremiah tossed a piece of wood toward a pile of debris.

"Ideas. Plans will come after we take stock and lick our wounds."

"And rebuild." Frank nodded and stared up at the sky. "Whatever it takes."

Jacob dropped to his knees by his wife. "Has she regained consciousness?"

"Several times," Asp spoke quietly. "There is a hell of a knot on her head. No doubt about a concussion."

Faith put a hand on his shoulder. He stared down at her. "What happened?" Her face was covered in bruises and her lips swollen, but she enunciated carefully so he could understand.

"We put the boys in the shelter. These men killed our teams. They jabbed me with a needle. We woke up on the airplane. When we landed, we broke away and ran. I lost them. They caught Tori. I hid in the house. Last place they'd look, right? I heard her screaming. I don't know what he did to her, but she was in pain. I shot two guards and tried to get her out." She waved a hand at her face. "They didn't like that. Gave me to the one you killed."

Jacob had to listen closely to understand what Faith was saying. Her missing teeth and swollen lips made it almost impossible for him to understand her, but he did. He stood and hugged her, but she pushed away. "Don't be nice. I'll crumble. Can I call the boys?"

"Yes, absolutely. Here." Jacob pulled out the cell

phone he'd been given. "Jewell's number is the second one. Call it and she can get the boys to the phone."

"Thanks." Faith took his phone and walked away.

He glanced at Reaper and dipped his head in Faith's direction, "On it." The assassin wandered in the direction Faith had walked. Jacob wasn't going to take any chances that a random asshole had survived or, if they were alive, hadn't broken their restraints.

He dropped back down and pushed Tori's hair off her face. Her eyes fluttered open. Her hand lifted, and she touched his cheek. "He told me you were dead. That he'd killed the boys." Huge tears formed in her eyes. "He killed my babies."

She fell into sobs so violent all Jacob could do was hold her and whisper, "No. The boys are fine." Dear God, what that animal had done to her gutted him. He held her, repeating the truth over and over.

Doc Zeke slid in beside him. "I'm going to give her something to help her relax."

"No!" Tori screamed and pushed away, her screams tearing through the air. Jacob grabbed her and slid her onto his lap, wrapping her in his arms.

He shook his head at the doctor and the man moved away, still eyeing them.

It took over an hour for her to come back to him.

"The boys?" she asked in a shaky voice.

"They are fine. We'll call them. They are at Lycos' mountain with Christian and Jasmine." He grabbed her hand and kissed the palm, then the purple bruises from the zip ties that circled her wrist. "I thought I'd lost you."

Tori stared at him. "I can't go back there. To Washington. I can't. I can't do this again. God help me, I just can't."

"You don't have to. We'll live wherever you want to live."

She took a shuddering breath and whispered, "Nowhere is safe. Nowhere. It's not safe."

Jacob shook his head, his heart breaking into a million slivers. He'd failed her. He'd failed to keep her safe. Never again. He'd never make that mistake again. "I'll make it right, babe. I'll find a way to make you feel safe again. I swear."

"Please. Please make it stop. I love you, Jacob." She closed her eyes again.

"I love you more." He wiped at a tear that dropped over his bottom lash. She'd need to talk with someone, to deal with the trauma, and together, as a family, they'd decide on their future, but when she was ready. Only then. He'd wait for her to find her balance because God knew she was his.

"Mom, are you okay?"

"I am," Faith enunciated as clearly as she could. "The little ones?"

"What's wrong? Why do you sound that way?"

"Well, I had a little accident. I lost a tooth." *Or four.* She rolled her eyes.

"Accident?" Reece's voice lowered. "Did someone hurt you, Mom?"

"It is nothing to worry about. How are Royce and Rogan?

"They are playing with the wolves."

"What?" She glanced around and lowered her voice. "What did you say?"

"It's okay, they are tame and Ethan's pets. They're really cool. Aunt Jasmine is here. Uncle Chad and Uncle Christian are with her, and everyone is playing outside. Are you sure you're okay, Mom? Have you talked to Dad? Aunt Jewell said he is still in Washington."

"No, I haven't talked to him yet. I'm flying home today. I'll see him then." Come hell or high water, she was going back to Washington. She didn't care if she had to hitchhike to Rapid City and buy a ticket in economy class, she was going to be with her husband.

"He's hurt. His back." Reece's voice quivered just a bit.

"I know. He's been through this once before. Before us. He'll be okay." She hadn't stopped praying for that since the man Jacob had called Reaper had told her what he knew.

"When can we come home?"

"Soon. Couple of days." She hoped. God only knew how long Jason would be in the hospital. Her team was gone. Dead. She had no clue if a new one would be assigned. So many unanswered questions floated around her. "I'll call after I talk to Dad, okay?"

"Please. Tell him I love him, yeah?"

"I will. I love you." She winced as her tongue hit her broken tooth.

"I love you, too. Talk to you tonight."

Faith lowered the phone and stared out across the pasture she was facing.

"Let me know when you're ready to go. I have a jet waiting in Rapid." Gabriel's voice behind her startled her.

"I'm ready." She stood and faced him.

"You'll need to see someone about your face and teeth." He offered her his elbow and she took it, letting him help her over a clump of dirt.

Her entire body hurt, and she didn't doubt that she'd need cosmetic dentistry. "I want to go home. Is it safe?"

"It is. Now. What remains of Lima Team will be waiting for you when you land." Gabriel sighed. "I can bring the boys back tonight."

"No. Not tonight." She shook her head. "I want to see Jason and see a doctor. I'm pregnant, or I was."

Gabriel stopped and stared down at her. "Let's get Eden Wheeler to do an exam before we fly you out. I told her to wait so you could talk. It would be just to make sure everything is okay. I would give anything to have stopped this."

She patted his arm and started walking again. "I know. I'll talk to Eden. I'm not bleeding, so I'm optimistic." She winced when her split lip caught on her broken tooth.

"It is best to know." Gabriel stopped. "Anything. I would have given anything."

Her mouth hurt horribly, and she was exhausted. "I know. The future is the only thing we can change. What we need now is a reason for Jason to get well. His family and his job. He'll need both of them."

"He has his job for as long as he's willing to do it." Gabriel walked with her toward the big house. "He's lucky to have you."

Faith stopped and looked up at Gabriel. "No. I'm the lucky one. He's been my rock, my salvation. Now it's my turn to be there for him. Love works that way, doesn't it?" She tried to smile, stretching her bruised lips, and regretting it immediately.

Gabriel smiled down at her. "It does indeed."

CHAPTER 26

J ared yawned so hard his jaw cracked but he shook it off and continued to type up the after-action report.

"You can leave that for later." Gabriel's voice behind him gave him a jolt.

"Hey. No, a good investigator always types up case notes when they're fresh in his mind."

"Where are you at?" Gabriel pulled out the chair Jade had used last night and took a seat.

Jared hit print, and the printer beside him spat out the report he'd been compiling. "I'm not one-hundred percent sure on the accuracy of the numbers in D.C. Cole Davis has been feeding them to me as they get reports from the rescue crews on-scene." He watched Gabriel's features harden and he knew he'd gotten the death toll. One hundred and twenty-seven known fatalities in D.C., the death toll at the ranch less substantial. Thirty-seven. The rest of the men were either being flown to detention centers awaiting interrogation or were under police custody in the Rapid City Hospital or points further out, depending on how severe their injuries had been.

The body of Richard Berkley was recovered, or, at least, most of it. Doctor Amari was also in a body bag, awaiting transport to the morgue Guardian had contracted to deal with the dead. The Rose was the primary point of contact for everything, and they'd been doing a solid job.

"Jason's surgery went well," Jared said as Gabriel put the paper down. "Maliki says the docs are hopeful."

Gabriel inclined his chin in acknowledgement. "Are you going back to D.C.?"

Jared blinked. Well, that was to the point. "I am. Christian's life is wrapped around that shelter. His work is so valuable to the kids that live on the streets. I have no qualms about running Dom Ops out of my home office until we can find another place."

Gabriel nodded. "You have room for Jade and Nic?"

"Lord, no. They can work from their house. We just need to have comms and video chat capabilities."

"Which is exactly what I've been thinking. Decentralize."

Jared nodded. "It makes sense. Nic, Jade, and I can keep Dom Ops going. Our biggest concern is any digital evidence we had stored at Guardian. There should be local copies, but that will be the first order of business. Well, that and pay. People will work with a promise of pay for a while, but sooner or later, they're going to need a check."

"I'm working that. I've got several options open. I'm glad you're going to stick with me."

"I don't think any of us are leaving you."

"Jacob may. Tori's taking this hard." Gabriel pushed the paper back across the desk to him. "You've done more than enough. I've got my jet landing at the ranch in an hour. Are you ready to go home?"

"God, yes. I want to check on Mom and Frank before I leave."

"They're out there. Jade is making sure Amanda is away from the messiest parts, but she was in the house. That woman has grit. All of them are holding up, but they don't have a place to stay unless they bunk with the kids, and no offense, I've tried that. So, I've purchased them a luxury RV from the dealership in Rapid. It's being driven up as we speak. They won't leave the ranch."

Jared stood up and stretched. "Did you think they would?"

"After what happened? Could you blame them?" Gabriel stood up. "I'll give you a ride out."

"Thanks."

He followed his boss out into the sunshine. The small little town of Hollister was wide awake, and the day was unfolding just like he assumed it had yesterday and the day before. He stared up at the bright South Dakota sky and drew in a lungful of clear, crisp air. They'd lived through the night and survived the morning. His family was hurting, beaten and bruised, but they'd survived.

Jewell closed her eyes again and soaked up the sun. The boulder she was sitting on was far enough away from the children that she wouldn't become involved in whatever game they were playing but close enough that she could hear their laughter. The sound was magical and just what the doctor ordered after the last twenty-four hours.

"Found you." Zane's voice beside her should have startled her, but she'd gotten used to his silent approaches.

She opened her eyes and smiled. "Was I hiding?"

"You're outside, so the answer to that would be yes." Zane lifted onto the rock, and she leaned into him.

He was her safe space. A place where she could just *be* and not worry about trying to explain or fit in. "What are we going to do?"

"Are you talking about now or in the future?" Zane's voice rumbled under her ear. She loved the sensation.

"Both."

"Well, first, we're going to soak up some vitamin D, and then we'll go take a long shower, some pain medication, and then sleep for a day or two."

She chuckled. "Yeah, that sounds good."

"It does. Then we'll reach out to Gabriel and find out what we need to do. Funerals would be first."

She opened her eyes and stared across the expanse. "I don't want to go. I don't want to say goodbye. They were my friends."

Zane dropped a kiss onto her hair. "And that's why you have to go. I'll be with you every step of the way."

"I don't know if I could..." She stopped. Was she being stupid? Selfish? Was she having some sort of PTSD? She pulled apart what she was going to say and examined it from each angle.

"Babe?"

"Hm?"

"You didn't finish your statement. You don't know if you could?" Zane prompted her.

"Oh. I don't know if I could work in a building like that again." She snorted. "I don't know if I'll be able to walk into an office building again without freaking out."

Zane was quiet for a moment. "You worked from here just fine."

"Because Lycos has nice toys."

"You have a very special toy all wrapped up and waiting for installation. Add that to what Lycos has here and you'd be set."

She sat up and blinked at him. "But Lycos lives here. You aren't being logical."

Zane winked at her and pulled her back down. "Play along. Could you live on the top of a mountain?"

"Technically, he lives *in* the mountain," she corrected him. Because it was important.

"Sorry. You are correct," Zane conceded the point.

"I could." She stared at the beauty all around her. "I would. I think it would be hard in the winter, but if you had enough stockpiled, you could do all right. He has solar energy. Jillian's invention is amazingly efficient. Yeah, I think it would be a peaceful place to live."

"No pizza."

"Oh, well that's a drawback." She sighed. "I guess ordering in would be out of the question."

"Probably," Zane agreed.

"Do you know how to make a pizza?" She tipped her head up. "Like, that's a thing, right?"

"It is. I think we'd have fun learning."

She nodded. "Yep. If you found me a magnificent cave house in a mountain, I'd live there."

Zane chuckled. "Good to know, babe. Good to know."

"Ground rules, Quick Draw." Joy paced back and forth. "First, you absolutely cannot act like I'm made of glass and I'm going to shatter."

"Fine. My first ground rule."

Joy stopped. "Why do you get ground rules? I'm the one who is pregnant."

"With my daughter."

"Son," she snapped back. She so was not going to have a girl. Not happening.

"Fine, one of each." Dixon smiled at her when she narrowed her eyes at him. "First rule, no killing people while you are pregnant."

"If I hadn't killed him, he would have killed Taty or Amanda."

"Keep me out of this. I wasn't in jeopardy," Taty said from the couch in the Pit where she and Mike were sitting.

"Thanks for the backup," Joy sniped in her direction. "Fine. No killing anyone while pregnant. Second rule, if I get a craving, you're going to get it for me because if I'm ever able to eat again, I'm going to be fucking starving." She'd consumed an entire box of graham crackers and three ginger ales today. When she could eat real food, she was going to be ravenous, and veggie fried rice sounded amazing at the moment.

"I will fly you to wherever the food can be found." Dixon crossed his heart with two fingers and kissed them. "My second rule. No knife, gun, or garrote training while pregnant."

"What? How am I supposed to stay in shape?" Joy slammed her hands onto her hips. "That's not fair."

"He didn't say sparring," Shae said from the same conversation area where Taty and Mike were sitting.

John rolled his eyes. "You're not helping, babe."

Shae shrugged. "Not sorry."

"No sparring either," Dixon amended quickly.

"I'm not an invalid!" Her voice echoed in the metal confines of the Pit.

"I didn't say you were. You can run, do weight training, calisthenics, anything you like, but no murder, mayhem, training, or sparring. Seven months. You can do that standing on your head."

Taty glanced at Shae. "He didn't say no standing on her head."

"True," Shae nodded. "Great for blood flow."

"Would you pah-lease stop," Joy groaned at her so-called friends and grabbed Dixon's hand, dragging him past their peanut gallery.

He spun her, laughing as he kissed her. When

he lifted her, she glanced back to the Pit's common area and whispered, "I wasn't going to spar."

"I know." Dixon pulled her closer. "I love you for who you are. I don't want you to change, just be careful."

"Always. Now, about you flying me. Shall we try for that ten, Quick Draw?"

"I think I hit a ten when I got you pregnant." Dixon leaned down and cupped her ass, lifting her up to his waist. She wrapped her legs around him.

"I don't recall. You'll have to try again."

Damn, this was going to be hard. Elliot Sawyer stood at the bottom of the stairs waiting for her. He looked up at her when she exited, wearing borrowed clothes and huge sunglasses. The swelling and bruising couldn't be disguised no matter how much makeup she'd applied. Lima Team's leader extended his hand to her. She hustled down the stairs and hugged the man that had been a big brother and protector to her for almost ten years. "Elliot, I'm so sorry. I heard about the rest of the team." Her mouth was so sore, but she tried her best to speak clearly.

He hugged her for a moment and stepped back. Always the professional. "Thank you, but *we* were supposed to protect *you*." He looked at her and shook his head. "After you finish at the hospital, I have instructions to take you to the dentist."

Faith sighed. "I must look horrible." She thought she was getting better at speaking; learning how to talk without front teeth was humbling.

"You are as lovely as ever. Come on, we'll take you to him."

"Thank you, Elliot. Do we have arrangements yet? I want to visit the families. Do they need anything?" She fell into step with him.

Elliot shook his head. "They are in mourning. Jason asked about them right after he asked about you and the boys. He's already told me to help in any way possible."

"That sounds like him. How was he?"

Elliot stopped at the hardened limo and opened the door. "He's worried about you, the family, us, the future. I can see the stress, but there was nothing I could do to alleviate it."

"Just being here takes so much off his shoulders."

"Then I'm at your disposal, as always." Elliot

gave her a little bow as she slid into the back seat of the car.

She leaned forward as Elliot slid into the front seat. "Have we heard anything about the pilots from the aircraft that was shot down? I know Jason will want to know."

"I was able to brief him about that earlier today. Both are doing well, but they have a long rehab in front of them."

Faith said a small prayer of thanks and sank back into the seat. There had been so much death. The trip to the hospital took only a few moments. Far too long in her opinion, however. As soon as the door opened, she and Elliot were through the hospital doors and heading to an elevator. "He's on the seventh floor. Room seven-twenty-three." Elliot gave her the information, but she doubted she'd remember. Her mind was on her husband.

They exited the elevator and headed down the hall. Guards stood aside and opened doors. "He's the only one on the floor?" She looked at empty room after empty room.

"Yes, ma'am," Elliot confirmed.

They turned the corner, and Maliki stood up from where he was sitting at the nurse's station and Nic turned. She hugged both men. "Thank you." She'd been told that they hadn't left Jason's side.

"Poet wanted to be here, too, but she's been taking care of Tippy and Tommy. They miss the boys."

"Thank you. You've all been so kind."

Maliki smiled and winked at Nic as he spoke, "It's what family does."

"Like you keeping me within your line of sight. I'm fine." Nic rolled his eyes. "Jade has called at least ten times."

Faith smiled and then winced. "She told me to check on you, too."

"No doubt." Nic laughed. "That's my woman. Bossy as hell."

"Indeed." Maliki stood. "Jason is right through there, but I want to give you a briefing on his injuries. He's had surgery, two procedures were done. The doctors performed a foraminotomy, which removed a large area of bone to expand the openings for the roots of the nerves. In addition, the doctors did a corpectomy, removing a disk and body of one of his vertebrae, then they fused the vertebrae to stabilize his spine."

"Will he walk again?" She wanted to know. She needed to be prepared.

"It depends on him to a degree and how his body responds and heals. He has sensation in both feet and legs, which is as close to a miracle as modern medicine can get. Jason will have to put in the time and the effort, but we're hopeful." Maliki smiled at her. "He's tough and a terrible patient. Go see him." Mal nodded toward the room.

Faith walked to the door and stared into the room. There were monitors and beeping noises and an IV stand beside the bed. Her feet froze as she stared at her husband. The man who'd rescued her from her past, who'd lifted her from the ashes of her life and had given her the wings to soar. He and her boys were her world. Seeing the strongest man she'd ever met like this tore her heart from her chest. She drew a deep breath into her lungs and lifted her chin. It was her turn to be the strong one. The love she felt for this man would be more than enough to shore up whatever defenses they needed to rebuild. They were a team, and it was on her to lead for a short while. She could do it because the love they shared made her stronger than the temporary or even long-term troubles they faced.

She stepped into the room and walked up to the side of the bed, placing her hand on his arm.

His eyes flickered open. "Princess."

His raspy voice was the thing that broke her. She leaned down onto his massive chest and cried. She shed tears of regret, fear, joy, and most of all, tears for those who'd lost this: the connection, the love, the other half of their soul.

Jason's hand stroked her hair as she was able to stop crying. "I'm s-sorry." She hiccupped the word.

"No, princess. I'm sorry. I should have been there to protect you."

She lifted her head and stared at him. She spoke carefully, the words hurt, but the communication between them was worth the pain. "Contrary to your opinion, you don't have a red cape and you can't fly. There was no way to know what was going to happen. This isn't on you." She drew a deeper breath and wiped at her tears. "This time, I'm taking care of you."

He narrowed his eyes and cupped her face. "What happened to your face?"

She took off her sunglasses and his eyes widened. "If that bastard isn't dead, I'll crawl to South Dakota and tear him limb from limb."

"He's dead. There was so much death."

"You shouldn't have witnessed any of it."

"But I did. I've seen what they did to the

building here in D.C., and what they did to the ranch. Guardian needs you as much as I do. You need to see the organization through this transitional time. It will keep you busy while you heal."

"You don't want me to dwell on the fact I can't walk or the fact I'm starting my sobriety over." Jason lifted an eyebrow.

"Who told you you couldn't walk? Not one of the doctors I talked to, they all said it was up to you. We've been sober for years, this little hiccup won't strand us. I'll take you to the meetings whenever you need to be at one. As long as I have you with me, we can manage. You and the boys are my world."

"It will be a long road." Jason used his thumb to stroke her chin. "I'll have to start my sobriety again. Walking and getting clean again *will* be a struggle. The doctors want me on painkillers for a while, and I need it. The tunnel, it was really bad."

"I can't imagine. I had no idea what had happened to you until after... you know, sunrise. But we will go through it together. I don't care how hard it is. I'll be with you every step of the way." She turned and kissed the palm of his hand. It hurt her lips, but it didn't matter. Her husband was going to be all right. She jolted.

Jason's eyes widened. "What's wrong?"

"Nothing. I just didn't have the chance to tell you. You were right, you knocked me up, while I was on birth control."

A smile spread across his face. "You confirmed it?"

"Yeah, at Tori's, before. Eden Wheeler did an exam before I left South Dakota." She stared at him. "I love you."

"You and the boys are my everything. I love you, princess. Forever."

CHAPTER 27

T*wo months later:*
"What do you mean, we have to move?" Bethanie blinked at her husband. "Ryan, you can't be serious. Nobody is going to come back here."

"But they all know where *here* is. Hell, Zane drove off the mountain three times before they went back to D.C. We had a rash of unwanted visitors."

"Stop. Zane isn't going to tell anyone. Besides, where would we go? What about this place? We can't just leave it. Dog and Lady? How are they going to adapt to new territory? You're being silly."

"Have you ever been to the Rockies?"

"As in the mountains? You know I haven't."

"I own a mountain there. The cave is twice the

size of this one, and the offshoots of the tunnel run forever. Think of the hydroponics you could grow. The challenge of building it together. What do you think?"

"I think it's going to be winter soon and we'd freeze to death." Bethanie stared at the huge fireplace in the corner of their front room. "Why move?"

"The floors and doors are done. It's sealed tight. Yeah, we'd have to rough it for a year or two until all the niceties are installed, but no one would know where we live."

She spun. "What about Ethan?"

"Nobody but immediate family. And Dog and Lady live in the freaking cave. They'd adjust to the new territory."

"What happens to this place?" She lifted her hands. "You can't be serious." Bethanie turned to her husband and stared at him. "You're serious."

He nodded. "I've been setting up drops for construction equipment. Denver is the nearest city, but there are several smaller towns. I can't stay here. I have to stay off the grid."

"We are off the grid, technically." She sighed and dropped back on the couch. "When?"

"Spring. Guardian has suspended recruitment

for the next six months. We can go out now, take measurements, decide what we want, and then start ordering supplies."

"Ethan comes with us for the walk-through?"

"If he can get away from school, absolutely."

"And this place? Our home?"

"Zane and Jewell."

Bethanie's mouth dropped open. "What?"

"Yep. Zane wants her away from D.C. They have satellite access here, off the grid, so she can do her computer shit and shield the equipment without raising suspicions."

"But they're city people."

"So were you, once."

Well, there was nothing she could say to that, was there? "I want twice the room for my garden."

"I thought three times the space." Ryan leaned in and kissed her.

"I'm still not sold."

"I know." He moved closer and kissed her again.

"You'll have to convince me." She wrapped her arms around his neck.

"As many times as necessary." He crawled over her and kissed her again.

"You just ran out of room here, admit it." She laughed as his eyes widened. He lowered to her again, and she whispered against his lips. "I'd follow you to the moon."

"I know." He dropped down onto her. "How about I take you there now?"

"These are the three locations I'd look at first." Dani wiggled the mouse and circled the three locations that she and Justin had located for the new, scaled-down Guardian headquarters. "One is in New York, another is in Miami, the third is in Denver. The Denver location is at the top of our list."

"Why is that?" Jared glanced at his brother's image on the computer screen.

"First, Denver is the closest city, this facility isn't in Denver proper, it is actually in the Rockies. We can build under the facility and, unlike D.C., we can have all operations underground, keeping the superstructure for appearances only. It is one story, spread over five acres. It would take a fifty-ton bomb dropped on it to destroy it due to the scope of the facility. The surrounding five hundred acres are for sale, so that would allow Guardian to put sensors out, preventing what happened in D.C.

and setting it up more like the Rose. Autonomous and independent. That was the marching order, right?" Justin looked up as he asked the question.

"It most certainly was." Jared nodded. "I'll send this on to Gabriel. Damn good work. What about our overseas locations?"

Dani answered, "We are flying to Europe next week. Australia in three weeks. The Far East is still iffy, Thailand and Hong Kong don't have the facilities or the landmass we are looking for. Sejong City, Korea, does, but buying land would be tricky. We're still researching. It will take time."

"Thank you for the work you're doing on this. I know you have an empire to run."

"I have people who make sure that happens. Nothing is more important than family." Justin shrugged. "Especially now that Dani is expecting."

"What?" Jared smiled like a loon. "Congratulations!"

"We just told Mom and Frank. Dani's dad found out about fifteen minutes before them."

"I'm so damn happy for you."

"Jared, tell him he can't break the baby, will you?"

"Lord, I was terrified, but Justin, the first time you hold that little guy in your arms, all those fears and worries disappear. You know you'd do anything to protect that precious life. You'll see. You'll be a great dad."

"That's what I told him, too." Dani leaned over and kissed her husband.

"I'm so happy for both of you. Are you making the calls to the rest of the family soon?"

"Yes. I'll call them as soon as we hang up." Justin chuckled, "I can't believe it."

"Believe it, mister. Morning sickness is a real thing," Dani laughed.

"Take care of yourselves." Jared said goodbye and leaned back in his chair. He stared out his office window and watched Christian and Marcus as they raked grass clippings. If Guardian transitioned to Colorado, they probably wouldn't follow. Christian's shelter was here. Marcus' friends, too. Jared smiled when Christian flopped into the pile of fresh clippings before Marcus dropped down on top of his dad. His life was here, his love was here, and working remotely was fine with him.

He closed his laptop and headed out of the house. Time to play.

Frank passed Gabriel a tumbler of the good stuff. "It's coming along nicely." He motioned to the ranch house.

"It is." Frank sat down on the bench outside the motor home they'd been living in. "The stonework was Amanda's idea."

"I love it," Anna said as she stepped out of the RV, Amanda behind her.

"The front will be different. We'll have a glass-enclosed room for the winter. It will be easier to heat and easier on my old bones," Amanda laughed and sat down by Frank.

"What construction crew do you have working?" Gabriel asked as he watched a double-cab truck with a stock trailer pull in by the barn.

"The same one as Drake and Jillian are using to build their house. Olsen and Son Construction. Local. Vetted." Frank had made damn sure he knew every person that came onto his ranch. Two months hadn't been enough to ease that stress.

"Mr. Olsen is very nice. His son has taken on two of the young men that Jillian and Drake have taken in. He's teaching them the trade. Both of them show an amazing aptitude for construction." Amanda pointed. "Terrence is right there, and

Bode is helping with the framing on the porch roof. Red shirt."

"Good kids. Hard-working. Appreciative." Frank liked them both. They were grateful for what they received and worked damn hard when given the chance.

"Speaking of hard-working kids, Deacon and Ronan are getting out of the service and coming to work for their old man." Gabriel lifted his glass. "I'm going to need another."

Frank laughed. "You ain't drank that one yet."

"Charley and Dan, and now Deacon and Ronan. Pretty soon, all of the young ones will be working for you," Anna chuckled and took a sip of her cold red wine.

"Ethan has expressed an interest in interning with Jewell. Of course, that won't be until we get her settled in her new location." Gabriel finished his drink, got up, and lifted his empty cup before he looked at Frank. "The good stuff still in the same place?"

"It is," Frank laughed as he watched his friend go into the RV.

"Did they find where they want to live?" Anna asked.

Amanda nodded. "I think so, but Zane has been

hedging. He said it was a surprise for Jewell. God only knows what that means. That little apartment they live in is wall-to-wall computers now."

"He said it was somewhere they could stretch their legs." Frank took a drink. That could mean anything, but he trusted Zane to take care of that girl.

"How's Tori?" Anna asked quietly.

"Better. Not well, but better. She feels safe at the Rose. Joseph and Ember being there helped with the transition, too. She's in therapy. The boys are loving it. Blake having cousins there is a relief for Ember. Jacob gave Talon a truck and he's been driving it all over the place. The only thing that is missing is sports, but Jacob and Joseph are keeping them active. Jacob is working out of the Rose and letting Tori get her feet under her. He said he'd stay there until she was ready to leave."

"Which may be never," Frank spoke as he stared at the horizon.

"Give her time." Amanda put her hand on his forearm. He smiled over at his wife. God, he loved her.

"Is Joseph still in a cast? I may have overheard him complaining about it the last time he called Gabriel." Anna laughed and took a sip of her drink.

"No, thankfully Ember took it off last weekend." Amanda laughed. "So impatient, that one, but he did a great job getting everyone here and set up. God only knows what would have happened if he hadn't coordinated the response."

"The right person for the job." Frank agreed with his wife. They'd discussed that day over and over. "Someone had to keep Jacob from coming in guns blazing. The only one who had a shot at keeping him in line was Joseph. Any other way and we would have had casualties on our side." Jacob needed Joseph that night, and Joseph stepped up.

"Grandma! Grandpa! We got Blue Ribbons!" Lizzy and Kadey flew up the path, long strands of blue ribbon streaming behind them.

Amanda stood up and waited for the girls. "Blue ribbons! Ethel and Lucy must have stolen the show!"

"They did. We couldn't enter them in the same judging, but they both got blue ribbons."

"Lizzy, Kadey, you have chores to do!" Keelee called from the corral.

"We got to go feed Ethel and Lucy and clean out the trailer. Can you keep these for us until we come back, Grandma?"

"Absolutely." Amanda took the ribbons and the girls scurried back.

She held them up. "Frank, how did they both get blue ribbons?"

"Different breeds of cow." He'd done that on purpose. "Couldn't have them competing against each other."

Gabriel stepped out of the RV and sat back down. "Do you remember the first time we stood on that porch together?"

Frank nodded. "You said our family was the tip of the spear." He recalled that day clearly.

"They still are. We've taken a hell of a blow, but it won't stop us from leaving a legacy. A Guardian Legacy. One our children will be proud to step into and carry on."

Frank put his arm around his wife and stared across his land. "A Guardian Legacy." He lifted his drink. "To the future. To a Guardian Legacy."

The Guardian Legacy Series is coming soon!

Author's Note: The Kings of Guardian **will**

continue on! I promise appearances of, and updates on, your favorite couples in future Guardian Stories!

Join my newsletter to get updates on all Kris Michaels releases.

To read Andrew's story, Click here.
To read Phoenix and Aspen's Story, Click here.
To read this Lt Evers' story, Click here.

ALSO BY KRIS MICHAELS

Kings of the Guardian Series

Jacob: Kings of the Guardian Book 1

Joseph: Kings of the Guardian Book 2

Adam: Kings of the Guardian Book 3

Jason: Kings of the Guardian Book 4

Jared: Kings of the Guardian Book 5

Jasmine: Kings of the Guardian Book 6

Chief: The Kings of Guardian Book 7

Jewell: Kings of the Guardian Book 8

Jade: Kings of the Guardian Book 9

Justin: Kings of the Guardian Book 10

Christmas with the Kings

Drake: Kings of the Guardian Book 11

Dixon: Kings of the Guardian Book 12

Passages: The Kings of Guardian Book 13

Promises: The Kings of Guardian Book 14

The Siege: Book One, The Kings of Guardian Book 15

The Siege: Book Two, The Kings of Guardian Book 16

A Backwater Blessing: A Kings of Guardian Crossover

Novella

Montana Guardian: A Kings of Guardian Novella

Guardian Defenders Series

Gabriel

Maliki

John

Jeremiah

Guardian Security Shadow World

Anubis (Guardian Shadow World Book 1)

Asp (Guardian Shadow World Book 2)

Lycos (Guardian Shadow World Book 3)

Thanatos (Guardian Shadow World Book 4)

Tempest (Guardian Shadow World Book 5)

Smoke (Guardian Shadow World Book 6)

Reaper (Guardian Shadow World Book 7)

Phoenix (Guardian Shadow World Book 8)

Hope City

Hope City - Brock

HOPE CITY - Brody- Book 3

Hope City - Ryker - Book 5

Hope City - Killian - Book 8

Hope City - Blayze - Book 10

The Long Road Home

Season One:

My Heart's Home

Season Two:

Searching for Home

STAND ALONE NOVELS

SEAL Forever - Silver SEALs

A Heart's Desire - Stand Alone

Hot SEAL, Single Malt (SEALs in Paradise)

Hot SEAL, Savannah Nights (SEALs in Paradise)

Hot SEAL, Silent Knight (SEALs in Paradise)

ABOUT THE AUTHOR

USA Today and Amazon Bestselling Author, Kris Michaels is the alter ego of a happily married wife and mother. She writes romance, usually with characters from military and law enforcement backgrounds.

Printed in Great Britain
by Amazon